CONS

CONS

Timothy Watts

SOHO

Published by
Soho Press Inc.
853 Broadway
New York, NY 10003

Library of Congress Cataloging-in-Publication Data

Watts, Timothy, 1957–
Cons/Timothy Watts.
p. cm.
ISBN 1-56947-034-0
I. Title.
PS3573.A88C66 1993

813′.54–dc20   92–31224
                               CIP

Manufactured in the United States
10 9 8 7 6 5 4 3 2 1

For Eleanore

CONS

CHAPTER

1

CULLY HAD A feeling in his gut. Cold. The thing was, it was familiar, it'd been there before. You'd see a guy, a pro football quarterback, somebody like that, walking out onto a field just before the game, and it would be the same thing. Cully, with his muscles tight and maybe a few butterflies in his stomach, but pretty determined. Walking down Bay Street, his shoulders hunched up because it had started to rain, cutting diagonally across the street and then starting to move faster, almost jogging, a little pissed off because he wasn't wearing a jacket and the water was running down his neck.

It wasn't like he was carrying a gun. He wasn't gonna do that kind of thing anymore. But the feeling was there, the iciness, flashing him back to his Jesse James days; young bad-assed dude, going into places with a pistol. It was good to know that he could still get it going. That feeling. Thinking about it: If you're gonna do something—maybe it's not the most pleasant thing—sooner or later you just do it. He was gonna walk into the bar and it didn't matter what happened. Because it wasn't like he had gone out in the rain, walking down the fucking street getting wet, so some asshole could tell him he wasn't gonna pay him his money.

A car went by, the headlights blinding him for a second, and then the tires hit a puddle, soaking his leg because he didn't see to step back in time, thinking too much about Dave Ross and his money. Cully let it go, though. It was gonna do a lot of good, maybe make him feel better if he shouted something at the car, said something rude? It's a carload of Marines headed out from Parris Island. Where was that gonna leave him?

What he was thinking was that it would be good to have a drink. He could almost taste it. Go into Casey's and sit down, have a couple of shots and a beer, see if maybe Jenny, the waitress, was on tonight. He could talk to her, work on it some more, because he thought maybe he was pretty close. The last couple of times he'd been in there, he wasn't sure, but he thought she was making up her mind. Laughing with him, but thinking about it, too, letting him know she was there. He could do that. But it wouldn't work. Tomorrow morning, he'd wake up and the money would still be bothering him.

He got to the front door of the bar and opened it. Walked inside and stood there, seeing Jenny behind the bar, with the other waitress, both of them wearing white blouses, with narrow black ties that came to just about where their belly buttons were. You look at them quickly, maybe you don't realize their hair was pulled back, Jenny's in a long ponytail, and maybe what would happen, you'd think they were guys dressed in suits. But give it a second. If they turned towards you, or stepped out from behind the bar where it was brighter, you'd see right away they're women. And then you'd see their legs, especially Jenny's. Wearing a short black skirt, balancing a tray of drinks and showing about six inches of thigh above her knees. It wasn't something you would be in doubt about after that.

Cully waited for a bit, looking at her while he brushed some water from his shoulders. Staring at her legs and the way her skirt hugged her ass until she looked over to see who had come in, seeing him and smiling. But not getting much back because Cully, now that he was here, was concentrating. Smiling at her a little, nodding, but then turning to look across the room, letting his eyes get used to the light. Thinking, Fuck it, here it was, so he might as well do it.

.   .   .

4

There were maybe twenty people at the bar. Nobody was ordering food, and most of the customers—unless they were on a date, maybe trying to impress somebody by ordering white wine or else something like a Beefeater's with a twist—were drinking beer. Having a couple of Buds and staring at the wide-screen TV over the bar. Watching Atlanta play the Chicago Cubs. Somebody had put some money in the jukebox. Had Tammy Wynette singing in the background, her voice mixing with the announcer's coming from the TV, so that a couple of times she sounded like she was cheering. Ryne Sandberg getting a hit off of John Smoltz and you'd hear Tammy singing away, sounding sad all of a sudden because her boys from Atlanta weren't doing so well.

The place was pretty dim, with most of the light coming from recessed spotlights in the ceiling, turned low, but with a couple of extra spots angled down from the ceiling over by the far wall where somebody had painted a mural of a baseball game. A cartoon, with all the ball players in old-time uniforms, the word MUDVILLE painted on their jerseys. Casey Jones up to bat, with a few spectators painted at the far side of the mural. When he opened it, the owner of the bar must have been trying to give the place a jock look. A huge baseball bat, maybe ten feet long, was hanging from a hook along the back of the bar. If you went there to eat they had things on the menu, Baseball Bacon Burger, Homerun Fries, shit like that. But who cared. You could turn the place into a stadium, what would you get, the same crowd. Young people, a couple of years out of high school, living in Beaufort but maybe working down in Savannah, at the paper mill. Or else Marines, coming into town from Parris Island or the air station, drinking beer and trying to get laid. They'd sit there at the bar, looking tough, checking out the women and getting into arguments with each other.

Cully stepped away from the bar and moved into the other room, where tables were set up. You went down a couple of steps to get there. You could sit down, get away from the crowd a little bit. Jenny, or the other waitress, would come down and take your order.

He saw Dave Ross right away, sitting with Earl Marsh. There was a pitcher of beer between them. Dave was talking, leaning towards Earl and speaking softly. And Earl, he looked blitzed. He had his elbows on the table, resting his chin in his hands. With that bleary look that Cully had gotten used to seeing when he worked with him down at the garage.

Behind Ross and Earl Marsh were two people at another table. Two men, one of them Latin looking, a Mexican maybe, or maybe an Indian. He had his back to Cully. The man on the other side of the table was white. Older, with a cowboy hat on his head, and a nice dress shirt on. He had a look about him that Cully had seen before. A guy like that, he went into a place and it wouldn't matter if maybe he'd never been there before. He'd act like he owned the joint from the minute he stepped inside. He was looking at Cully. And the other man, the Mex, he must've felt something, because he started to turn in his chair. Both of them staring at Cully now, with Cully looking back, waiting to see if maybe they knew Dave Ross and Earl Marsh. Waiting to see, were they gonna get involved in it? He gave it another couple of seconds and then decided, Fuck it, they were just looking at him.

He stepped down into the room and walked over to Dave Ross, coming up behind him and standing quietly, waiting for one of them to realize he was there. It wasn't that he didn't have anything to say, but he was thinking, what he'd do, he'd surprise them a little bit. They're in the middle of this conversation, leaning their heads together, not paying any attention to what was happening. And all of a sudden Cully shows up. Maybe it would help him out, let him get on top of the situation.

Dave Ross saw him first. He leaned back to take a drink and almost choked on his beer because there was Cully, standing right next to him and starting to grin.

Cully said, "See, I'm finishing up, closing the place up back there. Mopping floors, whatever. And I start to think about it. Where the fuck are you two? I get a picture in my head. Both of you, sitting here drinking beer."

Ross tried to smile. "You want a beer, I'll buy you one."

Cully shook his head. He was getting the cold feeling all over again. Happy almost, because this was something he could understand. Some of the other shit, trying to make a go of it with an honest job, it didn't always sit well with him. But this kind of thing—he'd been here before. He said, "You could do that. Buy me a beer. But what's bothering me, I might want to come in here sometime—maybe you're not around—I might want to buy myself a beer."

"Yeah?"

Cully asked him, "How am I gonna do that—come in here and buy a beer? How am I gonna do that if I don't have any money?"

Ross put his glass down and said, "Jesus, boy. You into that again?" He looked across the table at Earl Marsh. The big man was starting to grin, sitting there, drunk, watching Ross and Cully talk. Getting a kick out of it, Cully could see it. He watched Ross turn back to him and say, "I told you when I hired you. I said it'd be a little while before I can pay you."

Cully nodded. He took a step to his right so that he was directly between the two men and said, "Yeah, I remember. But I guess what I figured was a little while and what you had in mind were two different things."

Earl put his hands flat on the table. Cully saw him do it out of the corner of his eye. He was looking at Ross but seeing Earl's muscles bunch up in his arm as the man put some of his weight on them.

Cully told Ross, "I think what I want, you can pay me what you owe me. Do that now and we'll call it square. I can find work somewhere else." Waiting a second and then adding, "How would that be?" Still talking nice—slowly—letting them see he was still trying to be reasonable about it.

He heard Earl say, "Fuck that," slurring the words. So he put some of his weight on his toes, bringing his hands up next to his hips, but not closing them yet.

When he spoke it was almost a whisper. Talking directly to Ross because he knew Earl was too drunk to move fast. He said, "What about it? You want to make this thing easy?"

Ross looked at him and smiled, turning for an instant to Earl and winking. And then looked back at Cully and said, "You want a beer, I'll buy you a beer. If not, get the fuck outta here."

Cully gave it a couple of seconds, thinking, Shit, here it goes. Looking at Dave Ross and starting to grin. Shrugging his shoulders. Letting the man think he was gonna walk away. And then sweeping his foot out and catching the leg of Ross's chair. Seeing the look on the other man's face as he went down. And then turning to Earl.

Earl was not a small man. If you stood next to him, say you're average height, you'd realize that he's a couple of inches taller, like he'd go six two in his bare feet. Maybe two oh five, two ten, something like that. But with his muscles going soft from all his drinking. He'd been sitting there for a couple of hours with Ross, pouring beer down his throat and doing shots of Seagram's on the side, maybe seven of them—getting a nice glow, something he could work with, maintain for the rest of the night and still be awake when closing time came around.

What Earl did was, he'd wake up every morning, maybe lie in bed to see if he was gonna have to puke, push his feet out from under the covers, ready for it if he had to run for the toilet. If everything was all right he'd shuffle downstairs and grab a beer. Ice cold. Pour it down his throat and give it a minute. See if it was gonna stay there. More often than not, he'd do a couple of shots, holding on to the sink, breathing through his teeth, fighting to hold the whiskey in his gut. Wait for his hands to stop shaking and then have another beer. Cully would see it, every day Earl would come into work half lit. Drink a half a case of beer throughout the day. He'd be working on a car and every once in a while he'd stop. Go on back to the refrigerator in the back office and get a cold one.

It caught him by surprise, Cully moving like that, kicking the chair and then coming for him. Earl sitting there with Dave Ross, having a good time, seeing Ross give Cully shit and laughing about it. Not looking for a fight, but seeing it happen—watching Cully kick Dave's chair—getting up out of his seat and standing. Reacting to it finally but then moving right into Cully's punch.

When Cully kicked the chair he was already feeling it. The adrenaline, whatever, something extra inside of him. Taking over. It felt good, seeing Earl standing there, with an expression on his face like he just shit his pants. Cully, seeing things almost in slow motion, watching Earl stumble to his feet and measuring the distance between himself and Earl's chin.

He took his time about it, waiting until Earl was all the way up, standing there and looking like a goddamn target for Christ's sake. Still with the confused look on his face as Cully stepped towards him and swung his fist into Earl's face.

He felt it connect, knew right away that Earl wasn't gonna be a problem from there on out, and started to turn towards Dave Ross. By then Ross was getting back up, untangling himself from the chair and looking around the bar to see if maybe somebody was gonna help him out. Cully, moving his feet like a boxer, on his toes but not even breathing hard, turned to Ross and said, loudly enough for everybody in the bar to hear, "You gonna pay me or what?"

Ross looked at Earl Marsh, lying there on the floor like he was asleep, and then back up at Cully, seeing how angry he was, waiting there with his fists clenched to hear what Ross was going to say. He looked around the room. There were a lot of people there that knew him. Cully could see it: if Ross backed down now it would be all over town in a couple of hours. He turned back to Cully and said, "Fuck you."

Cully hit him three times, his fists little more than a blur, standing there and throwing quick little jabs that had a lot of power to them and then hitting Ross one more time, the knockout punch coming from somewhere down around his waist, catching Ross on the nose and dropping him.

He looked at the two men on the floor, both of them out cold, and gradually the sounds from the room came back to him. They were different, though. He could hear the TV, the Braves game, and the jukebox; he didn't recognize what was playing. But that was it. There wasn't any sound of people talking, just silence where a few minutes before there had been a continuous buzz. He looked around finally, towards the bar, where twenty pairs of eyes stared back at him. And then he turned his head, seeing the older white man and the Mex, out of their seats now and staring at him. He wasn't sure for a minute what was going to happen. Standing there, half crouched, in his fighter's stance, ready for it if these two turned out to be friends of Ross's.

9

The white guy took a step towards him and looked down at the two men on the floor and then back at Cully, holding the beer glass in his hand and then raising it slowly, until it was at eye level. Some kind of a salute. Smiling at Cully all of a sudden and saying, "Jesus, boy, you got a punch."

CHAPTER

2

THE BEAUFORT COUNTY lockup was in the center of town, on Charles Street. It was like a lot of small jails. Depressing looking, a brick building painted white, with a twelve-foot-high barbed-wire fence around the perimeter that had red plastic slats running through it at eye level so nobody could see in or out. The building itself was topped with razor wire and had brightly lit hallways running along the second floor where the cells were. If you're driving through town, a tourist from up north, something like that, looking at all the mansions, with the white pillars out front— maybe you're thinking of Scarlett O'Hara or Bill Sherman leading the Union Army up through Savannah and then into Beaufort on his way to burn down Sheldon Church out on Highway 21—the town seems so fucking historical. You come to the jail and it's right there. Ugly. You know what it is. You take one look and say, Oh, that's where they lock people up.

You walk in the first floor, down the hallway to Receiving. There's the sergeant sitting behind the big desk and the crackle of the radio coming from the open doorway behind him. The place smells of disinfectant mostly, with a touch of piss, and the sound of muted shouting runs through it constantly.

They put Cully in a cell by himself. The sheriff's deputies picked

11

him up after Dave Ross swore out a complaint against him. The deputies talked to Ross down at the county hospital while he was getting his nose taped up—the doctor getting a little irritated because Ross kept moving around in his seat and the deputies kept trying to get in front of him. Ross pushed the doctor away and looked at the two deputies, squinting against the pain and saying, "Fug him. Log the son of a bith up, I'll sign the pabers." Barely able to breathe because his nose hurt so bad.

The deputies—two of them, because by now everybody had heard about the fight, and what Cully could do with those fists of his—found Cully at his trailer out at the Live Oak Park. Cully had been more or less waiting for them and didn't make a fuss. They put him in a squad car and drove him down to the jail where they read him his rights and then locked him in a cell to think about things.

It was all right with Cully. It pissed him off but it wasn't the end of the world. He sat there, coming down from the adrenaline high of the fight and thinking things through, running it over in his head, what had happened in the four weeks since he got to town. They were gonna charge him with assault, which didn't sound too bad unless they decided to run with it, make a big deal out of him being an ex-con. If they just wanted to hassle him, well, that was something he could deal with. He didn't like being in the cell but he'd been in worse. He'd spent five years in Raiford Prison, fucking hellhole down in Florida that made this place look like a country club. If he could survive that, he could get through anything.

He wasn't sorry about the fight either. It was something that had to be done. He'd spent four weeks working for Ross—the man telling him he was gonna pay him any time, but then never showing him any money at all. Cully had let it ride, glad to get the work. But it had started to bother him after a while. He'd spend his days fixing cars, living on what was left of the money they gave him down at Raiford, putting brake pads on, or exhaust, shit like that, a thing that before he went to Raiford, before he ever pointed a gun at anybody, he used to do back in Florida. Cully, getting greasy all day long, and Ross, every afternoon he went down to Casey's, drinking sour mash with beer chasers and hassling the waitresses, and all the time Cully was waiting for his money.

He thought what he would do, after the fight, he'd move on out of town. Put some distance between himself and Ross. What he might do was what he'd originally planned, keep going north, head up to Pennsylvania and see if his sister recognized him after ten years. If they let him out. Because he knew how it worked. Ross was a local and Cully was new in town. It wouldn't matter that Cully deserved the money.

But he really did need the money. Sitting there in the cell, thinking about it, what was he gonna do without it? Over a thousand dollars coming to him for five weeks' work. It wasn't like he had a better plan, some other place in another town that was gonna pay him more money if he moved on. It got tough, after a while, trying to find employment. Anywhere he went, sooner or later they'd find out he was an ex-con.

He couldn't come up with any kind of an idea. He was stuck in jail, in Beaufort, South Carolina. In a cell that was maybe eight feet by six, with an open toilet right there, next to the mattress. You lie down in bed, stare at the ceiling, and all that happens is you breathe in the stink from a thousand other guys taking craps in here. It didn't matter, you could flush it a dozen times. It was still in your head.

He heard one time, some fucking psychiatrist down at the Dade County lockup, before he got processed through to Raiford, talking to him and saying, "The reason is, the reason you rob people, you *want* to be caught." Cully'd looked at the doctor, if that's what he was. The asshole had twelve pens in his shirt pocket. Cully had counted them, staring at the guy's pens and saying, "You think that's it, huh. The money, you think the money's got nothing to do with it?" Thinking, what a fucked-up way to be—go to school, come out and tell people robberies got nothing to do with trying to make a living.

But the motherfucker would take a look at him now, sitting in this cell, and get a hard-on. Stare at Cully through the bars and nod his head, maybe give it a minute and then write something down in a notebook.

But still, lying here, if the cops wanted to squeeze his ass, maybe make a big deal out of it, he could be looking at spending some time on a work gang, walking along the highway somewhere picking up trash.

He'd been out of prison for all of eight weeks. No parole because they'd made him do the whole five yards, the board turning him down for early release because he was listed as a troublemaker down at Raiford. They stick you inside a place like that and you've got to protect yourself, try to do quiet time, get through it without getting killed, or maybe have your asshole ripped open so far somebody would drive a truck through it by mistake. But it wasn't something that was easy. They see you walking in there, fresh meat, and it starts on the first day. What you got to do is maybe get a rep going so people wouldn't fuck with you. You do that or there's no way you're gonna make it.

The guards see what's happening, know what a person—especially a white boy, he's in there for his first time—has to do to survive. It didn't matter that most of the guards wouldn't last ten minutes, you take them out of uniform, take their shotguns away, and stick them in general population. They know all that shit and still they label you a hard case.

He was starting to get a little frustrated. Spend all that time in jail, five fucking years, and the whole time what you do is, you tell yourself, Never again. Cully had made a promise to himself, if he made it through Raiford he wasn't ever gonna steal another dime in his life. But what happens? He gets out and starts making his way north, gets away from Miami and tries to go straight. It made him laugh because what had happened, already he'd been cheated out of money twice. Once by Dave Ross, the man refusing to pay him the money he'd earned for fixing cars. And before that, down in Tallahassee, working for a guy that was gonna pay him a couple of hundred bucks cash for helping to clear a field—ball-breaking work under the Florida sun—and when it was done, the guy told Cully he didn't have the cash. Cully had let him go; what the hell was he gonna do? But still, the second time it happened, with Dave Ross, Cully couldn't let it slide.

His cellmate down at Raiford, a big Italian guy with yellow teeth and bad skin that everybody called Bobo—a cop killer—asked him, just before Cully got out, "What're you gonna do, you spent this time in here, now they're gonna let you out?"

Cully took his time about it. He didn't answer right away because even though it was something he'd been dreaming about for five whole years, he still hadn't come up with anything. He knew what he wanted. What was so hard about that? But if somebody asked him, Yeah, so how are you gonna get it? it wasn't something he had an answer for. He'd sit there, after lights-out, or else, if he was walking around in the yard, not bullshitting with the other cons, he'd let himself think about it, fantasize. What was he gonna do back on the outside?

He wasn't sure, but he told Bobo, "I can say this, I don't think I'm gonna get a gun, go into any more places and try to take people's money."

Bobo told him, "Shit. Everybody says that. First thing you know, they outside, maybe hurtin' a little. Start askin' themselves, how am I gonna make a little easy money?"

Cully asked him, leaning forward and looking at Bobo's teeth, "What makes you think sticking a gun in somebody's face—maybe they got a 12 gauge under the counter—is easy? I used to have to take a crap, couldn't leave my apartment, I knew I was gonna go out and rob somebody."

"Yeah, my man, but what else do you know?" Bobo looking at him, smiling and shaking his head.

Cully told him, "Maybe what I could do, I get out of here, I could open my own business. A place to eat, something like that."

Bobo started laughing before Cully even finished saying it, sitting on his bed and holding his belly, the breath whistling in and out of his nose, he was laughing so hard. He said, "Jesus, I can see it. A restaurant."

Cully had spent a lot of time listening to Bobo and he didn't really care one way or another what Bobo thought. It pissed him off, sitting there and having to listen to Bobo laugh, not able to do anything about it because they were friends. Telling Bobo finally, "Shut the fuck up," which he did after another minute. Cully was still mad, though, because Bobo was a pain in the ass a lot of the time. He was ugly, for one thing, and most times he smelled pretty bad.

But he was all right for a lifer, a three-time loser that'd killed a cop during a drug bust in Miami six years before Cully got to Raiford. Bobo told Cully one time—they'd bought some pruno and were sitting in their cell after lights-out one night, getting drunk and bullshitting—and Bobo said, "The worst thing I ever did, and I done some bad things, but the worst thing I ever did was pull my gun on that cop. I found out later he had a kid." He looked at Cully and said, with tears in his eyes, because he was feeling the pruno, "In here, you got to act like it don't matter. You got to act like you don't give a fuck—maybe you're just lookin' to kill somebody else. There's a lot of guys, they wouldn't think twice about killin' a cop."

Cully shook his head, not really giving a shit, but listening anyway. You see guys like Bobo, sitting there, you get them in the right mood, maybe a little drunk, and they'd tell you how bad it was. But none of them Cully'd ever met ever told you it was their fault. You tell any of them, Listen, somebody made a mistake, you ain't supposed to be here, they'd be nodding their head, agreeing with you and saying, Right on. Grabbing their shit and heading for the door before you finished saying it.

A couple of weeks later he was out of there, Bobo acting as if it were gonna break his heart, Cully leaving. But Cully knew Bobo was crazy for a guy that lived in a cell two tiers above them. He'd been saving his money so that he could pay to have the guy moved in with him. Bobo wanted to marry the guy, which was all right with Cully, as long as he was out of there when it happened. Cully thought that if somebody, a judge, say, ever told him he'd never see the outside of a prison wall again, sooner or later he would start looking around to see what was available.

When Cully got out he headed north. He stopped for a weekend to work the field for the guy that never did pay him and then got on a bus again. He wanted to put as much distance between himself and Florida as possible. He figured what he'd do was, he'd go back to Pennsylvania—see how his sister was doing. But halfway there he thought, Fuck it, and hopped off the bus in Beaufort.

He should have known better.

.   .   .

16

They let him sleep in the cell overnight and then came and got him the next morning. Cully's teeth felt like they had glue on them and he could've used a cup of coffee but he went along without a fuss, a deputy walking him along the tier of cells and then downstairs to a small office near the front of the building. There was a big man sitting behind a desk and another man, he looked familiar to Cully, sitting on one of the two other chairs in the room, with a hat, something like John Wayne would've worn, a Stetson, in his lap. There were two deer heads on the wall above the desk and another one, not a deer, one of those sheep, or goats, with the huge horns curled back from the head like the Los Angeles Rams' football helmet, on the far wall.

Cully took one look at the man behind the desk and knew he was somebody that could make trouble—sheriff, DA, something like that. A big guy that looked like he owned the whole fucking building, comfortable, sitting there looking back at Cully, with a weathered face and a big gut that might've fooled a lot of people in the past, they made the mistake of thinking his gut made him soft.

The guy on the other side of the desk was older, without the belly—in his fifties—a thin man with the kind of tan that looked like he got it at a salon and soft-looking hands. He had a cup of coffee in his hands, holding it, looking at Cully. Moving his fingers on the crown of the Stetson. Cully was sure now. He had seen him before. But he was too busy wondering what was gonna happen to worry about it.

He stood just inside the doorway with the deputy still holding his arm—no cuffs, but where was he gonna go anyway? After a minute the man behind the desk nodded to the deputy. The deputy shoved Cully into the room, over to the only other chair and pushed him into it, saying, "Sit your ass down," and then ambled to the door and walked out.

Cully turned in his seat and looked at the older man. He nodded slowly to Cully. Cully, feeling both men's eyes on him, with nobody saying anything, was beginning to wonder what was going on.

The man across the desk pulled a cigar out of his pocket, lit it, and looked at Cully. "Boy," he said, "you got any idea who I am?"

17

Cully said, "I get pulled out of my cell, dragged down here to see you. I got to figure you ain't my lawyer."

"That's right." The man laughed. "I ain't no goddamned lawyer. I'm the sheriff." He leaned forward. "I got something I want to ask you."

Cully shrugged and didn't say anything.

The sheriff looked at him in silence for about a half a minute and then said, "What the hell you want to do a dumb thing like that for? Go into a bar and, in front of maybe three dozen people, beat the piss out of a well-known member of the community?"

Cully said, "He owed me money." He smiled and said, "Still does." Thinking, what was this? The sheriff—if he wanted to play games, Cully was gonna go along with it until he found out where it was heading.

The sheriff asked him, "If I let you out of here, is that what you're gonna do? Go back out after Ross? Try to get your money back?"

"I don't know. Maybe Ross, he takes the time to think about it, maybe he'll come looking for me. Maybe after he thinks things through he'll see the error of his ways."

The older man snorted with laughter and the sheriff joined him and then said, "You see what I mean, Herb? I've met people like this." Talking as if Cully were no longer in the room. Saying, "I'm not sure you understand what you'll be getting into."

Cully looked at the man next to him, wanting to know who he was but not asking because he was getting a feeling. Thinking about the sheriff asking him what he was gonna do if he was able to walk out of here, and starting to wonder, maybe this guy next to him, maybe he was somebody that was gonna make that possible.

The older man spoke finally. He told the sheriff, "I think probably we can work something out." Smiling now, and turning to Cully with a little bit of a smirk on his face. Not offering to shake hands. Telling Cully, "My name is Herb Dorrance. I own a farm just outside of town. About six miles up towards Gardner's Corner. You know this area at all?"

Cully shook his head. "I've only been in town a couple of weeks."

Dorrance nodded. "That's what the sheriff told me." He waited a moment and then said, "I was in the bar last night. I saw the fight."

Cully remembered it then. He could picture the bar the way it had been the night before. Walking in and looking around for Ross. Seeing a few people, the waitresses—Jenny, the cute one, and the other, he couldn't think of her name. And then seeing two men sitting at a table with a couple of glasses in front of them. The Mexican. And this man, Dorrance. Lifting his beer glass to Cully. Making some kind of remark.

He nodded now and said, "I remember."

The sheriff spoke up. "Mr. Dorrance came in this morning to tell me that he'd seen the fight."

"That's right." Dorrance nodded.

"And," the sheriff continued, "he says that it was pretty much of a fair fight." The sheriff smiled slowly. "Matter of fact, Herb here told me that, even two against one, with them having the numbers, it was close as to whether or not you were being fair."

Cully didn't speak. He was waiting for them to get to the point. Cut the crap and tell him what was next.

The sheriff said, "Now I could put you back in that cell upstairs. Leave you there until I decide what else to do. Or you could listen to what Herb has to say." He looked at Cully. "What do you say?"

Cully shrugged, looking at the sheriff and then deciding to give it a push. Asking, "How about some coffee?"

The sheriff leaned forward and put his arms on the desk. "They didn't give you a cup? Room service, they came up to your cell without coffee?"

Cully shrugged again.

The sheriff said, "Uh-huh. You're just wondering, maybe you spent the night up there and we forgot you. Is that it?"

"Maybe."

The sheriff stared at him for a couple of seconds and then said, "Don't fucking wonder."

And Cully, giving in, because it wasn't worth it, nodded.

Dorrance cleared his throat. He said, "What I've got is a job for you. I need somebody out at my place. Kind of a chauffeur for my wife. Take care of the cars, keep them gassed up, and, if they need work, take them into town. See that it's taken care of. That kind of thing. And also, take my wife places. If she wants to go shopping, something like that." He stopped talking, looked at the sheriff and then back at Cully, nodding and leaning forward. Telling Cully, "You got a record. You like to fight. Rob people, whatever. Maybe a job like this, maybe you can't handle it. Too much responsibility." Dorrance, looking at Cully and smirking again, was enjoying himself from what Cully could tell. Saying, "I'm a guy that's willing to give you a chance here."

Cully gave it a second, thinking about it, because it almost sounded too good to be true. When they'd taken him out of his cell, he'd been looking at maybe getting sent to a work farm, or else getting nailed with a fine there was no way he could've paid. The two men, both of them looking at him now, waited for his answer. What was he supposed to do, fall at their feet with thanks? He said, "What's the job pay?"

The sheriff snorted. "Jesus." Leaning forward on his seat and saying, "Boy, this ain't no fucking interview. You want the job, want I should let you walk out of here? Don't be worrying about what kind of money are you gonna be pulling in, how long is it gonna be before you can retire."

Cully said, "I'm asking is all."

Dorrance nodded, saying to the sheriff, "It's all right, Pete. He's got a right to know." He turned to Cully. "It pays, on salary, two hundred dollars a week. But you get room and board. I've got a garage apartment, and the cook'll bring you all your meals. After hours, if you check with me, you can come and go as you like, use the car, unless my wife and I need to be driven somewhere. I'd let you know beforehand if that happens."

Cully decided to shut his mouth then. Hearing Dorrance talking about his cook and starting to wonder what kind of farmer he was, losing the image of dirt-poor sharecroppers and Willie Nelson singing benefit concerts. The guy wanted to give him a place to sleep, feed him, and pay him two bills a week. Plus getting him out of jail.

He said, "All right."

Dorrance smiled. "Good." He stood up and held his hand out to the sheriff. "Pete, thank you."

The sheriff smiled. "A pleasure." He picked up a folder from the desktop and said to Cully, "I had Florida fax me your sheet and I showed it to Herb. He still wants to hire you, that's all right with me. But don't you go into this thinking he doesn't know what you are."

Cully listened to him say it. He was thinking maybe he'd let it go. But it wasn't like he was back in Raiford where you give a guard shit, they throw you in a cell by yourself, leave you there with maybe an hour a day outside. Nobody to talk to, nothing to read; you sit there alone for the whole fucking day and after a while you start to go crazy.

He looked at the sheriff and said, "I can see it, county sheriff with a hard-on, you think everybody that's ever been inside, that's all they know." Nodding and saying, "Maybe I can even understand it. But it ain't something I got time to listen to right now." Feeling better because he'd told himself, getting out of Raiford, that he wasn't gonna take that kind of shit from anybody again. He gave the sheriff one more look, waiting to see if he was going to do anything, and then turned to Dorrance, waiting for the older man to start for the door and then following behind him.

Neither one said anything as they walked out into the parking lot, past the squad cards and over to a white pick-up that smelled like shit. Cully, wrinkling his nose, said, "Jesus, what the fuck is the smell?"

Dorrance grinned. "Cow shit." He waited a second and then said, "I get a kick out of it. All it is, it's fertilizer. I need it at the farm. But, see, you drive along with something like that, just sitting there, smelling something god-awful. And what happens? You pass some-body walking on the street and then look in the mirror. You see it in their faces. They look after the truck with their noses all wrinkled up." He laughed. "Or else, what they do, if they're not thinking about it, they lift their feet up, one by one. See if maybe they stepped on a dog turd."

Cully nodded. "Uh-huh." Seeing the manure now, in the bed of the truck, and thinking it was a pretty weird way for a grown man to get his kicks. Climbing in the truck pretty quickly because the smell wasn't that bad inside the cab. He looked at Dorrance and said, "Where're we going?"

Dorrance told him, "My place."

Cully thought about it and asked, "You mind if I stop out at the trailer park? I got a couple of things I need to pick up."

Dorrance hesitated and then said, "All right."

They looked at each other for a couple of seconds in silence and then Cully said, "Okay." Giving it a little smile, thinking he'd wait and see how things worked out before he made up his mind about anything. Saying, "Then you can show me your farm."

CHAPTER

3

DRIVING OUT ROUTE 21 towards Gardner's Corner, Dorrance asked, "You know anything about tomatoes?"

Cully shook his head. "Down at Raiford they grew corn. Some tomatoes, too. But I was never involved with it."

"Why not?"

Cully turned in his seat. "I was what they called High Risk. They didn't let us out in the fields." Watching Dorrance to see what kind of reaction he was gonna have, sitting in the car now, with the sheriff not around any longer and an ex-con in the passenger seat. Saying it casually, Cully letting him know that he was a bad dude, if that's what the man wanted to think. Maybe this was something he'd done a lot. Hire ex-cons so he could be around them. Hear their stories.

But Dorrance didn't say anything about it. He looked at Cully and said, "I've got twenty-four hundred acres. I grow tomatoes and peanuts mostly, and a few acres of tobacco. Every couple of years I'll throw in some corn. But mostly I stick to the peanuts and tomatoes. I sell the tomatoes to the soup companies, and the peanuts end up between two pieces of bread."

Cully said, "It sounds like a lot of land."

Dorrance shook his head and said, "It's not. Nowadays, that's considered a small operation." He laughed softly. "But what the hell. It pays the bills."

Cully waited a minute and then said what had been on his mind the whole ride. "And, what, you all of a sudden decided that you needed a chauffeur?"

Dorrance glanced at Cully quickly and then looked back out at the road. "It's something I've been giving some thought to."

Cully nodded. "I can picture it. You see me beat up a couple of people in a bar. You see me and say to yourself, Hey, he can use his fists, I wonder if he can drive a car, too?"

"More or less."

Cully asked, "You ever have a chauffeur before?"

Herb nodded. "A while back. It didn't work out."

Cully raised his eyebrows a little bit. "No?"

"No."

"Maybe there's something you want to tell me. Something you forgot."

Dorrance was silent for a moment but then he smiled. "No. Nothing I can think of. It's pretty straightforward." The man was quiet for a minute and then he looked at Cully and said, "Listen, I saw what the sheriff had in that file. I guess, what, you've been in a fair amount of trouble? If it's something you want to follow you around, maybe you can go out of your way to remind people of it. That's one thing. You want a job, a chance to get ahead. That's something else."

Cully took his time answering, saying, "It's as simple as that?"

Dorrance pulled the truck over to the side of the road and stopped. He shut the motor off and then turned towards Cully and gave him a look. He reached over to the glove compartment finally, smiling once and pulling a pistol out. He looked at the gun, not saying anything, and then lifted it up into the air, curling his fingers around the trigger, telling Cully, an edge to his voice, "It's as simple as this, partner. Basically, you don't have a fucking leg to stand on."

He rolled his window down, with the smell of the cow shit from the bed of the truck wafting in again and mixing with the salt air from the bay. He leaned his arm out, steadying the pistol, and then shot at a speed limit sign across the street.

It made Cully jump because he wasn't expecting it. He was used to gunfire, it wasn't something that usually made him flinch. But, goddamn, broad daylight and the guy was, what, shooting a gun off maybe a mile outside of town? The sound had to carry at least that far because there wasn't anything but salt marsh out there. Cully saw a couple of egrets, white against the sky, swing up into the air in alarm. Dorrance kept firing. He'd pull the trigger every couple of seconds, not looking at Cully but starting to talk at the same time. Interrupting himself every couple of seconds to shoot the gun again and then waiting for the sound to die down before he began again. He told Cully, "You can take the job, do things the way I want them done." The gun boomed. "Or I can turn around, take you back to your buddy the sheriff." BOOM. He hit the goddamn sign every time, too.

"I see that shit you were pulling with the sheriff. 'Where's my coffee?' You got an attitude, something like that." He pulled the trigger again, two or three times in a row, one loud bang, the noise of the shots so fast and loud that it shook the windows in the truck. He said, "What you want to do is lose the attitude. And quit asking so many fucking questions, maybe we'll get along." He pulled his arm back in, sitting there with the gun resting in his lap, the smell of cordite almost overpowering the cow shit.

Cully didn't think he seemed too concerned was someone gonna come along and ask him what was he doing, shooting the hell out of a traffic sign. Dorrance seemed to be thinking about something, looking at the gun in his hand and then smiling. Turning sideways in his seat and lifting the gun up into Cully's face before Cully could even move.

Cully sat there for a minute, looking down the barrel of the pistol, scared shitless all of a sudden because he didn't know the man at all, didn't have any idea what was in his head. But not showing anything, thinking, Fuck it, maybe it was some kind of test, like down at Raiford you got to stare down another con, guy gonna kick your ass or maybe cut you if you make the wrong move. Dorrance, a guy that shot up speed limit signs in the middle of the day, maybe all he was doing was proving some goddamn point. But to Cully it didn't seem real. More like Dorrance could pull a gun out and shoot a sign to pieces because there wasn't much chance the sign was gonna shoot back. But still, the man was sitting there with a gun pointed in Cully's face.

He made himself sit still, ready to move if he had to, but not giving anything away either, while Dorrance started to smile, licking his lips and then pulling the hammer back on the pistol, laughing a little. And then, without any warning, before Cully even thought to make a move, he pulled the trigger.

Cully almost hit him. He could feel it, the adrenaline pumping through his veins because he hadn't thought Dorrance was gonna go that far. The sound of the hammer falling on the empty chamber, with Cully holding his breath, seemed almost as loud as the actual gunshots had. He forced himself to relax, telling himself the man was trying to be a bigshot, thought that was how you dealt with excons. What Cully wanted to do, was drive his fist through the man's face. Take that pistol away from him and make him eat it. But he didn't. He took a long breath and smiled at Dorrance, saying, "See, people do shit like that, somebody could wind up hurt."

Dorrance looked at him for a few seconds and then smiled, giving Cully a look like he hadn't thought about that before. Saying, "Yeah, I guess they could."

He put the gun on the seat next to him and then started the truck up again, putting it in gear but then turning to look at Cully for a minute before pulling back on the highway, telling him, "But what the hell, maybe it's just you and me, we're getting to know each other. No harm in that." He pulled out on the highway laughing, right in front of a station wagon with a woman and kids in it, the other car swerving to miss them and the woman leaning on her horn.

Cully looked behind them, at the station wagon, now way back behind them, like the woman was scared to get too close. And then he glanced at Herb, driving the truck like he hadn't even seen it. Cully, sitting there with his new boss, wondering, was the man crazy or what?

Cully thought Dorrance's place looked like one of those pictures you saw in a travel brochure. You picked one up, all shiny, with a picture

26

of a beach on the front cover, or maybe a boat, and then you turned the page. Inside was a full spread of a working plantation, with the white-pillared house in the foreground. Out back, on both edges of the picture, you could see fields, with rows and rows of corn, or cotton. Maybe they have a couple of people in the picture. A few blacks working the fields—but smiling—they had to be smiling, or else somebody might mistake them for slaves.

Cully sat in the truck while Dorrance pulled off of Highway 21 onto a long paved driveway. The driveway was about a quarter of a mile long, shielded from the sky by a row of moss-draped oak trees, and Dorrance began to point things out to Cully as they drove along. Cully didn't say anything as Dorrance showed him the fields of peanuts and the long rows of tobacco plants. He nodded when Dorrance said, "That's the hanging shed," telling Cully that when they harvested the tobacco it was brought to the shed to dry and then shipped to the Philip Morris plant.

Dorrance pointed to a huge apparatus made of connected pipes with automobile tires attached to it every twenty feet or so. "Irrigation. I've got to be able to move that whenever I want. Get it to different parts of the property."

Cully nodding again, sitting up in his seat to get a better view of the house. Not really caring that much but a little curious, because he couldn't nail it down. Dorrance—sometimes he seemed rich, talking about servants, and other times, driving in his beat-up Ford pick-up, with the smell of cow shit sticking to the inside of your nose, you couldn't tell if maybe he was gonna go broke any minute. He sat up in his seat when he saw the house, though.

The house made Cully think that maybe Dorrance was doing okay. It was huge. Just like the pictures Cully'd been thinking of. A big white house with two-story pillars running along the front. The driveway approached it from the right and swung around in a big circle. Off to the far side, maybe a hundred feet from the main house, was the garage. From where Cully sat in the truck, with Dorrance turning the wheel now and beginning to slow down as they got close, he could see a tennis court out back and one end of a swimming pool behind the garage. There was a row of palmetto trees running from the house over to the garage, like some kind of giant hedge, with the tops rustling in the wind, making the whole row look like a bunch of crazy, upside-down hula dancers.

Cully couldn't help himself. He said, "Jesus. Farming this good?"

Dorrance stopped the car and turned the key, not saying anything for a moment. Then he turned to Cully and said softly, "My family left me a little money." Saying it quickly, with a little half smile on his face, leaving Cully to look around once more and wonder, a little money? How much was a little money?

They both got out. Dorrance walked to Cully's side of the car and touched his arm, saying, "Let me show you around," then turning towards the front of the house to where the door was opening and a small black woman was coming out.

Dorrance smiled and said, "Ah, Amelia. This is Mr. Cullen. Cully. He'll be staying in the garage apartment. Could you take his bag over?"

The woman nodded, giving Cully a quick look, and then taking the bag from him. The two men waited a moment, watching the woman walk towards the garage, and then Dorrance said, "That's Amelia. The cook. I promise you won't be disappointed."

Cully nodded, staring after the black woman for a second, and then turned to look back at the house. He said to Dorrance, "You wanted to show me around."

"That's right." Dorrance smiled and said, "I'll give you the grand tour. Then I'll show you where you'll be staying, let you clean up." As he walked away from the house, with Cully following, he began a running commentary.

"What I do, mostly, is just oversee. I've got a foreman, Billy Eagle. You saw him last night at Casey's. He's around here somewhere. You'll meet him later." Dorrance stopped and looked at Cully, grinning. "He's a half-breed Indian but he knows farming. Without Billy, I don't think this place would last two weeks. He's got a way with him. If he can't make something grow, tell you when to fertilize, when to irrigate, or just when to leave things alone, well . . ." He gave his quick smile again, walking around the side of the house away from the garage, with Cully following. Dorrance pulled a cigar from his pocket and lit it while Cully walked along with his hands in the pockets of his jeans, enjoying the fresh air and

28

feeling the heat of the morning on the back of his neck. Glad just to be out of jail.

They came to the far side of the house and turned the corner, walking slowly now, with Cully looking past Dorrance out into the back yard, seeing one end of the tennis court and the beginnings of a cabana on the other side of the court.

Dorrance said, "My wife likes to play tennis. I don't play."

Cully nodded, not saying anything. Watching while the court came into full view and looking past it to the pool, seeing the whole thing for the first time, with the water hurting his eyes because it was so bright. He almost didn't see the woman at first, just had an image of someone moving over by the water. But then he saw her clearly. Thinking that Dorrance hadn't said anything about a daughter, he kept walking, with Dorrance at his side, watching the woman as she looked towards them. Seeing, out of the corner of his eye, Dorrance lifting a hand in greeting and the woman beginning to walk towards them, wearing a black bikini that was cut high on the hips. She had long legs that were very tan, like she spent a lot of time sitting out by the pool, and a thin waist. Small tits, but nicely shaped from what Cully could see. She had dark glasses on, big ones with lenses that covered the entire area around her eyes. With the earpieces disappearing into her long blond hair. Cully thought she looked like a movie actress he'd seen in a picture once, he couldn't think of the name of it, something with Robert De Niro, where he played Jake La Motta, the fighter. The woman by the pool looked like the actress in that movie, except without the overbite. But the same cheekbones. And the kind of body that seemed to glide along the ground. Cully couldn't take his eyes off of her. Walking along with her father he tried to come up with something to say.

And then Herb Dorrance, surprising the shit out of him, said, "Cully, I'd like you to meet my wife, Michelle."

Cully, not believing it at first because the girl looked like she was half of Dorrance's age. Staring at her and then looking back at Dorrance, seeing a look in the man's eyes like he was furious. Turning back to the woman and hearing Dorrance tell her, "Why'n't you go put something on."

CHAPTER

4

WHERE IT WAS, it was out on State Road 16. They don't even bother to give it a name. Just a stretch of blacktop under the Florida sun. Most people, they take the trouble to drive out there, they're going to the prison anyway. They know where they are. Raiford State Penitentiary.

You drive along and there it is. Looking right back at you. Jesus. A mile long. With the administration buildings on one side and the prison—sitting there like some kind of dinosaur—on the other side.

If you had a minute, maybe looked along the edge of the buildings, you'd see the guards in their towers. Each one of them with a 12 gauge. Or else an M-16. The fuckers had orders. You cross that line, just make the attempt, and they were gonna shoot you down. It wasn't a place you went on purpose. Down here, they didn't fuck around. They killed people. Ted Bundy. People like that. They picked the wrong place to get stupid.

They walked Benny along the first floor hall of D Block. His last day there and they used two guards—neither one of them came up to his chin—and shackled his wrists to a chain around his waist. He was, what, gonna make a break for it? Maybe take a couple of guards out and then try to go over the wall? Jesus. Shiteaters bust your ass from the minute you got there to the second you left.

He was jumpy. Walking along in his Calvin Kleins, tight fitting, that weren't jailhouse issue—something that Benny had paid a lot of money for but knowing it was worth it. On the outside, what he used to do, every night before he went to bed, he'd think about what it was he wanted to wear the next day. Watch the Nashville Channel on cable, see what Kenny Rogers, or Hank Jr. might have on. Today he had on a white cotton shirt. It had stitching embroidered along the collar, a row of gold leaves running down all the way to Benny's waist, and a girl playing a guitar, about twelve inches high, on the back.

You spend four years in a place, they're gonna try to make you wear prison denims. No way. Benny, what he wanted, he wanted to look like a country music star. It pissed him off, the only thing he couldn't get in here, since he got sent down, was a pair of nice shoes. Outside, before he came here, he could always tell what somebody was like by their shoes. Were they chicken shit, maybe they didn't give a fuck about anything, they wore a pair of shitty shoes.

They kept him moving, guiding him down the tier. He was talking a lot—not to the guards, fuck that—but walking along the row of cells he exchanged jokes with some of the other prisoners, the ones that weren't too pissed off that it was him that was getting out. Giving them his country grin, Hey, lookit, this is Glen Campbell here, saying ya'll have fun. Seeing some of them, the ones he had given shit to while he was here, glad to see him going, but not looking at him—not gonna say anything to him because, you do something like that and what happens? Benny, he gets in trouble on the outside and he gets sent back. If he remembers you bad-mouthed him, where would that leave you?

Every couple of minutes one of the guards would shove him, put a hand on his back, give him a push and say, "Shut the fuck up." Benny'd look at him and say, "Hey, sport, this is my big day." Being polite about it, but letting the guard know it wasn't gonna do any good to try to keep him quiet. Then he'd crack a smile, show everybody he didn't mean any harm.

They walked him out of D Block over to Receiving, stopping

every hundred feet or so to go through a locked gate, with Benny reading the signs as they went—for the last time—the one just before Receiving that said, NO VISITORS PAST THIS POINT! and the other one, just before you got to the small canteen by the visitors' room—ALL PERSONS SUBJECT TO SEARCH! Benny felt like laughing because in a couple of minutes he wouldn't have to worry about shit like that. He told his guards, "What do you think, I get outside, maybe I go into a restaurant, like anybody else. You think, when I leave, I'm gonna forget where I am, maybe drop my drawers so the waiter can look up my asshole, see if there's any silverware missing?" Laughing about it, looking at the guard and explaining, telling him, "I'm saying I might be so used to it by now . . ." Seeing the guard's face and giving up. Shaking his head and saying, "Sport, what you need is a sense of humor."

When they got to Receiving, Benny couldn't keep still. He kept shifting from one foot to another. If you saw him there, a big son of a bitch with wavy blond hair, you'd think he was some kind of movie star. Good-looking, with a strong jawline and a little scar right above his chin—it didn't take anything away from his looks. Women, when they saw him—Benny would maybe be on the other side of the room, posing, but not making a big deal out of it—they'd want to come on over and talk to him. Get to know him because he seemed like he could be fun. The kind of guy, if you're at a party, he's the one making everybody laugh. Until maybe something pissed him off. Somebody said the wrong thing and he went off. Changed into something else right in front of your eyes.

The guard carrying his folder stepped into the small room in front of Benny and handed the folder to the clerk. He came back outside and looked at Benny, saying, "Stand still, goddammit." Benny told him, "It's all right, sport."

He could taste it now. Five minutes. Five fucking minutes and he was gonna walk out that door a free man. Not gonna ever, no matter what, take shit from another man as long as he lived. Go on out there, to the free world, man, and get himself a new outfit. A couple of them, the kind of clothes, people see him they're gonna know he wasn't a loser. He'd been thinking about this day for four years, playing their game and dreaming of the day when he'd walk out of here and go get what was rightfully his. Gonna be a rich fucking man. Gonna make some people pay.

The other guard reached over and touched his shoulder, winking at his partner behind Benny and saying, "Hey, Benny, sometimes what happens, we get all the way down here, you know, with a con thinks he's on his way out. And something happens. Paperwork gets fucked up. Something like that. Next thing you know, that con's not getting out. We got to take him back upstairs. Sometimes it takes weeks to straighten out."

The second guard nodded. "Happens all the time."

Benny gave it a minute, thinking, Fuck them to death, but smiling, saying, "Hey, I could go along with that. Put me back up in that cell, there's a new guy back up there. I mean, sport, this is a nice piece of ass. . . . Maybe what I should do, I should go on back up there, see if I can't get him alone somewhere. Welcome him to Raiford."

The guards didn't like it; the one pushed him toward the counter and the other one told him to shut up again.

The man finished writing the check and then pushed a paper over towards Benny. "You got four hundred dollars coming to you. You got to sign for it."

Benny couldn't help himself. "Four hundred! What the fuck're you talking about? Man, I got a lot more than that. I bust my ass out in those fields for four years, I got a lot more than four hundred dollars coming to me."

The clerk looked at him and said, "You want to argue about it I'll put you back in that cell upstairs and you can sit there until a review board checks it out." He smiled. "It's up to you."

Benny stood there for a minute. Picturing in his head, if he could someday find these sons of bitches on the outside, show them what it would be like to meet when Benny wasn't tied up like a hog. Let them give him some shit then, see where it got them. He remembered all the money waiting for him on the outside, all he had to do was go get it, and thought, Fuck their four hundred dollars. He said, "Hey, sport, I tell you what, if you say it's four hundred dollars, I got to figure you're right."

The guard to his left fished a set of keys out of his pocket and leaned down and unlocked the handcuffs from Benny's belt chain. Benny took the pen from the clerk's hand and signed the release. The guard pushed the check across to Benny and then handed him a cardboard suitcase that had Benny's jeans and shirt from the day he was processed in.

The two guards that had brought him down from D Block took his arms again and walked him out of the room and across a short courtyard to the main gate.

"Hey, Benny," the one on his left said, "how long you think before you're back?" He looked at his partner. "Whaddya think, George, a month?"

George was unlocking the cuffs on Benny's wrists. When he was finished he stood back up and looked at the first guard. "A month? I don't know. If Benny manages to stay out for a month, hell, I'll be impressed."

Benny stood there, rubbing his wrists, while the two assholes had their fun. Already he could feel it. The difference. He was still in the prison, wasn't even out the main gate yet. But he could feel it, like jumping in the ocean, a different sensation against your skin. Freedom. He squinted up against the sun, knowing the gate behind him was open and he could walk out, and then looked at the two men next to him. He said, "I'll tell you what, sports, I guess it all depends. First thing I'm gonna do, I'm gonna go rape your mothers. They catch me doing that, well, maybe I'll be back."

He turned away from the guards, seeing one take a step towards him but then stop, and walked on out of the gate, a free man. He kept on going until he got to the bus stop a quarter of a mile from the prison. He didn't know when the bus was coming. Didn't care. It would be there sooner or later.

He had all the time in the world.

CHAPTER

5

CULLY LIT A cigarette and looked out the window of his little garage apartment. It wasn't bad, the place they'd given him to live. Two rooms, a bedroom and a little kitchen, with a table, a small stove, and a refrigerator. Next to the bedroom was a bathroom. There was a phone on the wall in the kitchen and a door in the bedroom that led to a little deck overlooking the back yard. Down below was the garage itself, with a black Cadillac and a dark blue Porsche, a 928, next to it.

It was almost dark and he'd just finished dinner, waiting for it until Amelia, the black cook, brought it over from the main house. Fried chicken that was pretty good and some vegetables—beans, which Cully ate, and some okra, which Cully couldn't even look at. He'd wondered, was that what they were eating up at the main house? He'd tried kidding Amelia about it, saying, "I don't want to find out they're getting something special, maybe more beans than me." But she'd just looked at him, not giving anything away, telling him, "You got an hour to eat. I come back in an hour to get the dishes. If you're not ready, you can wash 'em your own self."

He'd taken the tray back to the house, hadn't waited for Amelia to come to get it. And then wandered back to the garage, thinking what he'd really like was a couple of beers, and wondering, could he take a car back into town and get a six pack. Should he ask or could he just do it?

He turned the TV on, watching a game show where the contestants had to guess the price of the prizes. Cully, sitting there, was doing better than any of the people on TV because he used to spend time with a lot of B and E guys down at Raiford. They'd know what all that shit was worth, always talking about it, what you could get for a stereo, television, something like that, and what it was worth retail.

He got bored with it after a while and turned it off, sitting on the bed and trying to decide what he wanted to do next. It startled him when the light from the pool went on. He stood by the window, watching, until Michelle Dorrance walked out of the main house and over to the pool. She was wearing a long white robe and sandals and carried a drink in her hand. She walked the length of the pool and stood by the deep end. Cully kept looking at her. Every once in a while he'd glance back towards the French doors to see if maybe her husband was going to join her. But nobody else came outside.

Michelle set her drink down on the diving board and then kicked her sandals off. She swung her head, her hair shiny in the beginnings of the moonlight, and then loosened the belt of the robe, letting it fall to the ground and stepping away from it in one movement. She was wearing a white bikini this time, the starkness of it standing out against the night. He couldn't get over it, how gorgeous she was. Married to a guy like Dorrance. Guy twice her age. What the fuck did she do around here, watch the tomatoes grow?

For a minute he thought about what it would be like to go on out to the pool and talk to her—find out what was going on around here. He could picture it. He'd walk on over and she'd start to smile, tell him, I was hoping you'd come on down. And then she'd lose the bikini, take him by the hand and help him undress. They'd go skinny-dipping, swim all around that pool, and then he'd grab her, take her back up here.

He stopped thinking about it because it wasn't gonna happen. He saw her look at the main house and then she stepped to the side of the pool and dove in.

When she hit the water Cully moved over to the door of his room and opened it, stepping out onto the little balcony and sitting on the one chair that was there. He stayed like that, smoking cigarettes and watching the woman, until he heard a car pull up to the front of the house. He swung his gaze away from the pool and looked out at the driveway, seeing a Ford Bronco idling in front of the house and the Mexican-looking guy, the one that'd been in the bar the night before with Herb Dorrance, pop out of the driver's side and walk around to the other side of the car.

The man appeared a minute later holding the arm of a woman, a good-looking girl in her early twenties. Cully could hear her giggling, a little unsteady on her feet, wearing high heels and holding on to the Mexican, both of them walking through a splash of light from the front porch and then disappearing into the house.

A minute later the Mexican—or maybe he was an Indian, Cully still couldn't decide—came back out to the Bronco without the woman. Cully could see him inside the truck, looking at the house for a few seconds and then putting the truck in gear. He waited until the truck had disappeared down the driveway and then looked back at the pool. Watching the woman in the water, her swimming laps and him just looking, until she finally quit. She got out in the shallow end and then walked slowly over to the diving board and picked up her robe, holding it in her hand and not bothering to put it on. She picked up her drink, standing motionless for a minute, and then looked up towards Cully, lifting her glass to him. Holding it for a moment and smiling. Letting him know she knew he was there.

He didn't move until she was inside, watching her walk across the concrete deck of the pool towards the house and then getting up out of his chair and turning to go inside his room. He was almost back inside, halfway through the little balcony door, when he heard the giggling again. He stood there, looking back out across the pool, seeing where it was coming from finally, across the pool area. From the balcony directly across from his. Herb Dorrance and the giggler. The girl with a drink in her hand and Herb, he didn't look like he had much on besides a pair of bikini underwear, walking out onto the balcony from inside and sliding his arm around the girl's waist. Grabbing a tit and then looking out across the pool. Cully wasn't sure, could the man see him, standing there in the dark? Wondering about it, the man with another woman, right there in his own house, and his wife coming into the house, too. What was going on? And then deciding maybe he didn't really want to know.

Herb Dorrance watched it happen from his bedroom window.

He'd married Michelle, taken some time out of his life to show her there could be more in the world than trash like her first husband or the guy he'd just hired, Frank Cullen. He'd met her the first time at the bank, going in and spending a little time chatting with her. Flirting. And then, when her husband had robbed it and gotten caught—and she got fired—he'd seen her a couple of times around town.

He'd caught her act a few times. Michelle singing with a couple of guys backing her up. The first time, at the Yankee Tavern, he'd just wandered in to get a beer and see what was happening. The place had been full of Marines—shooting pool and yelling at Michelle while she stood up on the stage and sang her heart out.

He couldn't believe it, how good she was. Had a voice like an angel, singing old Patsy Cline tunes and some newer stuff by Dolly Parton. He'd sat in the back and listened. Jesus, looking at her under the lights, her body moving differently while she sang. Like being up there on the stage, in a smoky room with a bunch of guys watching her sing—it didn't matter that maybe the place was a dive—it did something to her. Swaying back and forth and dancing a little bit to the beat of the song. It was as if she were stripping, making love to the fucking microphone, every verse of the song was like another piece of her clothes she was taking off. It had been weird because back when he knew her from the bank, he'd thought she was attractive. Somebody to flirt with when he went to the bank. But nothing special. When he saw her sing, though, he had to have her.

But watching her now, the dumb cunt, slinking along the edge of the pool and holding her glass up to the redneck cracker across the way, Jesus. What the fuck did she think she was doing? Did she think she could do shit like that and he'd let it slide? He wondered, who was it she saw do that in a movie? Maybe Bette Davis, somebody like that?

He took a sip of his Cutty, looking back into the bedroom at the other woman, the whore that Billy Eagle had dropped off. The girl was pretty young, he had to give her that. But cheap looking. And drunk. You look at her, standing there, the brown roots starting to show in her peroxide hair, with a short leather skirt on and heels, they had to be at least five inches. And a halter top. She had a cigarette going, the ash was about an inch long at the end of it and as Herb watched, it fell on the carpet.

He shook his head, thinking he'd say something to Billy Eagle tomorrow. Talk to him and tell him, Maybe you're wearing sunglasses when you pick these bitches up, you can't see what they look like in the light? He told the girl, "Get an ashtray." She just looked at him, swaying a little bit on her feet, until he had to step back inside and get her one himself, a big smoked-glass ashtray that he felt like hitting her with. The bitch was gonna take his money, she oughtta learn how to behave.

He let her make a drink and then told her to come on out to the balcony, looking at Michelle down there and then telling the blonde, "There, that's what you're gonna do." Watching while the woman looked down at his wife and then turned back to him and said, "Whatever you want, honey."

They watched Michelle walk back towards the house and then Herb stepped back into the room and took his bathrobe off. Standing there, naked except for a pair of silk bikini panties that belonged to his wife, hearing Michelle come into the house, listening to the sound of her bare feet pad up the stairs. Thinking about it, getting mad again. She wanted to flirt, maybe let other guys know what they were missing. What he had to do, every once in a while, he had to remind her who she belonged to.

He went back out onto the balcony and walked up to the blond woman, stepping up to her and sliding his arm around her shoulder and grabbing one of her tits, sliding his hand inside her halter top and squeezing her boobs. Looking past her at the garage and seeing the dim outline of Frank Cullen, still out on the garage balcony.

Motionless. He almost said something, knowing the man was looking at him, but then thought, Fuck it, let the asshole wonder what was going on. Seeing Cully step back into his room and then forgetting about him, because he heard his wife out in the hallway.

Michelle walked through the house with her bikini on, didn't give a damn if maybe she was getting the carpet wet. She dropped her robe on the living room floor and kept going, leaving footprints on the Oriental rug and then making her way upstairs, down the hallway to the room where her husband slept. Seeing Herb, all the way across the room, closing the doors to the balcony and stepping inside. Jesus, wearing a pair of her panties again, black ones that were tiny enough that they didn't even hold his pecker in that well, one of his balls was hanging out. It looked stupid, a fifty-year-old guy, he was wearing her underpants, with a nut hanging out. Giving her one of his smiles and walking across the room towards her. He had a look on his face she recognized, knew what it was that he wanted.

She forced herself to smile at him. Stretched her arms above her head and said, "Were you looking at me from out there? Watching while I took a swim?" Acting it out, for Christ's sake, but wondering, how could she get out of it? Get the hell out of the room and into her own bed.

He came back into the room and said, "I was getting some air."

"Uh-huh." She took a step into the room. Put more of a drawl in her voice, a southern gal who would just love to fuck him but was maybe a little too tired. Maybe he'd buy it, let her go to bed.

But he just looked at her. She should've known he wasn't going to let it go. She could see it, in a minute, what he would do, he'd have her going through the whole act. Do the same thing she'd always done since she had let him take her to that shitty little motel room the first time. She didn't feel like it at all.

Thinking, get it over with as quickly as possible, going through with it, she told him, "I can see it. You got that look in your eyes."

She walked towards him, gliding across the floor, until she was next to him. Reaching up to touch his face, running her hand along his cheek and beginning to sing softly, a song she heard Emmylou Harris do one time. Getting the words mixed up at first but then getting it right, stepping back from Herb, still singing, with Herb starting to nod as she gave it a little something. Feeling it, like the way it had been four years before. She'd be in a club, with a bass and somebody on drums, a lead guitar and maybe a steel string if they were lucky.

She moved further away from him, singing loudly now, like he wasn't even there, thinking about it, listening to her own voice. God, it was still good. Clear, with a nice country twang to it, a little bit like Crystal Gayle, or maybe even Emmylou herself. She wondered, maybe sometime, what she might do, she might go back to it. If she ever got away from Herb, what she could do was to see if maybe she could get a band going. It had been fun, standing up in front of the lights. You could pretend you were at the Opry instead of in some little bar.

She reached behind her and undid the bra of her bathing suit. Let it drop, seeing Herb's eyes widen. Coming to the end of the song, "My Dear Companion," that was the name of it. Turning away from him, like he wasn't even there. Pretending she was alone, because he liked it that way, liked to watch her move around the room without her top on, like he was outside the window. Like a goddamn Peeping Tom. She gave it another minute and then wriggled out of the bottom of her suit, taking her time—stripping—making it seem harder than it was.

She could see him out of the corner of her eye, coming over to her. She turned, with a surprised look on her face, putting a lot into it, because now that it had started it was hopefully gonna be over in about a minute. Playing her part, a housewife maybe, somebody alone at home and all of a sudden she sees somebody else is there. Saying, "Herb, what are you doing home?" Making herself forget how ridiculous he looked in her black silk undies. Playing the game and letting him squeeze her titties while she reached down and put her hand between her legs, arching her back. Letting him hear her moan and then touching him, getting mad all of a sudden because he was still soft. She looked down at his little shriveled-up pee-pee, hiding there underneath the black silk. The thing looked unconscious.

She said, "Shit." But then looked up at him quickly because it was a stupid thing to say. But he was grinning, doing it on purpose maybe, to let her know that it wasn't a big deal, he could stay soft because she didn't excite him that much. All part of the game he played. He was proving some goddamn point.

She told him, "Hey, hon, it's okay. All we got to do is wake it up."

He had that tone in his voice, furious, like he was gritting his teeth. Saying, "See, you're always doing that, complaining. Telling me it's okay, everything's gonna be fine." He smiled a little bit and told her, "You think, what, I'm going to make you work for it? Make you break a sweat when there isn't any need for it." He turned away from her and walked on over to the balcony and opened the doors. She felt like saying something. Maybe tell him she didn't feel like it anyway. They could try again the next night. Or maybe tell him there wasn't ever gonna be a next night, see how that went over. Getting the words together in her head because she really didn't want to do it, didn't want to touch him ever again. But then she saw the girl come in from the balcony.

Already Michelle was starting to shake her head, saying no. Talking to his back, saying, "Goddamn it, Herb."

Herb, ignoring her, walked the blonde over to his wife and then went back to sit on the bed.

Michelle said it again, louder, saying, "Herb, Jesus."

But her husband, reaching down to touch himself now, his pecker no longer sleepy, was already starting to smile at the two women, saying, "Ain't this nice."

The blond woman looked at Herb for a couple of seconds, waiting until he made a movement with his hands, looking at the whore and saying, "Come on." The woman turned to Michelle, standing there like she couldn't move, watching the whore's hand come up slowly and touch one of her tits, seeing the girl's face from close up, looking at a row of blackheads on the bridge of the woman's nose. And hearing Herb, in the background, say, "This is what you do, it's how you earn that money I give you."

Michelle, standing there, naked, with the other woman touching both her breasts now, wanting to run out of there but knowing she didn't have anywhere to go. Hearing the whore giggle and tell her, "Hey, you got a nice voice, you know that?"

The phone in Cully's garage apartment rang twenty minutes later. It startled him at first because he had forgotten there was a phone in the room. For a minute he couldn't think of who would be calling him but then he figured it must be someone from the main house. He picked it up, half wondering, maybe it was going to be Herb Dorrance telling him he'd better stop watching his wife swim. It was Dorrance all right. But all he wanted was to tell Cully to be ready to take his wife shopping in the morning. Cully listened to the man talk, his drawl, picturing him over in the main house with his wife and the other woman, the man in his black bikini underwear.

Dorrance said, "She's going to want to leave around nine o'clock."

Cully told him, "All right." Then he thought about it and asked, "Which car do I take?"

Herb sounded impatient. "The Cadillac. You'll find the keys to both cars hanging on a board in the garage. After you get back you can look around, get comfortable with what we have here."

Cully said, "Okay," but heard the click of the phone being put down even as he said it.

CHAPTER

6

THEY WERE DRIVING towards town, with Cully at the wheel of the Caddy and Michelle in the backseat, looking at him in the rearview mirror. Michelle asked him, "They call you Cully?"

He didn't know, was he supposed to say, Yes, ma'am, something like that? He'd gotten pretty used to doing it, down at Raiford, where you call all the guards Sir. But it bothered him, seeing her in the backseat, good-looking woman and him not sure how to answer. Finally he just smiled and said, "That's right, Cully."

"Short for Frank Cullen. Right?"

He nodded. "That's right."

She smiled now, letting a few seconds pass before she spoke again, and then saying, "Late of Raiford State Penitentiary. Is that right? Frank Cullen . . . Cully . . . ex-convict." Saying it slowly, with a lot of sarcasm. It sounded almost like a little kid calling somebody names.

He didn't say anything, couldn't think of a good reply. They were headed towards Beaufort because she wanted to go to a couple of different stores that morning. They'd just passed the Whale Branch River, on Highway 21, where the state was putting in a new bridge and the traffic was down to two lanes, with the oncoming cars whipping past Cully's window at sixty miles an hour. He had to concentrate on his driving.

Already he was a little pissed because she'd made him wait for almost an hour and a half this morning, telling him to be ready by nine o'clock and then not showing up until almost ten-thirty. He'd gotten up and gotten dressed—found a suit of clothes hanging in the short hallway outside his room. He didn't know when it'd been put there but it'd fit perfectly and he'd assumed it was his new chauffeur outfit. It felt strange, wearing a suit and tie. It bothered him, made him feel like he couldn't breathe, and before Michelle had even come out of the main house he'd loosened the tie and unbuttoned the top of the shirt. He walked around the Caddy, brushing it off with an old towel he found, smoking cigarettes and waiting for her. When he finished that he walked back inside the garage and did the same thing with the Porsche.

There hadn't been any sign of the other woman and when Michelle had finally come out she hadn't said anything to him except to tell him to drive into Beaufort, barely looking at him after she'd said good-bye to her husband. Cully had held the door of the Caddy for her and she'd walked right by him, wearing a short leather skirt and a white silk blouse, giving him a taste of her perfume and showing a lot of thigh when she slid into the back of the Caddy. Now she was asking about his name, letting him hear the scorn in her voice.

She didn't say anything else until they were across from the Marine Air Station. They were sitting at the light. Cully, glancing to his left, was looking at the three jet fighters by the main gate of the air station and trying not to look in the mirror. He could almost feel her eyes on him and didn't know what to do about it. It was starting to bother him. She could sit back there and make remarks all day long and what was he gonna do? If it was somebody else, another con back at Raiford, or else just somebody Cully had met in a bar, something like that, the conversation never would have gotten this far. Cully would have put a stop to it.

When the light turned green she learned forward in the seat just as he was hitting the gas. She spoke softly, almost in his ear, with him breathing her perfume and her saying, "Why is it, I wonder, that my husband hired an ex-convict to drive me around?"

He glanced in the mirror. Watched her settle back in her seat and then he shrugged. He didn't know what to say about her husband. Maybe if he told her he thought Herb was an asshole she'd get mad. So all he said was, "I don't know. I guess your husband's one of those people, he believes in giving somebody a chance."

He could see her raise her eyebrows. "Is that what you think it is? You don't think, maybe, what it is, he wants to surround himself with people he thinks are losers?"

Cully, trying not to lose his temper, shrugged, turning his eyes back to the road, not wanting to give her the satisfaction of an answer.

He slowed the Caddy down because they were coming to a speed zone. He drove past the National Cemetery and the public tennis courts and then had to hit the brakes because a Greyhound was making the left into the bus station and Cully didn't see it at first because he'd been looking in the mirror again. Cully, sitting there in the shiny black Cadillac, breathing bus exhaust and getting madder all of a sudden, thought, Fuck it, first he had to listen to the bullshit her husband had to say and now she was giving him this crap. He wheeled the Caddy around the bus and gunned it across the street to the little parking lot by the public tennis courts, sending up a cloud of dust because he locked the brakes, and skidded to a stop. He shut the car off and turned in the seat.

"Look, I don't know, maybe you got a reason to needle me. The thing is, I don't know you. I don't know your husband. He wants me to work for him, that's fine. He thinks I'm gonna drive you around, listen to your shit for two bills a week, it ain't gonna happen."

She didn't say anything for a minute, just sat in the backseat of the Caddy looking at Cully with a half smile on her face. Taking her time about answering. Cully could see it, she was playing some kind of game, like she was an actress, something like that. Waiting for the tension to build and then giving him a big smile and saying, "Cully, you take things too seriously."

She turned in her seat until she was facing the tennis courts, making a big deal out of it, leaving him to sit there uncomfortably, until he thought, the hell with it, started the Caddy up again, and pulled out onto Carteret Street.

Benny saw the Cadillac parked across the street from the bus station. But it didn't mean anything, he couldn't see who was inside, and besides, he was feeling like shit from sitting on the bus with a hangover.

He'd taken the bus from outside Raiford, going into Miami and then hopping a Greyhound, riding it all the way to Savannah the day before and then heading down to River Street, where all the bars were. Walking along River Street, remembering when he was younger, they'd come on down here from Beaufort, a bunch of guys maybe, or else Benny by himself. Drink beer all night and try to get laid.

If they couldn't get laid they'd go from bar to bar, looking for a fight. Benny would wait until he saw some guy alone, a loser, maybe with some slut, and then move up to the bar to stand next to them. Give it a couple of minutes and then nudge the guy's elbow, make the son of a bitch spill beer on himself, and then ask him, Was he gonna pay for Benny's jacket or what?

The guy would be looking at Benny, not knowing what to do because it was his jacket, not Benny's, that had beer on it. Pissed off maybe, but worried, too, because even back then Benny was pretty big. Benny'd give it another couple of seconds, enjoying it, and then deck the guy. Put a couple of moves on him, like that guy in a movie he'd seen once, Chuck Norris. Son of a bitch knew how to fight. Benny would kick the shit out of the guy while the girl stood there screaming, looking around to see if somebody was gonna help her faggot boyfriend. He liked it, watching the girl scream, while her boyfriend lay on the ground.

He walked along the street outside the bars and watched the crowds, waiting for his chance. Seeing a guy finally that looked good. Looked pretty easy. The guy looked like he had money, too. All dressed up in pre-washed jeans and a nice sweater. With a leather jacket on his shoulders. Benny didn't care about the jacket, it looked too small anyway. But the guy had on a pair of boots, cowboy boots, that Benny kind of liked. The kind that looked like they were made out of lizard skin, with real pointy toes and two-inch heels.

Benny went up to him after a while, smiling, being nice, but already wanting to do him because the guy was an asshole. He had foam above his lips from the drink and kept looking past Benny, looking around the bar to see if there were any girls and not paying any attention when Benny said hello. Benny stood next to him, getting a beer, and then turned, smiling like he was seeing the guy for the first time. And then telling him, "Hey, sport, those are some slick boots." Asking, "Where'd you get 'em?" The guy didn't give it much, looking at Benny finally and saying, "I bought them." Being rude about it. But Benny had to know, thinking he was right but asking, "Yeah, what size are they?" Thinking the guy was gonna tell him to fuck off. Make Benny do it right there, which would've pissed him off because then he couldn't take the boots. But finally the guy told him, saying, "Eleven," and then walking off. Benny finished his beer and followed, smiling, thinking, Hot dog, eleven.

He did the guy in an alley, walking up to him when the guy was pissing, getting rid of all those fucking piña coladas or whatever they were. Not even seeing Benny until he hit him, smashing him in the kidneys as hard as he could and then hitting him in the head a couple of times, letting him go down and then pulling the boots off and trying them on, smiling because they fit. Going through the guy's pants and grinning, saying, "Hot dog" again, because he had a couple of hundred bucks in his wallet. Benny almost walked away then, thinking that he'd let the guy go but then he went back and tried out his new boots, kicked a couple of field goals with the asshole's face because he'd been rude back there in the bar. Standing there in the alley, rubbing the boots with the guy's sock to get the blood off and saying, "All I was doing was being nice, being polite, back there in the bar, sport. And all you are is rude. And lookit you now."

He walked back out onto River Street and blended into the crowd, going into a bar further down and getting pretty drunk on Seagram's whiskey. Pretty happy about it, smiling at people and being polite, now that he had some money, making friends and finally picking up a junkie whore, taking her to a motel and giving her fifty dollars. He made her take it up the ass, enjoying it, because he could tell she didn't want to, but she was hurting, needing the money. Saying all right finally and then almost screaming when Benny did it. Benny taking his jeans off to fuck the girl, but putting the lizard-skin boots back on, digging the toes into the mattress while the girl yelled. They were pretty nice boots.

Now he was in Beaufort, a little hung over maybe, but it didn't matter. He was here. No more waiting, no more bowing to guards and watching his ass all day long so some psycho jig didn't stick a knife in it. He was gonna hang around just long enough to get his money. There was no way anybody was gonna stop him.

The first thing he had to do was find a place to stay. He could go on down to the garage, look his brother up and maybe stay with him. But he wanted privacy. After four years of living with a couple of thousand other men he wanted to be alone for a little while.

He left the bus station and started walking down Carteret Street towards Dave Ross's garage. He hadn't heard from his brother Earl for a couple of months. But he couldn't imagine Earl had left town. What he'd do was, he'd look him up, borrow some money against that four-hundred-dollar prison check.

He watched the Cadillac go down the street, admiring it, the sleek shiny lines of the big car, smiling, thinking it was what he would buy. A big car like that, maybe get somebody to drive him around, sit in the back, maybe with a bar. With a tape deck in it, put some Randy Travis on it and roll the windows all the way up, let the fucking thing blast. And maybe a couple of ladies, one on each side of him, holding on to him and pressing their titties up against his arms.

Smiling because it was all right, he could think like that now. He was back and all that money was waiting for him. Putting him in a good mood.

He looked across the street, seeing a store that sold clothes. He crossed over and looked in the window. And then he went inside, seeing a nice-looking woman come over to him, a little old for him, midforties, maybe she was somebody's mother, had a part-time job while the kiddies were in school. Still, she was pretty good-looking, with a nice figure and a pretty dress on. Benny liked it, he figured it was nice to see a woman who tried hard, maybe worked out to Jane Fonda on video a couple of times a week. He said, "Hey, hun-bun." She smiled at him and he said, "I like it, you go into a men's clothing store, and instead of some guy coming out, maybe he doesn't know what'll look good on me, I got you." She smiled even more, saying, "Well, that's a refreshing thing to hear." Benny took a step closer to her and touched her lightly on the arm, telling her, "Hun-bun, I'd rather have a woman help me dress any day." Winking at her because she wasn't moving away from him and she was beginning to laugh. Saying, "Especially a pretty gal like yourself." Giving her his best smile. Benny, standing there with his teeth sparkling because that was one thing, you spend time in prison, all that free dental work, you come out with a nice smile. Asking, "You got anything that'd look good with lizard-skin boots?"

When he came out he started to walk towards Dave Ross's garage again. Not paying any attention to anything around him. Not seeing the Ford Bronco sitting on the other side of the Greyhound lot, with Billy Eagle in the driver's seat, an Atlanta Braves cap on his head, looking at Benny as he walked down Carteret Street. Billy, thinking Herb had been right, telling him to come on down here and see if Benny showed up, had sat there all morning, waiting for the first bus from Savannah. Not seeing Benny on that one and then going to get breakfast, taking his time, eating eggs and grits, seeing a couple of people he knew down at the Huddle House and then coming back to catch this bus, the only other one that came in from Georgia that day. Being patient about it, because he could still remember Benny, knew what he was like and figured if he was gonna come back to town, which Billy was pretty sure he was, it was gonna be on a bus.

Billy Eagle started the Bronco and pulled into traffic, driving past Benny and taking a look at him, seeing him the way he had been four years before. Mean. Only now, spending that time on the work farm, with four years to think about it, Benny was more than likely gonna be even meaner.

Billy figured the thing he should do was tell Herb Dorrance that Benny was back in town. Mr. Dorrance would know what to do.

Cully watched Michelle, thinking that she acted like a queen. He'd drop her off outside a store and she'd walk in. He could see, through the windows of the stores, she'd enter and within seconds she'd have two, maybe three clerks fighting over her. He'd sit out in the Caddy, listening to the radio while she tried things on. After a little while she'd come on out, followed by a salesman carrying boxes. Cully would get out of the car, go on around and unlock the trunk and put the packages in.

Finally she told him, "I'm thirsty." She'd been shopping for about three hours, and she came out and got in the car, with him holding the door for her and waiting for her to tell him where to go next. She said, "I need a drink." She told him where to drive, directing him back Route 21 to the Ramada Inn and telling him to pull into the lot.

When he parked she opened the door for herself and then leaned back into the Caddy and said, "You gonna sit there or are you gonna come in and have a drink with me?" He'd looked at her, thinking what he'd like to do was to tell her to fuck off. But he had to go to the bathroom and he could use a drink and maybe something to eat. He got out and followed her across the parking lot.

Inside the Ramada Inn it was air-conditioned. The bar was dimly lit, with a bunch of plastic plants in the corners and more hanging from the ceiling. There were a man and a woman at a table over in the corner and a couple of men, serious drinkers, at the bar itself. He followed Michelle to a table in the center of the room. She sat down, lit a cigarette, and smiled at him. They were getting some looks, Cully in his suit, and Michelle, turning heads when they walked in and then sitting down like she owned the place, not even looking at the bar, knowing the bartender was on his way over.

Cully was wondering, was this something she did a lot? Go shopping and then stop to.have a drink, not getting past the cliché: a woman coming into a bar by herself, what was she really looking for? Before they put him in Raiford, if he walked into a bar, maybe he was only there to have a couple of drinks, but it was always in the back of his mind—if he saw a good-looking woman by herself, he'd give it a try.

The bartender took their orders, Michelle asking for a Manhattan and Cully, after thinking about it for a minute, saying he'd have a beer. Michelle kept smiling at him and finally said, "See, back there in the car, when you got pissed, all it was, was me trying to find out about you." She leaned forward in her chair, putting her elbows on the table and showing Cully a little cleavage, the white shirt she was wearing opening up just enough for Cully to see the tops of her tits and some kind of silk thing, a teddy, he thought it was called, underneath. She told him, "What do you expect. I'm going to be driven around by someone, I oughtta get to know them."

Cully was thinking it was gonna be hard to stay ahead of this woman. She was gonna keep changing, be a bitch one minute, come out sounding like a concerned friend the next. Playing some kind of game, maybe just bored, living on the farm with the tomatoes and her older husband. He took a sip of his beer and said, "You want to find out about me, all you have to do is ask." But smiling at her, not willing to let her do the same thing she had done at the tennis courts, let her piss him off again.

She told him, "But that's what I was doing." Nodding her head and smiling. She took a sip of her Manhattan, holding the liquid in her mouth, swirling it around and then swallowing, smiling in satisfaction and then looking at Cully. She said, "You ever just get the feeling, maybe it's the middle of the day, and all you can think about is how good it would feel to have a drink?"

He nodded. "Sure."

She took another sip; already the level in her glass was low. She looked at it, holding the glass up and then finishing what was left, looking towards the bar, where the bartender was already coming around, walking towards her and taking the glass from her hand. She waited for him to bring back a fresh one and then turned to Cully.

She took a sip and then said, "I want to ask you something."

"Go ahead."

She smiled. "I don't know, I want to ask, but I think maybe you'll get mad at me again." Saying it with a little bit of a laugh in her voice, teasing him.

He said, "How about this—you go ahead and ask. Instead of getting mad, if I don't want to answer I just won't. How would that be?"

She laughed softly. "That'd be fine." She moved in her chair and for a second Cully could feel her leg against his. She made no sign that she noticed but then she moved again and the pressure of her leg was gone.

She said, "What'd you go to jail for?"

"Prison."

She looked at him. "What?"

"Prison. Jail is where they put you if you have too much to drink on a Friday night. They catch you driving your car DUI, maybe you hit a stop sign or run a red light. Something like that. They put you in jail. Prison is a different idea altogether. Got a whole different feel to it."

She was staring at him, nodding a little. He could feel it. She wasn't playing with him now. He could see the fascination in her eyes. It wasn't the first time. It had happened before. Some women, it didn't matter who they were, they find out you've done serious time and it turned them on. Or at least they were interested. They wanted to know all about it. Wanted to ask you things like what was it like to spend all those years behind bars? Wanted to know about sex, ask you, What'd you do?

He took a sip of his beer and looked at her. "You want to know why I got sent to Raiford?"

She nodded. "If it doesn't make you mad to tell me."

He thought about it, wondering why would he want to tell her, because he knew that he did. Sitting there at the table, with Herb Dorrance's wife. He wasn't even sure was he doing the right thing. Was it part of his job, if she wanted a drink, was he supposed to go with her, have a few beers while she had her lunchtime Manhattans? And why was it he wanted to tell her anyway, maybe he wanted to impress her? If she was gonna try to make fun of it, act snotty about him being in Raiford, maybe he'd tell her what it was really like.

He said, "I robbed places."

"With a gun?"

"That's right. I'd go into a place, a liquor store, someplace like that, show the people a gun and they'd give me their money."

"And you got caught?"

"Eventually."

"What happened?"

He thought about it, remembered coming out the back of a bar and seeing all those cops. He'd gone in, knowing it was stupid, because a bar was a dangerous place to rob. Worse than banks. Too many chances of things going wrong, somebody with a little too much booze in them, maybe they'd decide to play hero. He remembered how it had been, sticking the .357 in the bartender's face. Seeing the man's whole expression change, like all of a sudden he could see life from a different perspective. Both of them scared. Cully, because it always scared him. And the bartender, because the barrel of that .357 looked like a fucking cannon from that close.

And then going out the back. He had scored maybe four hundred dollars and then run right into the cops. They were waiting for him because he hadn't seen, back by the bathroom inside the bar, some asshole on the pay phone, talking to his girlfriend. The girlfriend had heard what was going on, the sound of Cully's voice loud enough for her to pick up over the line. She'd called the cops and they'd been waiting outside. With their guns out, wanting Cully to try something. Ready for it, he could see it in their faces. All they wanted was for Cully to move, take a step in any direction, and they were gonna blow him away. He'd dropped the .357 and stood there, not even fucking breathing.

He looked at the woman across from him. There was a sheen of sweat above her lip. He didn't know, maybe she was just a little hot, sitting there in the air-conditioned bar at the Ramada Inn and perspiring. He said, "What always happens. I was in the wrong place at the wrong time."

She looked at him. Her eyes were a little funny; maybe she was feeling those Manhattans on an empty stomach. It was like she couldn't quite focus. Before he could move she reached across and touched him, letting her hand rest on his for a second and then

54

moving back, picking up her drink and tasting it before asking him, "What did it feel like? Going in to those places. With a gun. What did it feel like?"

He gave it a couple of seconds, made it seem like he had to think it over even though he didn't. You could make a lot of money, you had the balls to go into a place with a gun. Sometimes it didn't work out. If you went into a bar, or maybe a 7-Eleven, someplace like that, and business had been slow, or else maybe the owner was dumping most of the night's take into a one-way safe, maybe then it wasn't worth it. Even if the cops weren't waiting for you, you'd only get maybe two or three hundred dollars and that wasn't worth the risk.

But other times—Cully had to admit, a lot of times—you go on in, wave a pistol around—try to be nice about it but, still, let the people know who was in control—and you were liable to walk out with anywhere from one to two grand. Twenty minutes' work, which wasn't bad if you figured it as an hourly wage. But the thing was, sitting there, in the Ramada Inn, sipping his beer and looking at the attractive girl across from him, seeing her eyes a little shiny with the thought of it, the romance, maybe she thought he was some kind of Robin Hood, except he didn't give the money to anyone. But from the first time he'd ever done it he'd always felt the same thing, always had the same feeling in his gut, walking into a place and reaching down to his belt to pull his magnum out. It'd never changed.

He told her, "It scared the shit out of me."

CHAPTER

7

WALKING BACK OUT to the car she told him, "I want you to meet someone." She was weaving a little bit, not enough so a stranger would notice but Cully, walking next to her, could see it. She was carrying a plastic glass with a Manhattan in it; the bartender had given it to her. Twice on the way out to the Caddy she brushed against Cully, both times smiling and looking up at his face. He held the door for her and then walked around to the front of the car.

She said, "Go through town and across the river." And then she'd sat there, while Cully wheeled the big car around and headed back into Beaufort, coming to the Beaufort River finally and crossing the bridge. He drove along Route 21 across Lady's Island, past the Winn-Dixie supermarket and then onto St. Helena's Island, watching the stores disappear behind them, occasionally looking in the mirror where Michelle was sipping her drink and humming softly to herself. He didn't know where they were going, but he thought maybe she wanted to go to the beach, which was gonna be the only choice they had pretty soon. But he didn't care. She wanted to drive around all day, it was okay with him.

But she sat up finally. He could see the bridge to Harbor Island, the one just before the state park, maybe a mile ahead, when she suddenly sat forward and said, "There. Pull in there," pointing towards a little seafood restaurant that was the last building on the road before you hit the Harbor Island bridge.

He slowed the Caddy and pulled off onto the dirt-covered parking lot at the restaurant. It was a little place, painted gray, with olive green shrimp netting hanging on the walls outside the building and a big slab of wood over the door where somebody had carved THE SHRIMP BOAT in big letters.

Cully got out and waited for Michelle to come around to his side of the car. She smiled at him and said again, "I want you to meet someone," taking his arm and leading him up the steps to the screened-in door.

It was the kind of place where you went up to a window, ordered your food, and then ate it sitting at one of several benches along the wall or else at one of the tables in the center of the room. There were only two other people inside, an older couple sitting by themselves over in the far corner. As Cully and Michelle walked in, the couple got up and, carrying their trash, walked past Cully. The man dumped his trash and gave Cully a nod. Cully smiled at him and then turned to Michelle, saying, "You hungry?" Not sure why they were there.

She ignored him and went up to the window, leaning down and yelling, "Kristin" loudly. Giving it a second and then yelling the name again. Cully thought she was pretty drunk because it didn't seem to bother her—she looked like a million bucks in her short skirt and her silk blouse, wearing four-inch heels on her feet—yelling in public and making a little bit of a scene.

A moment later a door against the far wall opened and a woman walked out. Cully didn't even have to think about it; he knew it was Michelle's sister. A couple of years older, maybe, but with the same good looks, the same cheekbones and long blond hair. She was dressed in blue jeans and a man's T-shirt and had a white apron tied around her waist. And she had bright red lipstick on, with a couple flecks of it on her teeth. It didn't look right, didn't go with the apron and the jeans. The apron had spots of cooking grease on it and what looked like patches of bread crumbs sticking to it in a couple of places.

The woman glanced at Cully and then walked towards Michelle. When she spoke Cully could hear something in her voice, he didn't know what it was, anger maybe, or else just worry.

She walked over to Michelle and said, "What are you doing?" But giving it a little smile.

Michelle said, "I'm driving around town." She laughed and looked at Cully, saying, "Not driving. Being driven. And I thought I'd stop by." She put a hand on her sister's arm and said, "I wanted to introduce Cully to you." She turned and pointed at Cully. He was standing there, feeling a little foolish because he didn't know what to do.

He said, nodding at the sister, "How're you?" Feeling a little bad because the sister gave him a look, staring at him for a second like she could tell Michelle was drunk and it was Cully's fault.

Michelle took a step towards Cully. She said, "Cully, this is Kristin. Kristin, this is my chauffeur, Cully."

Kristin nodded at Cully and then took her sister by the arm, leading her over to the table and saying, "I was going to have a cup of coffee. How about it? You want to have a cup of coffee?" She turned towards the window and said to someone in the back, "Grace, can we have two coffees out here?"

Cully stood there, feeling out of place, watching the two women sit down and then seeing a huge black woman come out from the back with two Styrofoam cups in her hand. He cleared his throat and said, "I'm gonna go wait in the car."

Michelle gave him a look, he thought maybe she was going to argue, but her sister just nodded, not really paying any attention to him. She was busy, leaning towards Michelle and ripping open a couple of packets of sugar, stirring them into her sister's cup and beginning to talk softly to her.

He walked out to the Caddy, hearing the screen door slam behind him and feeling the heat of the sun on the back of his neck. He saw a pamphlet stuck underneath the windshield wiper of the Caddy and pulled it out. Loosening his tie, he opened the door of the Caddy and looked at the pamphlet, seeing it was an advertisement for a circus that was going to be in town for the next week. He glanced through it, trying not to look over at the two women and wondering what it would be like to have a life where all you had to do to enjoy yourself was go to the circus.

After about twenty minutes, the women walked out to the car. Cully hopped up and opened the door for Michelle. He stood there while the two sisters said good-bye and then closed the door. He waited for a second, wanting to say something to Kristin, but nothing came to mind. Finally he just nodded. He was stepping away from her, ready to go back to the driver's seat, when she touched his arm. He turned and found himself pinned by her eyes. Big beautiful eyes. Cully looking into them, seeing a strand of hair in front of them, a loose blond tail, coming down from her forehead and moving in the wind, wanted to touch it, reach out and push it back from her face.

She looked at him for another second and then smiled, saying, "Thank you."

He didn't know what to say. He stood there, waiting, until she turned back to the restaurant and started up the stairs. He shrugged, getting back in the car, looking in the mirror and asking, "Where to?" Waiting for a reply but not getting one.

He gave it another minute, looking at her as she sat curled in the backseat, finally meeting his eyes and saying, "Home." Then she started to sing, not sounding drunk at all, her voice surprising the shit out of Cully because it was so good.

He looked in the mirror, seeing her back there with her eyes closed and her head thrown back, getting a little louder now. Going through a whole bunch of songs, "My Dear Companion" and "I'm Willing." Cully recognized those, and then a couple he didn't know. She sang "When a Man Loves a Woman," which was one of Cully's favorites, and which he would've said no woman could do right, except it didn't sound bad coming from the backseat of the Caddy. She did "Too Much to Ask," with a catch in her voice like Kelly Willis would've had. And then she opened her eyes, looking at him in the mirror and saying, "I can do rock," closing her eyes again and singing, "Will You Love Me Tomorrow" by the Shirelles and "Crimson and Clover," making her voice deep, sounding almost like Tommy James.

She'd sing a little of one and then get tired of it, or else forget the words, Cully couldn't tell, keeping it up almost the whole way home, taking a break every once in a while, with her eyes closed. Cully would think maybe she was gonna take a nap, see her there with her eyes still closed. And then she'd start singing again, not paying any attention to him, until he could see the driveway to the house maybe a quarter of a mile ahead and suddenly she was leaning forward in her seat, breathing on him.

He could smell the liquor on her breath, looking at her in the mirror and hearing her say, "My husband, you think he's doing you a favor, giving you this job?" She met his gaze in the mirror, pointing with her thumb to behind the car, and said, "Back there, that's what you said. You said, 'Maybe your husband, he believes in giving somebody a chance.'" She laughed in his ear and then said, "Un-uh, he ain't giving you nothin'. He's gonna fuck you over. One way or another. It's what he does."

CHAPTER

8

BENNY WALKED RIGHT into Dave Ross's garage like he'd never been away. There was a new guy out front by the pumps, putting gas in a Chrysler with Virginia tags on it and when he saw Benny head into the service bays he stopped and came on over, walking up to Benny and saying, "Whaddya want?"

Benny gave him a look—little chicken-shit gas pumper gonna try to stop him from walking into a place, it wasn't gonna happen. He said, "Where's Earl Marsh, sport?"

The attendant must have seen something in Benny's face because he swallowed and when he answered his voice had a different quality to it. All the meanness was gone and he was almost polite, pointing over to the side of the lot and saying, "Earl's over there, by the red Datsun. The one with the hood up."

Behind them, out by the pumps, a horn sounded. Whoever was in the Chrysler was getting impatient. Benny spat on the floor and said, "Assholes." He turned and looked at the attendant and said, "Fuck that. Make 'em wait."

The attendant grinned. "You're right. I ought to."

Benny spat again and looked at the attendant, saying, "Why the fuck don't you then, sport?" He walked out the bay door and over to the red Datsun, with the attendant looking after him, rubbing his hands on an oily rag and shaking his head slowly.

Benny felt like what he ought to do was sneak up to the red Datsun and maybe lean on the horn, scare the crap out of his brother. He could picture it—Earl with his head buried in the engine compartment, trying to work on the car, and he hears that horn go off all of a sudden. Jesus, he'd shit his pants. He almost did it, but Earl looked up just before Benny got there. Earl, younger than Benny by about four years. And dumber, too. All his life he'd been following Benny around like he was some kind of fucking prince. Benny would do something, steal something, maybe take a car that didn't belong to him, and Earl would think it was the greatest. Next thing Benny'd know, Earl would be trying to do it, too. Except he'd fuck it up, pick a car with no gas, something like that. Or else get caught by the owner, if he was that drunk, get the shit beat out of him.

But Earl could fix cars. Benny had to give him that. It didn't matter, drunk or sober, you give Earl some piece-of-shit car, it didn't matter if maybe it hadn't run for a couple of years. Tow it in on the back of a truck and let Earl fool around with it for just a little while, look at the plugs, play around with the carb, maybe take the top off and clean everything out. He'd have the thing running. Except if it was fuel injected. It pissed him off; they had to go and fuck with things, take the carburetors out of automobiles and put in fuel injection. He used to tell Benny, "Why the fuck they want to do that? What, carburetors didn't work?" He'd shake his head and ask Benny, "The cars wouldn't run anymore so some dickweed hadda invent fuel injection, is that what happened?" It would piss him off if somebody brought in a car that had fuel injection in it. He'd look at the customer, maybe spit, or wipe his hands on a rag and tell them, "I was you, I'd take it back to the dealer, they're the ones supposed to know how to fix it."

When Benny was down at Raiford, Earl used to come down once a month. He'd hop on a bus, make the eleven-hour trip on Saturday, sipping bourbon out of a pint bottle of Wild Turkey, be there in time to see Benny for a couple of hours on Sunday afternoon, and then have to make the trip back by Monday morning. Benny told him after a couple of times of doing that, "Why you want to put yourself through this bullshit every month?" And Earl had looked hurt, his face clouding up and him saying, "Don't you want visitors?" Benny had told him, "Yeah, but not every fucking month."

When Earl moved out from under the hood of the Datsun and saw Benny, his whole face lit up. He gave a whoop and rushed towards his brother with his arms wide. Benny saw it coming and took a step back, not even smiling, and knocked Earl's hands down. He said, "Take it easy."

Earl stopped short, still smiling but with a confused look on his face. He said, "But you're out."

"Yeah, I'm out. Big fucking deal." But then looking at Earl, smelling it and saying, "Jesus." Because Earl was drunk again. Standing there, outside in the sun, trying to fix somebody's car—two o'clock in the afternoon and he had a load going.

His brother said, "What's the matter . . . ?" But then he stopped because Benny was giving him one of his looks, staring at him with his lips pulled back a little bit. Not like he was smiling. Earl knew what a smile looked like and this wasn't it. More like Benny was getting ready to start yelling. The kind of look Earl used to see on Benny's face right before he would beat the crap out of somebody that'd been hassling him in a bar.

Benny said, "I need a car."

Earl nodded. "You can use mine. My Camaro." He started to grin, saying, "I reworked the whole thing, pulled the engine, put oversized pistons in it. . . ." But then stopping because Benny was giving him the look again.

Benny said, "Does it run?"

"Yeah, it runs."

Benny nodded. "That's all I need to know." He looked around the lot and then back at Earl. "Where is it?"

"Out back, behind the garage."

Benny stood there, waiting, until finally he had to ask, "You got the keys?" And Earl, looking sheepish, put a hand in his pocket and came out with a set of keys. He took one off the ring and handed it to Benny.

"You'll be careful with it, huh?"

Benny nodded. "Don't worry about it." He seemed to notice Earl's face for the first time, looking at the bruise on Earl's chin. "What the fuck happened to you?"

Earl grinned. "I got in a fight."

"You win?"

Earl looked away. "The guy was pretty big."

"Jesus. What'd I always tell you, sport? You got to fight some guy, he's bigger than you, pick up a fucking baseball bat, something like that."

Earl said, "I didn't have time."

Benny shook his head and said, "Shit."

He started to walk away when Earl called out. "Benny?"

Benny turned around. "Yeah?"

"You gonna be around? Maybe come by the house later?"

Benny shook his head. "I don't know. I got some stuff I got to take care of."

Earl jogged the ten steps over to his older brother and said, "You gonna go see Michelle?"

Benny reached out and grabbed his brother by the shirtfront. He said, "Don't ever fucking ask me am I gonna do something that don't concern you. You hear me?"

Earl tried to twist away, saying, "I was just asking."

Benny shoved him away. "Don't ever just ask." He walked away, going past the service bays and around the back, seeing his brother's silver Camaro behind the building and getting in it.

He started it, revved the motor a couple of times, and then popped the clutch, burning rubber and whipping around the building, hitting the brakes when he got to Earl and rolling the window down. He leaned out, holding a cassette tape in his hands, saying, "What the fuck is this shit, don't you have any Randy Travis, something like that?" Earl started to answer but Benny said, "Shit," disgusted, like he couldn't believe Earl'd drive a car that didn't have at least some country music on tape. He pulled out of the station lot, fiddling with the radio. Leaving Earl standing there and waving at him.

.   .   .

Herb, standing on the front porch of his house, looked at Billy Eagle and said, "So he's back, huh?"

Billy nodded and told his boss, "Looks the same as when he went away."

"Yeah?"

"Swear to God. I seen him down at the bus station. Going into that place on Carteret that sells clothes."

Herb nodded and said, "So what did you expect? Benny, what, spends his time in jail, he's gonna come out and forget why he got sent there?"

Billy shook his head. "It's just kind of strange, seeing him again."

Herb glanced at him. "Yeah, were you impressed?"

Billy shrugged, looking away from Dorrance and saying, "No."

"Bullshit." Herb, laughing, moved out into the sun. He saw his Cadillac turn into the driveway a couple of hundred yards away and start to head towards the house. Cully and Michelle back from spending more of his money. He gave it a minute and then said to Billy, "He's a loser. A punk." Looking back at the Cadillac for another few seconds and then saying, "What Benny is, is a dead man. He just doesn't know it yet."

When they pulled in, both Herb Dorrance and the Mexican-looking guy from the bar were standing outside by the front door. Cully pulled the Caddy up and parked right in front of them, getting out and going around to open the door for Michelle. Dorrance moved forward a little to meet his wife, and Billy Eagle just stood there, watching Cully walk back to the rear doors of the Caddy.

Cully wasn't sure what was gonna happen when she got out. He half expected her to stumble or say something wild. But she surprised him, giving him a quick look while he held the door for her and then saying, "Thank you, Cully," in a nice voice and turning to her husband and saying, "Whew, what a day. I'm beat." Not showing those Manhattans at all, giving her husband a quick kiss and then saying to the Mexican, "Good afternoon, Billy."

Billy smiled at her and then moved aside so that she could walk past them up to the front door.

Herb Dorrance waited until she was gone and then turned to Cully, saying, "What do you think?" Startling the hell out of Cully because for a second he thought Dorrance was asking what Cully thought about Michelle, but then Dorrance said, "First day on the job, how'd it go?"

Cully gave him a little smile and said, "Fine. Hardest part was dealing with the traffic."

Dorrance nodded. "Good." He turned to the man standing next to him and said, "Billy, this is Cully. The one I was telling you about." He introduced Billy to Cully by saying, "He's probably the only Seminole Indian you're ever likely to meet." And then looking right at Cully he said, "Thing is, the reason Billy and I, we get along so well, is cause Billy here knows which side of the bread his paycheck is gonna be on. Ain't that right, Billy?"

"Yessir."

Herb said, "Billy here, I met him same way as I met you. Coming out of jail. On parole out of the state correctional facility up at Columbia. Gave him a job and all." He looked at Billy. "And it worked out, didn't it?"

Billy said it again, "Yessir," the sound of the man's voice starting to get on Cully's nerves a little bit.

But he went ahead and shook hands with Billy, the man's grip pretty dry, with a lot of power to it. Cully thought the man was putting a lot of effort into it, though, showing something to Cully. Cully didn't mind. The guy didn't look too bright, standing there and nodding at whatever Herb Dorrance said. And maybe the Indian couldn't help it, it was just the way he was, hard from working fields all his life.

But it was starting to bother him, the way Dorrance was, the kind of guy—Cully had seen them in prison—they always had something to prove. Spend their life walking around letting people know they were important.

He was getting a feeling, starting to wonder, was he gonna be able to stick around and put up with this shit for very long? But he was thinking, too, was it just that he wasn't used to it? Maybe prison life, and before that, robbing places, it made him forget what it was like to work for somebody that paid you.

66

Cully smiled and tried to make small talk with the two men. Nodding when Billy said, "Some fight the other night." Being polite but holding something back, like he was only being nice because his boss was around. Cully wondered about it—Herb, talking a lot, filling in the spaces that would have been there if it was only Cully and the Indian. Cully had a feeling, like he wanted to tell Billy Eagle, I'm doing my job, that's all. Like the Indian was pretty loyal to Dorrance and maybe had a hard-on for anybody that he thought might cause trouble. Cully couldn't figure it out at first. Was it because he was an ex-con, the Indian giving him that blank stare because he'd spent some time in jail, too? Or was he always like that, just something he'd learned. Maybe somebody told him sometime, Indians are supposed to never show anything, especially to a white man.

Cully was getting pretty tired of it by the time Dorrance finally looked at his watch and said, "Well, I think I'll get cleaned up for dinner." He looked at Cully again and waited while Cully shook Billy Eagle's hand again and then the three of them separated, Billy getting in a Ford Bronco and driving off.

Dorrance stood there for another second and then said to Cully, "See, things'll work out if you just concentrate on doing your job." He turned away then, walking back up to the house. Leaving Cully, tired, looking after him, wondering, was the man gonna push it *all* the time? He watched the older man for a couple of seconds and then shook his head. Turned and made his way slowly back to the apartment over the garage.

He stayed there, watching a little television until Amelia brought his dinner tray over. After he finished eating he took a short walk around the property. He saw Herb Dorrance leave after a while, the man wheeling the dark blue Porsche around the driveway and then heading out on 21 towards town. Cully watched him go and then went back to his apartment. He turned the TV back on but couldn't keep his mind on it. He kept thinking back to the afternoon, driving Michelle around. He could picture both of them, Michelle and her sister, Kristin, trying to decide which one was better looking and giving up finally because they seemed somehow too different. Michelle, with her tight clothes and flashy looks and her sister, quieter somehow, walking around her restaurant with her dirty apron on and not letting it bother her a bit.

After a little while, just as it was getting dark, he walked out onto the balcony and sat in the chair facing the pool. He stayed there, telling himself he needed the air, until Michelle came out of the French doors down by the pool wearing the same white bathrobe, but this time not wearing a bathing suit underneath, making Cully sit up when she took the robe off because she was naked. He watched her, saw her stretch slowly in the moonlight and then look up at him, smiling from fifty feet away, before she dove in the water.

Michelle woke up because she had a headache. At least it felt like a headache, or something wrong with her face—the whole side of it cold, almost numb, a feeling you'd get if you went to the dentist and he loaded you up with Novocain.

She couldn't figure it out at first. Was it a dream or was it really happening? She told herself she must still be asleep but then realized that her eyes were open. She was lying on her back and looking up at Herb, his face flickering because he had a candle in his hands, the only light in the room, still feeling the coldness on the side of her face, but not knowing what it was until Herb lifted his hand.

It was a butcher knife, the blade maybe twelve inches long. Flickering in the candlelight while Herb turned it slowly from side to side, smiling in the light. Drunk. She could tell—could smell it and see it in his face.

She tried to move, to slide a little bit away from him but act like everything was okay at the same time. But he reached down and put the knife against her face again.

He said, "Don't."

She stopped moving, almost not breathing, making herself smile, act like everything was normal and maybe he'd quit. Saying, "What's the matter, Herb?" But a little mad at herself because her voice was shaking and it would only make him push it more if he noticed.

He said, "You have a good time tonight?"

She tried to nod slowly, aware of the knife against her face. He pushed it against her a little more and said, "I hear things. Stupid things. Somebody tells me you're out at the pool. Skinny-dipping. What am I supposed to think? It's something—I got a feeling—it's something even you wouldn't be dumb enough to do it."

When she spoke it was barely a whisper, wondering who saw her, Amelia, maybe even Billy Eagle, if he had come back unexpectedly. But it wasn't like it mattered who had told him. She whispered, "I did go swimming."

"Uh-huh." He started to slide the side of the blade back and forth on her cheek. Smiling at her. "I can understand that. You got a nice pool out there. It's pretty warm out. Maybe you decide, jump in and cool off. Something like that."

She waited a second, scared to death, because it could go either way. And then told him quietly, "Yes, that's what I did."

He was silent for almost a minute, looking down at her and holding the knife without moving it. Finally he said, "If somebody maybe told me you were out there, you forgot to wear your suit, you went in naked, maybe the new guy, Cully, he's up there watching you, they'd be lying?"

She couldn't look at his face when she answered, "Yes."

"Uh-huh." He stood up all of a sudden, the candlelight making the whole room swim in front of her eyes, and walked to the door. When he got there he turned and looked at her, grinning and saying, "The thing is, I believe you. Cause what else am I gonna do? I think you did do something like that, it's not like I'm gonna wake you up. Hell, no, I'd just come in here and cut you."

She sat up in bed after he left, hearing him laugh as he walked down the hall. Her whole body shaking now because he scared the shit out of her. But furious, too. Because he could do whatever he wanted. She wasn't even safe anymore. A guy like that, he brings hookers home, that was bad enough. He wakes you up in the middle of the night with a knife and a candle and it was time to get the fuck out of there.

CHAPTER

9

CULLY WOKE UP the next morning, lying in bed—not quite ready to get up, but with the racket of a couple of chain saws running pretty close to his room. He got out of bed and walked over to the window, pulling the curtain out of the way and seeing, about fifty feet away, next to a big chipper truck that said OASIS TREE SURGERY on the side, a couple of guys cutting up an oak tree that had just been felled. He said, "Jesus," to himself and walked over to the bathroom and took a piss.

Somebody started to pound on his door. He swore again and began to walk towards it. He got halfway there, still wearing nothing but his underwear, when Amelia came into the room, moving quickly, with her eyes wide as if she were scared. She came to a stop, seeing Cully standing there in the middle of the room in nothing but his shorts.

He said, "Amelia, honey, I had no idea." Grinning and trying to make a joke out of it, but knowing something was wrong. He kept waiting for the black woman to say something but she was out of breath. Finally he had to ask, moving towards her, "What's the matter?"

The black woman nodded, seemed to come to her senses, walking up to him and touching his arm. "They're fighting. Mr. Dorrance and Benny. I think he's hurt." She pulled at his arm and he almost stumbled.

He said, "Wait up. I got to get dressed." He moved to the chair and grabbed his jeans, hurrying after Amelia as he was pulling them on, moving across the floor in bare feet—following after the black woman as she hurried down the stairs and wondering who the fuck was Benny?

When they got to the door of the garage and then stepped out onto the front lawn, Cully could see, about seventy feet away, Herb Dorrance, his wife, and another man. He guessed that was Benny. Herb Dorrance stood with his hand on his face, holding himself like he might be hurt, Cully couldn't tell from this far away.

He could tell what was happening, though. Feel it in the air. The tension. It wasn't like he hadn't seen it happen before. Down at Raiford, where all of a sudden it'd get real quiet. Seven hundred cons out in the yard and suddenly you could hear a person fart from across the field. The feeling of violence about to happen. And then all hell would break loose.

He stepped away from Amelia and glanced over to where the men were cutting up the tree. They had ear protectors on their heads and heavy plexiglass face shields. Each one had a chain saw in his hands, running, with the racket making them unaware of what was happening over by the house. Next to them, on the ground about halfway between them and their truck, was another saw and a two-gallon jug of gasoline. Cully walked on over to where they were working. He picked up the chain saw and turned back to the house, setting the choke as he was walking and then pulling the cord. He had to try it again because it didn't catch at first, but then he got it right, feeling the smooth power of the saw and looking down at the eighteen-inch blade. He heard a shout behind him and turned to see one of the tree workers looking in his direction and pointing for Cully to put the saw down. Cully held up one finger, saying, "One minute," and then turned back to where Amelia was waiting for him.

When he got up to her, she said, shouting to make herself heard over the saw, "What the hell you doing?"

He grinned. "I'm gonna go talk to the folks over there, see what's going on." Asking her, "Where's Billy?" And her answering, shaking her head and saying, "He went into town." And then Cully, not sure how far he was willing to go, but thinking, Fuck it, turning and walking over to where the little group was clustered. All of them were looking in Cully's direction now, even the newcomer.

Cully was awake now and feeling pretty good, not worried that he was maybe missing breakfast. Thinking instead that it was a different way to start a day—seeing things clearly, like the script was already written and all he had to do was follow it—getting closer to the little group of people on the lawn. He smiled at Michelle, seeing her frown a little bit, and then looked past her at her husband, nodding and seeing that he had a puffy lip and a little trail of blood going down his neck.

He kept on walking, right up to Benny, getting a good look at him as he did. It took about three seconds, once Cully got close to Benny, for him to see that the man had been in prison at some point. His first impression, though, looking at the man, was he was a guy who made his way through life smiling at people. Giving them that pleasant look. Standing there, maybe you'd meet him for the first time, if he wasn't punching somebody, and you'd think he looked like a movie star. Somebody, maybe they were famous, but trying to be cool about it. Casual looking, in his designer jeans and his lizard-skin boots with the nice spit shine to them. Cully figured he was the type he could charm anybody, get a lot of women, with his Glen Campbell looks. Walk into a place, if you look like Benny, maybe you'd give everybody a smile. And the women, what they'd do, they'd turn around and take a second peek.

He had big shoulders and arms, with the veins popping out of them like he'd spent a lot of time pumping iron, and jailhouse tattoos running up both arms and disappearing inside the cut-off sleeves of his blue work shirt. There was something about Benny's eyes, too. Something that Cully had seen in a lot of guys' eyes down at Raiford. Not in people like his old cellmate Bobo, who got drunk and cried about killing a cop. But in the ones that killed people and didn't give a fuck afterward. You look in their eyes, you see that same flat look.

Cully didn't even wait, didn't say anything to the guy. What was he gonna do, walk up carrying a chain saw and ask Benny what he thought about the weather? Instead he spit one time, right at the guy's boots, and then hit the throttle of the saw. He felt the blade begin to spin and gave it a little more gas, heard the roar it made and then lifted it up into Benny's face, feeling a coldness in his belly, a sensation he was familiar with. You get to a point where words aren't gonna do you a whole lot of good. Maybe you're trying to get along with people, doing quiet time, like Cully tried to do at Raiford. If it doesn't work, what are you gonna do? Maybe back off. Or else say, Fuck it, go ahead with whatever you have available and see what happens.

Benny had been standing there, watching Cully along with the rest of them. But when Cully pushed the saw towards him, let the blade flick through the air maybe an inch and a half from Benny's cheek, he yelled and stumbled backwards. Saying, "Hey" loudly. And holding up his hands. Giving Cully a look like, What was this? Letting Cully see it in his face. Saying it again, "Hey, sport, what are you doing?" Smiling at him and telling him, "Jesus, you don't understand. All I want to do is talk to the folks." Backing up. Telling Cully, "Sport, you got the wrong idea."

Cully kept walking. He followed Benny across the front lawn, with the little group of people, Herb Dorrance and Michelle following him. He could hear Herb behind him, starting to yell. Saying, "Cut him. Goddamn it, cut the son of a bitch." Amelia was a few steps behind them. And further away, coming over from the side lawn next to the garage, the two tree surgeons, without their chain saws, both of them watching Cully, neither one of them yelling about their saw anymore. Just watching, like everybody else. Cully ignored all of them, concentrating on the saw and the man in front of him. Pretty calm about it, walking Benny back to the silver Camaro, taking a swipe at his face every couple of seconds to keep him moving.

Benny started to swear. It was kind of hard to hear over the roar of the saw, but he pointed at Michelle and then at Cully, saying something that Cully couldn't understand. He never took his eyes off the saw in Cully's hands, reaching behind him for the door latch when he got to the Camaro and pulling the door open—sliding into the seat and reaching up to the key with one easy motion. Looking at

Cully for a long couple of seconds, nodding his head, calm now, not yelling. Giving Cully a grin as Cully let the throttle on the saw go, watching Benny smile. Leaning out of the window of the Camaro, Benny said, "This is something, sport," pointing. "The saw, it's something you probably shouldn't've done."

Benny gave it another couple of seconds and then started the car and popped the clutch, throwing dirt behind him and spinning the Camaro in a circle—gunning it down the driveway at about fifty miles an hour.

Cully killed the chain saw. He heard Herb say, "Jesus, why didn't you cut him, let him know you were serious?"

Cully couldn't believe it—let him know he was serious? What the fuck did they think he was, shoving a saw into somebody's face. Do something like that and you're being pretty serious. He set the saw on the ground and turned to the group behind him, seeing Herb Dorrance, his face red like he was gonna have a heart attack. Breathing hard and staring at Cully. And next to him, his wife, scared looking, maybe from what had happened with the guy in the Camaro or else because her husband was working himself into a rage. Cully couldn't tell.

Dorrance said, "Man, I tell you to do something, you'd better learn to do it."

Cully started to say something but Dorrance interrupted him. "I ain't fucking around." He pointed at where the Camaro had gone and said, "That boy's a dead man. Come on to my house and pull shit like that." He walked up to Cully and said, "And you don't do what I say next time, I'm telling you, you'll be back in that fucking jail so fast you won't know what hit you."

He stalked away, with Cully looking at his back, thinking, what he should have done was stay up in his garage apartment. Let whoever it was in the Camaro beat the shit out of Dorrance. He stopped looking at Dorrance after a bit and turned to the others, looking at them all for a couple of seconds and then asking, "Who the hell was that?"

Finally Michelle said, "His name's Benny Marsh."

That's all she told him. Cully had to ask. "I chase a guy off of your property with a chain saw and all you're gonna tell me is his name?"

Michelle took a step towards Cully. He could see she looked more at ease already. She stepped up to him with a trace of a smile on her face and repeated, "Benny Marsh." Letting the words hang in the air, drawing out each syllable as if it were some kind of chant. She took another step towards Cully and touched him on the arm, saying, "I used to be married to a guy named Benny Marsh." Her back was to the others and only Cully could see her face, see the look she gave him before she turned away, letting her hand linger on his arm for another couple of seconds, while her gaze traveled across his bare chest—leaning towards him and closing her eyes, opening them again after a second and looking at the chain saw and then up into Cully's eyes. Saying, "Jesus," softly, like she was seeing him for the first time.

For a moment Cully forgot that there was anyone else there. But then she stepped back and shook her head. Gave him a big smile then, looking back up into his eyes and saying, so that everyone could hear, "Thank you, Cully."

She turned away and walked over to Amelia. "Why don't you make some breakfast. Will you do that, Amelia? Get Mr. Cullen some breakfast." Looking one more time at Cully and then walking back to the house.

Cully watched her go. He looked around the yard and then turned back towards the house, to where Michelle and Herb had gone, shaking his head slowly and saying, "Shit." He didn't know if he said it because of the confrontation with Benny, or what Herb had said or if it was because of the feeling in his groin from Michelle. He shook his head again and picked up the chain saw, walking with it back to the garage. Halfway there he handed it to one of the tree surgeons, saying, "Thanks" and nodding while the man looked at him with wide eyes and didn't answer.

An hour later Herb Dorrance came over to Cully's apartment above the garage. Cully saw him coming, watched Dorrance walk across the lawn and was waiting for him when he got to the top step.

Herb told him, talking a little slowly because of the cut on his lip, "You and me are gonna have a talk." He was carrying a brown paper bag in his hands and he set it on the floor and then walked over to sit on the one chair in the room.

Cully sat on the bed. He waited a second and then said, "If you're gonna tell me I should've cut that boy, I won't do it."

Dorrance smiled. "I'm gonna tell you a couple of things."

Cully looked at the other man, not saying anything. Sitting there, in his little apartment waiting for Dorrance to get to the point.

Finally Dorrance said, "I'm gonna paint you a little picture. A guy, say he's pretty well established in town. You know, people respect him." Herb laughed softly. "It ain't like he's the guy you hit in the bar the other night—folks know somebody like that, his word is no good." Herb was still smiling slightly, looking at Cully and telling him, "No, this fellow—respected—he decides to give an ex-con a chance. People are gonna say what a nice thing to do. Maybe, who knows, maybe they'll say it's a little foolish, taking a chance on a guy been in jail for five years. Used to stick people up. You know how people are."

Cully was already getting the picture, turning away from Herb to look out the window because here it came.

Listening to Dorrance tell him, "Say all of a sudden, this fellow, the one that hired the ex-con, he goes into town and tells the sheriff, Hey, this guy, this criminal, he stole money from me." Dorrance laughed again. "Or maybe, maybe he tells the sheriff, This fellow tried to rape my wife. Get Michelle to swear that you did." He reached across and touched Cully on the leg. "You think I couldn't do that, get my pretty young wife to say that you made advances on her?"

Cully looked at him and said, "Maybe you could."

Dorrance shook his head. "Ain't no maybe about it, son."

Cully said, "Uh-huh."

"You getting the picture?"

Cully nodded. "Let me guess. I decide, fuck you, I decide to take off, you swear out a warrant, say I stole money from you. Something like that."

"See that, you're sharp as a tack. You and I, we're gonna get along real good long as you follow the rules."

Cully said, "Uh-huh. Let me ask you something."

76

"All right."

"That's your wife's first husband? What's his name, Benny?"

Dorrance nodded. "Benny Marsh."

The name rang a bell in Cully's head but he couldn't quite place it. He stood up from the bed and walked to the window, looking out at the pool and saying, "This guy violent?" He turned to look at Dorrance, who shook his head.

"He's trash. Every once in a while he'll call Michelle. Be abusive. Or he'll come out here, yell a little bit."

Cully asked him, "You gonna press charges? Go to the cops?" Wondering about it. Dorrance, he was buddies with the local sheriff. It didn't seem like something that he would put up with, Benny coming onto his property and causing trouble.

Dorrance looked away from Cully, staring out the window, and said, "There's no need to go to the cops." He got up out of the chair and walked across to where the brown paper bag lay on the floor. He reached into it and pulled out a pistol, holding it for a few seconds and then tossing it to Cully. He said, "I want you to carry this."

Cully caught the gun and said, "Maybe if I meet Benny again, if he comes looking for me or your wife, or maybe you, then I'll be prepared?"

Dorrance nodded. "I like that, it's like you're reading my mind. I don't even have to tell you these things. You figure them out on your own."

"Jesus." Cully looked at the pistol, a .38 with a stainless steel barrel and walnut grips, and then back up at Dorrance, wrapping his hands around the pistol's grip like it was the most natural thing in the world. Looking from the .38 to Dorrance and saying, "What the fuck you got in mind? I run into Benny and maybe he says something to me. Insults your wife, something like that. And, what, I take this thing out and maybe shoot him? Is that what you want?"

"You got it."

Cully shook his head. "Herb, you know what I went to prison for?"

Dorrance nodded. "I read the file Pete Williams had."

Cully shook his head. "You read a fucking file. That doesn't mean shit. It doesn't say in there what it is to carry a gun around with you.

Cause if you do carry one," he held the pistol up so Dorrance had to look at it, and then continued, "if you do walk around with one of these, maybe stick it in your belt so you can pull it out pretty quick, you got to be ready to use it. It ain't like you're shooting at some goddamn sign. You pull something like this out, stick it in Benny's face, or somebody like Benny, you aren't ready to use it, they're gonna take it away from you and stick it up your ass." He tossed the pistol back into the bag and said, "Herb, I ain't ready to use it."

"It ain't up to you."

Cully said, "Jesus." Then he looked at Herb. "What makes you think I won't turn around, maybe use this on you?"

"Cause I did read that file. You never used one before. You'd stick a gun in people's faces, that's one thing. But it didn't say anything in that file Williams had about you shooting anybody." He waited a second and then said, "See, I don't think you got the balls to do something like that." He smiled and said, "Unless, say, you hadda make a choice. Either use it to stay out of prison, or else I go to my buddy the sheriff, maybe you'll find yourself back inside that cage you just got out of."

Cully said, "You're telling me to kill Benny."

Dorrance laughed. "Hell, boy, I ain't said that. All I'm saying is, you got to be prepared. Case the need arises. See, Benny, he might feel he's got a score to settle with me. It ain't any of your business why. All you got to concern yourself with, you got to learn to do what I tell you. You do that and you'll find I'm all right to work for." He grinned. "Just ask Billy Eagle."

He got up to leave, walked to the door, and then turned to stare at Cully for a few seconds before saying, "I've got to leave later this afternoon. I'm supposed to go up to Fayetteville and look at a couple of tractors. Stay there until at least tomorrow night." He kept staring at Cully, not looking away, and finally he told him, "I just want you to be aware, I don't want to come on back and find out you been a disappointment while I was away."

Cully asked him, "What do you think is going to happen?"

Herb waited for a second, like he wanted to think about what to say. But then he just shrugged and said, "I'll tell you what better happen. Nothing."

Cully let him get to the stairs and then he called out. "Herb?"

Dorrance turned. "What?"

"Benny have a brother?"

Herb nodded. "Yeah, he does. Name's Earl. I thought you knew that. He's one of the guys you beat up at Casey's." He turned to leave, clumping down the steps, leaving Cully still sitting on the bed, with the .38 sitting on the mattress next to him, thinking about what Herb had told him. Wondering what was he gonna do? Was it all that time he spent in Raiford that made him take this shit from Herb? Maybe, what had happened, he'd gotten so used to taking orders that he didn't know how not to. It made sense. But then he decided that it wasn't that at all. He could see through Herb, the man was ready to use him for whatever he wanted. It didn't sound like Herb was telling the truth about Benny either, at least not all of it. The thing was, Cully decided, he didn't have a lot of choice right now. Didn't have a dime of his own money, and the only way he was gonna get any was to stick around for a couple of weeks until Herb paid him. Get together a couple of hundred dollars and then get the fuck out of town.

CHAPTER

10

BENNY WAS DRINKING a Budweiser, pacing around on the cement floor of Dave Ross's garage after closing, taking big gulps from the can and swearing. He'd walk a few feet in one direction, drinking beer, and then stop, saying, "Motherfucker," and then he'd turn around again and walk back. His brother Earl and Dave Ross watched him—sitting on a bench a couple of feet away—Earl still with a bruise on his chin and Dave Ross with a wad of adhesive tape on his nose.

When he finished his beer he threw the can on the floor and got another one from the case on the workbench in the corner of the bay. He looked at his brother and said, "That motherfucker put a saw in my face." When Earl didn't say anything, Benny yelled at him, "What, is that something you think is funny?" Looking at Earl and taking a step towards him, thinking of that morning—some asshole comes out of the garage with a chain saw, waving it around in his face. He told Earl, "It's all right, some son of a bitch wants to stick a fucking chain saw in my face?"

Earl held up his hands. "I didn't say it was all right." He looked at Ross and then back at Benny. "If you want, I'll go with you right now. Teach Cully a lesson." Earl waited a second and then blurted out, "He's the one that busted Dave's nose."

Benny stopped pacing and looked at the two men. "This is the guy? This Cully? A guy like that, he busts your nose and knocks you out." Benny looked from Dave Ross to Earl. "And you're gonna forget about it?"

Dave Ross shrugged. "Whatta you want me to do? I got a business to run. I can't go looking to get revenge on some guy just because I got in a fight with him."

Benny said, "Jesus." He looked at Earl and said, "What about you?"

Earl told him, "I told you, you want to go get this guy, it's okay with me. I'll go along."

Dave Ross said, "Besides, from what I hear, you got other things to worry about."

There was dead silence as Benny turned towards Ross, staring at him for a second. He knew what Ross was talking about. He'd known, sitting up at night back at Raiford, that there were gonna be some people, give them enough time and they'd come sniffing after the money. He didn't think anybody'd have the guts to talk about it to his face, though.

He smiled now, looking at Ross and shaking his head slowly. Acting friendly, with a nice grin on his face, saying, "Dave, I don't know, maybe you're getting ahead of me. Maybe you're talking about things you oughtta let alone."

Dave Ross looked at Benny. "Maybe."

Benny turned to Earl. "There's something going on here, Earl, maybe something you want to tell me?" He wasn't even thinking about Cully anymore. He was looking at the two men in front of him—his brother Earl, weak little son of a bitch, and Dave Ross. Ross was so nice he just gave Earl a job, kept him on here all the time Benny was in jail? Was that what it was? Or maybe Ross, he figured to keep an eye on Earl, see if he'd lead him to the money. He said to his brother, "Earl, maybe a couple of times, you and Dave here, you'd close up the shop, have a few beers and get to talking about things that didn't concern you."

Earl looked at Benny, his eyes wide because he could remember all the times before Benny'd get that look in his eyes, the crazy look, Earl used to call it, like he didn't give a fuck about anything. He said, "Benny, I didn't say anything. I don't know anything."

Benny laughed, the meanness going out of his eyes as he took a drink of his beer. He said, "That's right. You don't know shit. Because I didn't tell you shit." He looked at Ross. "You got something on your mind, you want to come sniffing around, maybe see if you can find all that money I'm supposed to have stashed away somewhere? You go ahead." Looking at Ross and not trusting him a bit. Not trusting anyone. Not Ross or Earl. He had spent four years in a fucking prison, with all that money out there waiting for him. He didn't talk about it up there and it wasn't like he was gonna start now. He tossed his beer can at Ross's feet and walked to the door, opening it and looking back at Ross. "You fuck around with a thing like this, it'll get you killed, you son of a bitch. That's what it'll do."

When he left, Dave Ross picked up the beer can and threw it into the trash. He walked over to the half-full case of Budweisers and brought two of them back to the bench. He handed one to Earl and then popped his own, giving it a minute, letting Earl settle down and take a few swallows before he said, "Tell me about the money again, Earl."

Earl looked at the door, like Benny was going to come charging in any second. "Are you nuts? Didn't you hear him? He'll kill you. He'll kill both of us."

Dave spit on the floor. "Fuck that. He ain't gonna kill anyone. He's got something else in mind, being stuck on that prison farm for four years, watching guys fuck each other in the ass. All he wants is to stick his dick in his ex-wife."

Earl said, "That's not true."

Ross leaned forward and touched Earl's knee. "You want to tell me why, the first thing he does, he gets out of that jail, the first place he goes is out to her house?"

Earl shrugged. "I don't know."

"I'll tell you why. He's got pussy on the brain. All that cash out there, it's just waiting for him. He's the only one that knows where it is. And all he can think about is his ex-wife."

Earl shook his head. "He don't care at all about her."

"Earl, I don't know. I guess maybe you're trying to convince yourself."

"No, I ain't. He don't want nothin' to do with her. She's trash."

Ross laughed. "Is that what she is? How come, if she's trash, how come when she drives that Caddy in here, wants to fill it up with gas, you drop everything you're doing and run out to the pump? Looking at her with your moon eyes, like she was the queen of fucking Sheba."

"I'm doing my job. That's all." But he looked away from Ross, taking a sip of his beer and looking outside.

Ross asked him, "Earl, if you had a choice, say you were in your brother's shoes, what would you do—go back, mooning for that woman, or else, if you had all that cash, or knew where to get it, take the money and get the fuck outta town? Go somewhere with all that money. Someplace where you can find a hundred girls like Michelle."

Earl gave Ross a sly look. "Who ever said that there was all that cash out there?"

"Jesus, boy, you did. You come in here, the day after the robbery, bragging about your brother. And when he got caught, what'd you say? You said Benny Marsh was too smart to let them find the money."

"John Lewis took off with all the money."

Ross snorted. "John Lewis was a half-wit. Your brother conned him into going into that bank with him. And then, when Benny knew he was gonna get caught, with the cops banging on his door practically, what does he do? He cops a plea and blames it all on John Lewis."

"Well, Lewis took off, didn't he?"

Ross leaned forward again and said softly, "John Lewis took a swim, is what he did. Your brother took him out in that old boat of his, put a couple of bullets in his head, and dumped him over."

Earl stood up. "That's bullshit."

Ross shook his head. "No, it's not. I can't prove it. Nobody can. But it's what happened."

Earl sat down and took a drink. They sat there in silence for a couple of minutes until Ross spoke again. He said, "Where's the money, Earl?"

"I don't know. You think Benny'd tell me a thing like that? Even if he knew, he wouldn't tell me."

Ross said, "I think your brother's up to something here."

Earl said, "You don't know that. Neither of us knows what he's doing."

Ross waited a minute and then said, "Well, why don't you do this, Earl," waiting again until Earl was looking at him and then saying, "why don't you find out?"

Herb Dorrance left for Fayetteville the next day at around eleven o'clock in the morning. He came over to where Cully was washing the Cadillac to say good-bye, making bullshit small talk while he moved his feet on the driveway. After a couple of minutes he told Cully, "Well, I've got to be going. Billy is probably waiting." He looked at his watch, making a show of doing it, and then said, "You remember what I told you, hear?" He looked back at the house and then at Cully, saying, "You might want to think about it. Sheriff Williams, I go fishing with him—deep sea—maybe a half a dozen times every summer. Have him out to dinner every once in a while. I tell him you're giving me trouble, he ain't even gonna think twice. He'll squash your ass."

A horn blew up at the house, Billy Eagle in the Bronco and ready to go. Herb ignored it. "My wife might want to run into town. . . ." Not saying anything else, but looking at Cully to see if he might have a comment.

Cully made himself grin and told him, "She wants to go anywhere, shopping, or whatever, I'll drive her. Make sure it's okay."

Herb didn't say anything for a couple of seconds. Then he nodded. Cully could feel it, Herb coming on down to talk to him for one last time, make sure Cully knew what was expected of him. Trying to be natural about it; he had to go on a business trip and all he was doing was checking with the help before he left, giving a couple of last-minute instructions. But still, he kept pushing it.

Cully watched him walk back to the house and get in Billy Eagle's Bronco. He kept watching them as they drove out of the driveway, holding the hose in his hand and then glancing up at the house, wondering what Michelle was up to. Thinking about it for a couple of seconds, not sure if he really cared, and then shrugging and turning back to the half-washed Cadillac.

Billy Eagle, driving towards the Frogmore Airport, headed out to Lady's Island with Herb—they were going to pick up a four seater and fly up to Fayetteville. He gave it a little while before he said to his boss, "You all right with this thing?"

Herb, either acting stupid or not thinking about it right, said, "The tractors?" And Billy Eagle had to shake his head, take his eyes off the road for a couple of seconds and say, "Back home, leaving Cully there."

Dorrance shrugged. "Do I think he's a crook, something like that?" Shaking his head and smiling at Billy Eagle. "I mean, I know he's a crook. Hell, boy, it's why I hired him."

Billy nodded and waited for his boss to continue.

Dorrance told him, "See, I know guys like Cully. They act all hard, nobody's gonna tell 'em what to do." Dorrance laughed. "You know what the truth is?"

Billy asked him, "What?"

"The truth is, they're weaker than shit. They *want* somebody to tell them what to do. Maybe they don't know it. But that's what they want."

"Yeah?"

Dorrance nodded, pulling a cigar out of his shirt and saying, "A guy like that, he's got a lot of aggression. And he finds out he ain't gonna make it on the outside, not by going straight. Where's that gonna leave him?"

Billy said, "Yeah, but giving him a gun?"

Herb nodded. "See, it's all right, I do something like that, what am I really doing? I'm giving an ex-con a gun. Telling him to carry it. He ain't gonna use it against me. I know that. It's not his style. But something happens between him and Benny. Maybe I even make something happen. Benny comes back at me because maybe he's got the mistaken idea that I got something that belongs to him. I point Cully in his direction, get him a situation where he feels like he's got no choice. What happens if Cully uses that gun? I can tell the sheriff, Hey, I didn't even know he had it. Son of a bitch must've stole it from me."

Billy Eagle thought about it. It was in his head to tell the man to get rid of Cully. But it wasn't his place to say it. He asked Dorrance, "You're sure?"

Herb snorted. "He's a small-time cowboy, guy spent his time robbing liquor stores. I can't handle somebody like that?"

Billy nodded. "Yeah, I know. You want somebody if Benny Marsh turns out to be a problem, maybe comes back again. Only this time he thinks about it a little more. Maybe makes better plans. You want somebody there to help out. Take care of your wife."

Herb turned in his seat so that he was sitting sideways, with one leg drawn up on the seat, looking at Billy Eagle and saying, "Fuck my wife. I want somebody, if Benny Marsh comes back, which I think he's gonna, I want somebody that'll kill the son of a bitch. Somebody, say they get hurt in the process, maybe we got two dead people on our hands, it won't matter if that happens." Dorrance shrugged. "That's all it is."

Billy said, "Uh-huh." He was quiet for a minute, coming up to the Frogmore Airport, putting his turn signal on and waiting for a truck to go by before making the left. He pulled the Bronco into the airport lot, parking it about twenty feet from the little one-room terminal and getting out, walking around the back to get their bags, locking up afterward and then joining Herb Dorrance by the side door. He looked up at the sky for a minute and then said, just as Dorrance was reaching for one of the bags, "Well, you got your eye on Cully. Working on him. Maybe you're gonna make him do something about Benny. Set it up so it looks like he did it on his own. Am I right?"

Dorrance nodded and said, "I don't know exactly what I'm gonna do. But, yeah, it's there. The possibility that I might have to do something like that. What I'm thinking is Benny doesn't exactly deserve to be walking around. The man's an insult to me."

Billy said, "I can see that." Waiting a second and then adding, "So while you're working on Cully . . ."

Dorrance said, "Yeah?"

And Billy told him, "How would it be, while you're doing that, why don't I keep an eye on Benny, make sure he doesn't do anything we don't appreciate?" Waiting a second and then saying, "How would that be?"

And Dorrance gave him a look, saying, "What the fuck you think I pay you for?"

At about five o'clock Cully wandered down the driveway looking at the fields of tomato plants and tobacco. He wondered, what would it be like, to have a place, all this land, for yourself? If it was his, he didn't know if he'd even be able to grow anything on it. He'd spend all his time walking around, with a feeling in his gut because it was his. Maybe never get around to planting anything.

He drove into town around three o'clock, careful not to take too long, in case Michelle wanted to go somewhere, but wanting to get a case of beer and some smokes. Heading back to the house he decided maybe he didn't envy Herb Dorrance so much. He had a nice place, a lot of land. And a pretty young wife. But, thinking about it, it wasn't like Dorrance was overflowing with happiness. You meet the man and right away he's got a point to prove. The kind of guy, he goes through life telling people, we're gonna do things my way or not at all. Cully had the feeling that Dorrance liked it, liked pushing people, making them squirm just so he could watch how they reacted.

Cully drove back up the driveway, still thinking about it and not even seeing at first that the garage door was open and the Porsche was gone. He stopped the Cadillac in front of the garage and shook his head, saying, Shit, out loud. What was he supposed to do? Michelle wanted to go somewhere, nobody could stop her. It wasn't like Cully could go inside and call the cops. Get the sheriff on the phone and tell him, Hey, the woman I work for, I'm supposed to watch out for her, drive her around, and now she's driving herself. But still, until he could get away from this place, get a little money and take off, it wasn't gonna sound too good if he told Herb when he got back from Fayetteville that he had lost track of Michelle the evening Herb left town.

He put the Caddy in reverse and turned around in the driveway, heading back out to Route 21 with no more of an idea than that maybe if he drove around he could find her. What he was gonna say if he did find her was something else altogether.

He drove towards Beaufort slowly, thinking of all the places he'd taken Michelle the day before and finally remembering her sister's restaurant.

He drove across the bridge and kept on going, turning his headlights on because it was getting dark. Driving past the little one-room cinder-block bars where the young island blacks hung out, laughing among themselves but looking Cully over as he went whipping by in the Caddy. He had to swerve once to miss a deer, pulling the wheel to the right, getting only a second or two to react, seeing nothing but dark road ahead of him and then the buck, a six pointer, jumped out into the road. He felt the wheels hit the shoulder of the road, could feel them start to sink into the sand, and yanked the wheel back to the left, thinking, for a second, that he wasn't going to make it, but then getting control again, punching the gas and heading towards the restaurant.

When he got to the Shrimp Boat it was closed, the lights turned off and a big padlock on the outside door. He sat there, looking past the restaurant eventually to the little ranch house behind it, seeing that there were some lights on in the house and wondering if maybe that was where Kristin lived. He could either find out or else go back to the farm.

He got out of the car finally and walked over to the house, half expecting either Michelle to answer the door or else somebody he didn't know would answer it—it would turn out that Kristin didn't live there at all, somebody else owned the little ranch house behind the restaurant.

He knocked and waited, turning to look at the darkened restaurant one more time and then hearing the door of the house opening, turning back and not saying anything at first because Kristin was standing there, holding a dish towel in her hand and looking at him. Not smiling but not acting like she was sorry to see him either.

CHAPTER

11

BENNY WAS PLAYING with Michelle's tits. He kept reaching across her—she was lying with her back to him—and he'd reach across her with his left hand and grab one of her tits, rub the nipple for a while just to see it get hard again. Michelle would groan a little bit, move her ass against him, and maybe reach up with her free hand and touch his fingers.

He couldn't believe it. Michelle, she was, what, four years older than when he got sent down to the farm? He figured that a lot of times, you take an average woman, maybe she was pretty good-looking, something like twenty-six or twenty-seven, and then you don't see her for four years. She'd be liable to be a lot older-looking when you came back. But not Michelle. If somebody would've shown Benny a picture of her, maybe make it look like it was cut from a magazine, without the face so he couldn't tell who it was, he would have said she was twenty. Tops. It didn't matter, you could take a picture of her tits, her ass, none of it sagged.

He grabbed her tits again, pulled her onto her back, so that she was lying on his chest, and started to rub them. This time he didn't quit. He kept it up until she was really moving, thrashing around on the bed, with him getting hard again because she was rubbing her ass against his crotch. When he couldn't stand it any longer he flipped her around. Pushed her face down into the pillow and came into her from behind. He pushed as hard as he could, grunting, and hearing her say, "Jesus," and then pulling almost all the way out to do it again. He kept it up for a while, longer than the first time because now he was more in control. Not like when he'd first walked in the motel room, with her lying naked on the bed, smiling at him, like it'd been all she'd thought about for four long years.

She'd called him and said, "I'm sitting here, in a motel room, and there's nothing on TV, nobody to talk to. What am I supposed to do?" Using her sweet voice. Her fuck-me voice they used to call it, back when they were married and they used to do it two, sometimes three times a day.

It was all right, coming here to this motel room and fucking her. Hell, he had, what, a big choice? Sit back at his own motel room, or maybe he could go on over to Earl's house, sit around and drink beer with his ding brother and they could talk about cars, pretend nothing had ever happened and Benny hadn't just gotten out of prison.

So he'd come on over and found Michelle. Same as always, lying on the bed with the door unlocked and him walking in to find her naked, like a cat in fucking heat, giving him that bedroom look, like she'd already been playing with herself. Like she couldn't wait for it, thinking about Benny and she had to touch herself down there. Grabbing him and pulling at his clothes, biting him, telling him yes, closing her eyes and tearing at him.

It was fun, he had to give her that. She had the kind of body, what it was made for was fucking. She'd walk into a room, there could be twenty girls there, some of them better looking, and still, if there were any guys around, they'd end up staring at her.

So it was okay, like old times almost, holding her down on the bed and slamming into her. And her telling him, afterwards, Jesus. Looking at him and saying, I can't get enough of you.

He reached across her to get his shirt. Pulled out his cigarettes and lit one, blowing smoke past her and squinting up against the overhead light. Thinking, Fuck her, and saying, "That was almost as good as what you'd get down at Raiford."

She moved away from him. Sat up on the bed and looked across the room while he lay there and blew smoke at the ceiling. He wondered about it—was she thinking it was gonna be the same as before? He could picture what was going on inside her head. It was like a part in a movie. The director would come in and tell her, Okay, what we're looking for is some emotion. Telling her, You're hurt, that son of a bitch hurt you, said something nasty and now you're gonna react. Benny watching her, and seeing it differently than he had before he got sent to jail. The last time he fell for that look they put him in a fucking cage for four years.

He was getting a kick out of it, watching her turn slowly towards him, fucking Greta Garbo, with her eyes a little wet. Not quite looking at him, her eyes focused on a spot right above his head, like it was too difficult for her to even talk about. Giving him a look and saying, "Benny," in a soft voice. But careful not to cover up her tits, leaning forward with her weight on her arms, the inside of her elbows touching her ribs so that her tits were pushed together. They were the closest things to Benny. If he felt like it, he could reach maybe six inches towards her and grab one of them.

She said, "Why'd you have to do that? I haven't seen you, been alone with you in five years, you have to go and say a thing like that."

He told her, leaning back on the pillow, with one arm behind his head and the other, with the cigarette in it, pointing at her as he spoke. Saying, "I don't know. You're gonna get all worried if I say something. How's that gonna work? I've been in jail for a long time and I get out. I'm not supposed to be mad?" Letting a couple of seconds go by and then telling her, "I'm not supposed to be listening for you to tell me you got something belongs to me?"

She said it again, shaking her head slowly and then looking at him. Saying, "Benny . . ." softly and then reaching over to touch his chest. Jesus, he couldn't believe it, she was stalling. Telling him, "I've been waiting for this day for a long time."

He laughed. "Waiting. This is what you call it, you divorce me when I get sent to jail. I get out, you're married to some old fuck grows tomatoes for a living." Looking right at her now. "What about me, I've been waiting for my money now for what, four fucking

91

years. You and me made a deal. I go down, spend some time in that fucking place and when I get out you have the money for me." He moved closer to her and whispered, "You gonna tell me it slipped your mind?"

She got up out of the bed and walked across the room to the dresser. Looking at him in the mirror and playing with her hair. Turning around finally and looking at him. "I don't have it."

"What?"

She said it again, "You heard me, I don't have it." She held up her hand before he could say anything and told him, "Hey, I watch you get sent away, I don't know am I ever gonna see you again. Anything can happen. So there I am, alone all of a sudden. I got the cops looking at me like did I have anything to do with the robbery. Trying to put me in jail too. What was I supposed to do?" Taking a deep breath and saying, "I gave it back."

He started to raise his voice, "Hey, what the fuck are you saying?" He started to get up out of the bed but then stopped. "We're talking about something that I went to a lot of trouble for."

She wouldn't look at him now. Turning her head away from him and staring at the door of the motel room. "I know, but it wasn't gonna do any good me winding up in prison too. They came looking for it and I gave it to them. Acted like I found it and didn't want anything to do with it."

He shook his head, almost too mad to do anything right away. Looking at her across the room and saying, "Jesus Christ." Thinking about it, what would she do if he got up and walked over to her, started to bounce her off the goddamn walls? Taking a couple of breaths instead because he thought maybe he wanted to hear the whole thing, find out how much she had really fucked him. He asked her, "And then what happens? Some old motherfucker starts noticing you. Before he knows it, you catch on and you're hanging out, letting him see the tops of your titties every once in a while. Maybe playing him along for a while, then when you think it's time, maybe you give him a piece of your ass. You got to be careful, though; you rush into something like that, that old fart'll have a fucking coronary."

"Is that the way you think it happened?"

Benny shrugged. "See, it doesn't matter do I think it happened one way or another."

"It does to me." She came back to the bed, walking slowly, and then kneeling down on the edge where his feet were. She touched his toes. Started to massage them and said, "Four fucking years. That's what I was looking at. And what am I supposed to do if something happened to you down there?"

"You got to look out for yourself, right?"

"That's right." She started moving her hands up Benny's leg, working her way up his calf, kneading one leg with both hands and then moving over to the other leg. She said, "You think all I've been doing, I marry Herb and it's only so I can get ahead. Is that it? That's what you're thinking?"

Benny said, "Hun-bun, if you tell me it's true love I might start laughing. Maybe you'll get offended." He waited a couple of seconds and then said, "I got to tell you, there were some times—I'd be sitting in a cell down at Raiford. Maybe I'd be wondering what you were doing. And then, when I heard you'd married Herb, I used to think, imagine what it would feel like if I got out of there and came on up. Went on over to that fancy house of his and put a bullet in his brain."

She pushed his leg away, looking at him like he was being stupid. Saying, "And then where would you be?" She didn't give him a chance to answer. "And if you're going to worry about who's gonna offend who, then you and I aren't gonna get anywhere."

"Are we going someplace?" Trying to be sarcastic, but he couldn't help himself, he sat up and looked at her. Pushing the cigarette down into the ashtray and watching her. Remembering back to when they were married, he'd hear that tone in her voice, maybe they'd be fooling around, joking, and all of a sudden she'd get serious. And her whole voice would change. He said, "What've you got in mind?"

She walked back to the dresser and picked up Benny's shirt. Held it up to her nose and smelled it, looking at him for a second and then holding it against her chest, rubbing it on her tits and smiling. "Benny, when you went into that bank. You went in there and picked up the cash."

"So?"

"And I made sure you knew what day to go in. When they'd have the most cash lying around."

Benny moved to the edge of the bed. "I don't know, I hear you saying all this. You're not telling me anything I don't know."

She came over and sat down next to him. "Benny, when you saw all that money they were giving you, what were you thinking? Was it going through your mind maybe I was misleading you?"

Benny acted like he had to think it over. He gave it a couple of seconds and then shook his head. "Right then and there, looking at those fucking bills and seeing you across the room trying to act all scared. No, I'd have to say I wasn't thinking anything like that."

She said, "I set it up. Told you go in there, and then what? You weren't gonna decide, halfway through, maybe I should call it off."

Benny said, "Hey, hun-bun, I already had a gun out, what was I supposed to do? All that money just sitting there."

"So, it wasn't anything *I* did that made you go to jail."

He shrugged. "Hey, what do you want? Maybe I should apologize. Except, who was it that spent four years in jail?"

She said, "Uh-huh." And then touched his face. "Let me ask you something. Now that you're out, what did you have in mind? You gonna get a job?"

He shook his head, "It's not something I can see myself doing. Work for somebody else. Fuck that."

She nodded, "That's right. Fuck that." She looked up in the air like she had to think. "What if I told you I knew where you could pick up something that was worth a lot more than the money you got from the bank?" She looked back at him and said, "What if I said I knew somebody, maybe they had something, something worth a lot, they don't want anyone to know about it. Where are they gonna keep it?"

Benny smiled. "I don't know. Under their mattress?"

"Jesus." Shaking her head and saying, "A safety deposit box. You put money in a safety deposit box, maybe it's there because you don't want to pay taxes on it. You're saving it for a rainy day. What happens? You take it out, maybe ten years have gone by, and it's worth what, if it's cash? Maybe two-thirds of what it was worth when you put it in."

"Inflation?"

"It's like burying it in your back yard. You lose money by doing something like that."

Benny said, "Uh-huh." Getting it now, but still not seeing what it meant. Asking her, "So what's in the box?"

"Diamonds."

"Diamonds?"

"That's right. There's no such thing as inflation, you're talking about precious stones."

Benny leaned forward and touched her face. "I'm sitting here, listening to you explain this thing to me. And I'm wondering why. You're telling me about diamonds and I can't help but remember, didn't I listen to you tell me about a score once before? Where'd that get me?"

She shrugged. Started to say something else but Benny held up a hand. "Wait. I'm wondering, you're trying to make this sound easy, teasing me with it. Telling me it's a lot bigger than what we tried before."

Michelle got back off the bed and walked over to the dresser, turning slowly and looking at Benny. "I never said it would be easy." And then she told him, "There's a problem. . . ." Pausing for a second like it wasn't something she wanted to tell him. Benny, sitting on the bed and watching her, was thinking, Uh-oh, here it comes. Seeing a look in her eyes and recognizing it. Little bitch in a tight spot was gonna try to talk her way out.

He said, "I got an idea. Why don't you just say it. That way, we can cut the shit. I don't like what you have to say, we can deal with that, too."

She nodded. "All right." Staying at the dresser but beginning to tell him, "The diamonds . . ."

Benny said, "Uh-huh." Sitting up straighter.

"They're my husband's."

"Herb's?"

"Yeah."

"So, go get them. You're his fucking wife. Walk into the bank, wherever they are, you can do it tomorrow, walk in and get them." He smiled. "You do that, bring them here to me, I think we can forget about me spending all that time at Raiford."

She shook her head. "See, I'm telling you all this and you say something like that. If I could do that, you think I wouldn't?"

"Why not? You're his wife."

"I'm his wife, but he made me agree when we got married. It's a private box. Not something that we can both get into. I want to put anything in there, or maybe take something out, he's got to be there." She waited a second and then told him, "Look, you just got out of jail. Where the hell you think I am, stuck here, I'm married to a guy—all he wants to do is see me suffer."

"You're gonna break my heart, sugar."

She got a little mad, he could see it. "Benny, I'm not fooling around. Herb, you think, what, you meet him and he seems like an all right guy? It's bullshit. He's a fucking psycho. He finds out I'm even thinking like this and he'd kill me." She stared out into space for a moment and then said softly, "He may kill me anyway."

Benny said, "You're telling me you know right where they are. And you can't touch them?" Shaking his head and saying, "Jesus," because he was getting mad again.

"Benny, I can't." Giving him a look, though, being a fucking actress again. Dramatic about the thing. "But somebody else could."

It took him a couple of seconds, hearing her say it and not getting it at first. But then pushing her away from him and yelling, "Wait a fucking second. You're telling me why don't I go in there and take them? I've maybe had some practice at it, did it once before, so it should be a fucking piece of cake." Looking at her, not even that mad anymore because he was starting to think she was crazy. Saying, "Jesus Fucking Christ." Getting up off the bed and starting to pull his jeans on, standing on one foot and looking around the room, trying to find his lizard-skin boots without falling over.

She stayed where she was, watching him, until he had his pants and boots on and was looking for his shirt, clearing her throat and showing him that she was still holding it. She said, "What I was wondering, you got a box full of diamonds, sitting in the bank. Not doing anybody any good. It's a shame."

He took the shirt from her and started to put it on. "It ain't as much of a shame as going to jail."

She nodded. "Uh-huh. But they could only put you in jail if you took them. Right?"

He stopped buttoning his shirt and looked at her. "So?"

"So what if we got somebody else to do it? Somebody else to take them for us." Stopping him when she said it, because she made it sound so simple, sitting on the bed looking satisfied, like the first act in a play she was in had gone well, she knew her lines and the critics loved it.

He looked at her, came back over to the bed and sat down, staring at her and finally saying, "We maybe advertise, take out an ad in the *Beaufort Gazette,* say something like, 'Bank Robber Wanted.' Maybe ask for references."

"No, that's not something we'd have to do."

"Yeah? You got somebody in mind? Somebody already lined up?"

She nodded. "You met him already."

He thought about it, watching her face. Seeing her smile and getting it all of a sudden, starting to smile himself because after knowing her for seven years it didn't sound that crazy. Seeing it, and knowing how her mind worked, knowing how far she would go. "The guy with the chain saw. Right?"

"Cully."

He thought about it. "I can almost see it."

She reached over and put her hand on his leg. Told him, "It's what he does."

"Rob banks?"

"Banks, stores, bars. Anyplace where there's money."

"He does that now?"

She shrugged. "I don't know." Waiting, giving him a look, leaning forward and then speaking quietly. "I've got something you aren't going to believe."

"What's that?"

"Our boy, Frank Cullen. You wanna guess where he was eight weeks ago?"

"Why don't you tell me."

She nodded. "All right, I will. He spent some time, just got out of a place, maybe you know it, Raiford State Penitentiary."

"Holy shit." He grabbed her hand. "Are you kidding me? He's a Raiford boy?" Running it over in his head, did the man seem familiar? He didn't think so. He told her, "I might have passed him a dozen times. It's a big place. But I got to believe I ran into him at some point."

She shrugged. "Maybe."

He ran his hand through his hair, thinking about it. "You never know. It could happen. There's a lot of people down there, I didn't know them all." He thought about it a little more, seeing Cully with the chain saw, almost proud of him, because it was something he might have done. "Jesus, I can see it now." Looking at her and asking, "And you think, we tell him what we have in mind, you think maybe he'll help us out?"

She frowned. "I don't think it's something he's planning to do, no. I think he's got it in mind that he's retired."

"Gone straight?"

She nodded. "I think so."

"So?"

She smiled. "So maybe I can change his mind."

He smiled, too, reaching down to touch her hand. Picking it up and looking at it. Saying, "Maybe."

She said, "What you have to do, you have to let me do it the right way. Not go out to the house and hassle him. Or Herb. We aren't gonna tell him anything. You let me do it. Let me work on him."

Benny nodded. Seeing it in his head and thinking she could probably do it. He said, "What about your husband? We're gonna take the man's money, what're you gonna do then?"

She sighed, looking at him like he was stupid. "Benny, you have any idea what it's like, sitting out on that farm listening to him talk about the weather, asking me do I think it's going to rain soon? All the time, it's all he thinks about. And the games he plays, running around in my underwear, maybe some nights he gets his asshole buddy Billy Eagle to pick up a hooker. Bring her home so he can watch her fuck me. You got any idea what it's like?" She waited a second and then said, "Besides, you think Herb's gonna sit by and take it if he found out we robbed him?"

"I imagine he'd be kinda pissed off," Benny said.

"Jesus, I think, if he knew it was us, I think he'd kill us." After a second she said, "I got a feeling he doesn't need much of an excuse to kill you anyway."

Benny thought about it. "So you and me, we take the man's diamonds and then we split."

"That's right," Michelle said. "This time we do it right. Get Frank Cullen to do it for us."

Benny was silent for a minute. But grinning because it might work. Looking at her and beginning to nod. Saying, "I can see it, put it on the son of a bitch. The cops, they take a look at it and say, Dude's back to his old tricks."

"That's right."

Benny said, "Hey. You know what we could do?"

She shook her head.

"We get that money, go on down to Nashville. Get you a record contract." He thought about it for a minute. "Shit, they don't want to give you a contract, we'll buy a fucking studio." Smiling at her and saying, "How would that be?" Going with it for a second, thinking it through. It would be something. Get her to do a couple of songs, a demo. See if anybody would be interested.

She smiled at him. "We could do that."

"Yeah." Benny thought about it, maybe they could. Even if they didn't, they'd have all that money. Do whatever they wanted. He pictured Cully with the chain saw. Son of a bitch had it coming.

He said, "Motherfucker threatened me with a chain saw."

Michelle nodded. "That's right, he did."

Benny said, "He did, didn't he?"

She looked at him for a couple of seconds and then said, "Why'n't you take off those jeans."

99

CHAPTER

12

CULLY HAD NEVER seen so fucking many cats in his life, maybe a dozen of them since he walked into Kristin's house. It was a pain in the ass, sitting at the kitchen table, they kept jumping into his lap. At first, if she was looking at him, he'd make an effort, pet it for a while. But then he got tired of it. One'd jump up in his lap and he'd give it a push, boot it back onto the floor and another one would take its place. He was starting to worry. What would happen if maybe two or three of them jumped up, maybe they started to fight, he's got a cat fight going on an inch away from his pecker.

He couldn't believe the way she looked. Wild. Wearing a long skirt, some kind of thin material, if he had to make a guess he would've said cotton. The thing touched the floor. She was wearing sandals; he'd get a peek every once in a while of her toes underneath the skirt. And a sweatshirt that said Duke University on it. The thing was, it was all right, he guessed, she wanted to dress casually to lounge around the house, that was okay. But she also had earrings on, and her hair was done up. Cully couldn't think of what it was called where the hair hung down from her head in a whole bunch of braids, like Bo Derek in that movie. He thought maybe it was called dreadlocks but wasn't sure—was that only if it was a black guy doing it? Bob Marley, somebody like that?

She had a big flower pinned into her hair, too. With big white petals that took up a lot of that side of her head. And she was wearing make-up—not a lot—but he could tell, maybe she put a little rouge on and a touch of eyeshadow. He couldn't figure it out. Did she think she was gonna go out, get halfway ready, and then change her mind? Still, if someone had asked him, besides the outfit being a little weird, did he think she was good-looking, he'd have to say yes.

What he was doing, sitting at the table with all the goddamn cats, he was trying to see through her dress, get a look at her figure. Every once in a while, if she stood between him and the light from the other side of the room, he'd get a glimpse, see the outline of her legs underneath the skirt. Looking at them and deciding that she'd look pretty good, you get her out of that dress and maybe put her in something normal. Or just get her out of the dress.

He was sitting there, telling Kristin how he was trying to find Michelle because he'd promised her husband that he'd keep an eye on her while Dorrance went up to Fayetteville to buy the tractors. He told her about Benny coming out to the farm but didn't mention the part about the chain saw. He acted like it had just happened. Benny, he'd come on out, had a few words with Herb and Michelle, and then gone on back into town. Looking at her, sitting across the table from him, watching him talk, not saying anything much, but nodding her head like she was interested.

He asked her, "The thing is, how far am I supposed to take this? Your sister, if she wants to go somewhere, it's not like she's not allowed."

She looked at him. "Well, you're trying to do your job. But you're right. I don't think you're supposed to drive around for hours looking for her. She's a big girl."

She reached across the table and pulled a leather purse over to her, feeling around inside it and pulling out a pack of cigarettes. She lit one and then looked at Cully, taking a drag of the cigarette and blowing a stream of smoke at the ceiling, shrugging and telling Cully, "Michelle's always been this way. You expect maybe she's going to act one way, do something a certain way, and she does the exact opposite."

Cully asked her, "What about Benny? He comes out to the house and gets in an argument. Is that something he does a lot?"

She gave him a look, like she was surprised he'd be asking something like that, taking a drag of her smoke and then leaning back. Touching the flower in her hair and telling him, "Benny doesn't go out to the house."

"He did today." Leaning forward in the chair and putting his elbows on the table. He picked up her cigarettes and shook one out of the pack without asking, sticking it in his mouth and lighting it, turning the lighter over in his hands, playing with it and saying, "Herb told me he comes out every once in a while. Gets drunk, something like that, and calls Michelle up. Or else he shows up at the door. I figured that was mostly why he hired me."

Kristin shook her head. She touched her hair, pushed the flower a little higher, and sighed, blowing smoke past his head. She told him, "He might've hired you because he thought Benny was going to *start* coming out. But otherwise, he's lying. Benny's never been out there before. He couldn't of."

Cully thought it over. Benny—it wasn't like he'd seemed drunk. Mad, yeah, shouting things at Herb Dorrance and slugging him, knocking him down before Cully showed up with the chain saw. Seeing it again in his head, Benny standing there, with his cut-off work shirt and his tattoos.

Herb had been lying to him. Telling him that Benny made regular appearances at the house. Thinking about it, the coincidence, saying, Jesus, softly and then looking at Kristin and saying, "Benny just got out of prison, didn't he?"

"I thought you knew."

She told him a little about it, sitting there, talking softly, with Cully having a little trouble concentrating because he was beginning to see, from what he could tell, that maybe she was even better looking than her sister. Listening to her, yeah, but with a part of him wondering what would it be like to spend a lot of time with someone like this? You get rid of her cats, maybe take them out to the bay and drown them, something like that, and maybe talk to her about her clothes.

Kristin said, "Benny had this idea, I don't know when he got it. But he must have figured he could just walk into that bank, take the money, and everything would be all right." She shrugged her shoulders, looking at Cully like it was too unbelievable to understand. "It was like he didn't even plan it, like he decided one afternoon that that was what he was going to do. Him and another guy. His partner. Drive into town and rob a bank."

Cully could almost see it with what he knew of Benny. Hottempered, storming out to Herb's house the day after he got out of jail. Probably the same way he robbed the bank. Go in there with a gun, it didn't matter maybe they had guards, cameras, shit like that.

"Just all of a sudden, do it?"

She nodded. "You have to understand Benny. I don't think he was playing with a full deck. He was like that guy, the one Al Pacino played in that movie *Dog Day Afternoon*. Where Al Pacino's character, he's doing it all for his boyfriend. So he can have that operation. I guess Benny figured, I don't know, everything would work out." She waited for a second and then said, "He was strange back then. He used to pretend a lot of the time."

"Pretend?"

"Yes. The day I met him, Michelle brought him over. He told me he was big in country music. Knew all these people. Kenny Rogers. People like that."

"And then he goes and robs a bank?"

"Yeah."

He asked her, "They catch him right away?"

"No. He got away, at least for a couple of days. Acted like nothing had happened."

"And then what? The police pick him up?"

Kristin held her hands open. "That was the weird thing. He turned himself in. He could have taken off, maybe headed across country. He still had time."

"What about Michelle? They were married at the time, right?"

When Kristin nodded Cully said, "And now Michelle's married to Herb." Maybe it was as simple as that. Benny, he had a grudge against Herb, because he used to be married to Michelle.

Kristin said, "They've been married for almost three years now."

"And Benny, he goes and robs this bank and then just hangs around town like nothing had happened?"

"Uh-huh."

Cully leaned forward, interested. Thinking about it, what would he have done? Saying, "He didn't take off? He turned himself in?"

She nodded. "*He* did, yes. Not his partner, a guy named John Lewis. Nobody's seen him. I heard he took off. But nobody knows." Saying it softly. Cully could hear something in her voice. He wasn't sure what it was, but it was there. Like it bothered her to talk about it.

After a couple of seconds he asked her, "And what happened to the money?"

She shrugged. "He spent some of it. And then gave the rest back for a lighter sentence. Worked something out with the police." Pausing for a few seconds and then saying, "It wasn't a lot. I heard something like seven thousand dollars." She looked at Cully and said, "I mean, for a bank, seven thousand dollars doesn't seem like much."

Cully frowned. "Not a whole lot. But banks are tricky. A lot of times you don't get a lot of cash. You only hear about the big ones; somebody walks off with fifty, a hundred grand, you hear about those." He waited a moment and then said, "Or else . . . maybe that wasn't all of it."

"What do you mean?"

"Maybe that was all that was left. Maybe he spent it. Or maybe he hid it." Starting to think about it, seven grand, it was possible. Sometimes, you go into a bank, that's all they had. Maybe they give you only what's in the top drawers, you're so nervous they could give you Monopoly money you wouldn't know the fucking difference. Or else they give you a stack of money, you go running out of the bank and the fucking thing explodes in your face, turns you purple. All the cops have to do is follow the color. They find you covered with purple dye, you're gonna tell them, what, you fell in a can of paint?

She was staring at him, frowning a little bit. "This is something you know about?"

Cully thought for a moment, not wanting to get into that because he had just met her and things were going pretty good. He smiled and said, "You hear things, is all." And then he said, "So Benny, he robs this bank, gets a little cash, not much, and then he turns himself in. Is that what happened?"

Nodding. "That's it."

Cully wondered what would he have done, if he hadn't been caught, down there in Miami, with his armed robberies. There was no way he would have turned himself in. If the cops hadn't been waiting for him outside that bar, what would he be doing now? Still sticking guns in people's faces probably. He said, "This guy, Benny, he's not impressing me. I picture him doing these things, and I'm thinking, we're not talking about a very bright guy here."

She lifted one hand in the air, almost pointing at him and saying, "Well, that's what I meant, about Al Pacino in the movie. You know, doing it for someone else. I think that Benny, what he was trying to do was impress his wife."

Cully couldn't see it. "He goes into a bank with a gun. Gets caught. That's gonna impress his wife?"

She shrugged. "I guess he thought so."

"Why do you say that?"

"Well, for one thing"—giving him a little smile, like maybe she knew he was gonna like it—"she worked at the bank."

He figured out what it was, the thing he heard in her voice. The two of them getting to know each other and talking about bank robberies. One minute he was looking at her, not sure what she was thinking and the next minute, he could see it, hear it in her voice. She liked talking about it, thinking it through and trying to figure out how Benny had screwed up. She sounded like it made her a little mad, too. But also, maybe she liked thinking about it, what would she have done differently.

She was quiet about it, talking to him calmly, telling him what had happened four years before, but every once in a while she'd stop talking and look at him. He'd watch her think about it, run it over in her head, and maybe she'd see him watching, catch him looking back at her, and she'd smile at him.

He asked her, "So what's she do, he comes running into this bank with a gun. She looks up and there's her husband. Committing a felony."

"I don't know. She told me afterwards that he'd said he was gonna do it. Bragging about it. But she never took it seriously."

"It was just Benny talking?"

"Uh-huh." She thought it over for a second, and then said, "At least I think so. I could never make up my mind whether or not she knew."

Cully nodded. "It would be one way to do it. Have somebody on the inside, telling him when to do it. What to look for."

Kristin said, "I don't know. She doesn't talk about it much." She sighed. "I don't know what it is, she's married to this guy, this was only, what, four years ago. And he goes out one day and robs a bank."

"And maybe she knew, maybe she didn't?"

"I don't know. I could see where it could happen. You're married to someone, living with them, whatever. And they do something like this. Catches you totally by surprise."

Cully nodded. "It could happen."

She looked at him for a second and then got up from the table, carrying the ashtray over to the sink and then coming back, sitting down and staring into space. Finally, nodding and saying, "Well, the guy he did it with, John Lewis . . ."

And Cully nodding. Saying, "Yeah?" Waiting for it, because he could hear something in her voice again, leaning towards her, close enough that he could see a tiny scar next to her right eye, a little slash of white against her tan. Wanting to reach out all of a sudden and touch it but asking her instead, "What about him?"

She gave him a look, surprised almost, like she couldn't believe what she was going to say. Shaking her head a little bit and saying, "I was living with him at the time." Giving it a second and then saying, "The thing is, I had no idea it was going to happen." Nodding and telling Cully, "So I could see where it could happen. Michelle, she might not have known."

Cully said, "Or maybe she did."

She nodded. "That's right, maybe she did."

.   .   .

Later, she made coffee, carrying the cups to the table and sitting down next to him. He spent the time, while she was making it, looking at her. Wondering about it, because he was feeling pretty comfortable, sitting in her kitchen, not really knowing her too well, but feeling pretty good about it.

He could see, now that he had a little more time to look at her face, that she was a little older than her sister. Her face had a few lines in it. Nothing much, but Cully liked it. He thought it gave her a little more character than her sister. Made her seem just a little more mature. She was still beautiful, though. He'd look at her and see the resemblance to Michelle. You couldn't help but see it. But he liked the way she looked. Not as flashy as her sister. But somehow calmer, more relaxed with herself.

She wasn't like any of the girls he was used to talking to. She didn't even look like any of the girls he used to dream about when he was down at Raiford. Down there, you're stuck in a cell, you didn't want to picture yourself with a girl that looked like her, standing in her kitchen with her long skirt on. Fuck that. He used to dream about girls, the kind maybe you'd see in a show in Las Vegas or Atlantic City. Or else in a fuck flick. Girls with their tits jammed into push-up bras that were too small for them. And garter belts. With five-inch heels that would tighten up their legs and make their asses stand higher.

Maybe before, when he was into his robberies but hadn't been caught yet, he'd see a woman on the street, a housewife, something like that. And he'd look at her, see her going into the Winn-Dixie, maybe a little dolled up to flirt with the bag boys. And he'd wonder, what would it be like? Get married, work all day while your wife was out doing the grocery shopping, and then what? Come home every night and maybe twice a week, you'd give the old lady a shot? Back then he'd sit in his car, maybe casing a place in a mall, and watch the women shoppers. Later he'd go into downtown Miami and forget about it. Go to a bar, maybe see a few people, and then, if he felt like it, pick up a hooker. Keep it simple.

But looking at her now he thought maybe he could see what she was really like. He'd seen her twice for maybe an hour all told and already he thought maybe he was getting a lock on it. He could picture her in her restaurant, serving food. Or else, maybe outside, working in a garden or riding a horse. Something like that.

She sat down again and said, "How's your coffee?"

"Fine."

"I'd offer you something else, I don't know, a beer, something like that. But there's none here."

He nodded. "This is fine."

"You're sure?"

He nodded, thinking about the case of beer in the backseat of the Caddy all of a sudden and asking her, "Would you like a beer?"

"You mean go out for one?"

"I mean go out to my car for one."

She started to laugh. "You brought beer with you?"

He told her, "I never had time to unload it."

She stopped smiling and looked at him for a couple of seconds, running her hand through her hair and then saying, "All right." Waiting a second and then telling him, "I'd like that."

He left her there, going out to the car and taking a six pack out of the case and bringing it back in. She was walking back from the kitchen sink with a baggie in her hand. It took Cully a minute to realize that it was pot. He sat at the table opening the beers while she rolled a joint. Watching her do it, her tongue sticking out while she concentrated on it. He liked it that she didn't think she had to ask him was it okay. She was being careful about it and doing a pretty good job. Licking the joint and then holding the lighter to it for a second to dry the paper. Taking a drag and then handing the joint to Cully.

He took it, taking a hit and trying to hold it in but coughing. He took a sip of his beer because his throat was killing him. Shaking his head when she offered it again. The two of them quiet for a while while she smoked her joint and Cully finished his beer.

She reached across the table and poured another for him. He sat there and watched her open the bottle and then hold the glass on its side, with the lip of the bottle touching the glass.

When she handed it to him he took a sip and said, "Like a date."

She looked at him. "What do you mean?"

He shrugged. "It's like a date." Saying it calmly, but thinking he'd better not push it. "I don't know, sometimes if I'd take a girl out, maybe we knew each other pretty well, we'd end up just going out and having a couple of beers." He stopped talking but then felt a little uncomfortable so he said, "It wasn't a big deal."

She smiled at him. "A beer date." Teasing him a little, he could see it, but maybe having fun, too. She took a sip of her beer and said, "We don't know each other, though. Do we?"

He shook his head and said, "It reminds me of it. That's all."

She was still smiling, reaching across the table and taking his beer bottle and pouring the last bit into his glass and then doing the same with her own.

He said, "Let me ask you something."

"All right."

"I see you, you're running that restaurant. You've got this nice little house here. And then I look at your sister. . . ."

She smiled. "You want to know how come, if we're sisters, how come we're different?"

"I was wondering."

"Let me ask you something. You see us, Michelle and me. You think we're different. Right?"

"More or less."

"How do you know?" She took a sip of her beer. The glass was almost empty and she twirled it in her hands, looking at him and waiting for an answer.

He said, "I don't know. It's what I would have said. But you've got a point." He picked his glass up and walked with it over to the sink. When he came back to the table she was looking up at him.

He said, "I'm gonna go." Smiling, wanting to say more but not sure what. Finally he just nodded and said, "Good night."

When he was halfway to the door she called his name, saying, "Cully." Surprising him because he wasn't even sure that she remembered it.

He turned around and saw her leaning against the kitchen door. He smiled and said, "What?"

"What about your beer?"

He grinned then, taking a step towards her and saying, "Why'n't you keep it. I'll come back sometime and finish it." Feeling good about saying it, walking out to the Caddy and looking back once, seeing her standing in the doorway, giving him a wave as he got in the car.

Going back to the house, he thought about Kristin, and then her sister, Michelle. Thinking they seemed different. But not sure. Michelle, he could see it now, what she was doing. Playing with him. If somebody asked him did he think Michelle loved her husband, was she happy living out on the farm, growing tomatoes and maybe going into town a couple of times a week to shop, he couldn't have said. But he thought Michelle would be happier around a lot of people. Someplace maybe where they had casinos, something like that, where she could be seen. In the middle of the action.

He thought about it, picturing her in the car the day before, him driving her into town and the things they'd talked about. Playing games with him. Driving the Caddy back through Beaufort, with the streets pretty deserted and the whole town looking different, quieter, in the dark, he caught himself smiling, enjoying himself, thinking about Kristin now. He had spent, what, an hour with her? It wasn't enough to get to know her. But he had a picture of her in his head, seeing her sitting at the table in her kitchen, not really knowing him, but being nice. Talking to him and sounding like she was interested enough to listen to what he had to say. But maybe it wasn't as easy to figure as that. He knew one thing. If he had a choice, somebody asked him was that somebody you'd like to see again, spend some time with, he'd have to say yes.

Thinking about it, before he got sent to Raiford, and trying to come up with a name, any name, of a woman he wanted to spend time with. A woman who he wanted to do more than fuck. He couldn't do it.

CHAPTER

13

HE PULLED THE Caddy into Herb Dorrance's driveway finally, not even thinking about Michelle anymore, just driving slowly up to the house and wheeling the Cadillac around to the garage and then seeing the Porsche sitting outside.

He got out slowly, not sure what to do, thinking he'd just head upstairs to his apartment and maybe act like he'd never gone out looking for Michelle, not give her the satisfaction of knowing it.

He was going to do it, was walking across the driveway to the garage, when he heard music. He stopped to listen, knowing where it was coming from already but telling himself he wasn't sure. Starting to walk towards the back yard, the pool, even though he wasn't sure it was what he wanted to do. He walked through the gate, by the big live oak tree on the side of the house closest to the garage, hearing the music better now, something by the Rolling Stones. He couldn't remember the name of the song, but it sounded familiar, with a driving beat that reminded him of Raiford, where you'd sit in your cell and hear a hundred different songs at once, everybody turning their boom boxes up as loud as they could, until you didn't hear any one song but the beat of a hundred.

She was swimming. Moving the length of the pool while her arms churned through the water and her feet kicked up little fountains of spray. With the light from the pool flickering against the trees, making the whole place seem like some open-air dance floor. The music seemed almost to keep time with the light.

Cully walked the length of the pool, watching Michelle as she swam, matching her speed as he walked over to the table where her robe was. There was a bottle of whiskey on the table, Seagram's, with ice and some 7-Up next to it. He made himself a drink, wondering, all this money that seemed to be floating around here, you'd think they'd be drinking Chivas. He sat down and lit a cigarette, looking at the woman in the pool, running it over in his head—what was it he was going to say to her when she stopped swimming?

She kept it up for about another five minutes, moving slowly through the water while Cully watched her. It was all right, sitting there was kind of relaxing. He could smell the salt in the air from the marsh not too far away. He remembered, when he was younger, down in Miami. It was always there. The salt smell. You'd get used to it, wouldn't notice it after a while. But then, if you went away and came on back, there it was. Tangy. And you'd walk around aware of it for a couple of days until you got used to it again.

Michelle stopped swimming finally, by the wall at the shallow end of the pool. She was still for a minute, with her arms on the coping of the pool and her chin resting on her hands, her back to Cully.

He was going to say something, maybe clear his throat to let her know he was there. But she surprised him by saying, without turning around, "If you're going to drink my husband's liquor you might as well make me one." Turning then and looking at him, not smiling, but with a look on her face, like she'd been waiting for him.

He told her, "I've been wondering. When I'm up there on the porch, and now, down here, maybe I'm trying to sneak up on you. But you seem to know when I'm coming."

She smiled then, lifting herself away from the edge of the pool and beginning to walk through the water toward him. "I can just tell sometimes. Somebody watches me, after a while I get a feeling."

"Like somebody's burning two little holes in your back?"

"Something like that."

He liked the way she looked, sleek, with the water still dripping down her shoulders, and her hair, plastered flat now, slicked back and darker. The light from the pool, bouncing back off the trees and onto her face, made her seem even younger. Took a couple of years off of her features but gave her an exotic look, too. Cully, sitting there, sipping his Seven and Seven with a mystery woman.

She said, "You make me that drink yet?"

He started to, reached for a glass but stopped and handed her his own instead. She took a sip, pulling the glass away from her lips for a second to smile at him, and then finished the drink. She said, "You went out."

"I wanted to see the sights. Get the feel of the Caddy." Not saying anything about looking for her because he knew it was what she wanted. He reached for the glass. Took it out of her hands and started to make another drink, seeing out of the corner of his eye that she was moving towards the stairs, climbing out of the pool and coming over to the table. Putting on the robe.

"You have fun?"

"Well," he handed her the glass and waited for her to sit down, "I don't know if it was fun. Driving around. You go downtown, maybe pull into the mall, and what is there to do? You can watch the kids go into the movie theater. Something like that."

She asked him, "What about women? Don't you know any girls in town?"

He thought about Jenny, the barmaid, and then about Michelle's sister, seeing her waving to him as he pulled out of her driveway. Looking at Michelle now and shaking his head, thinking he wasn't gonna say anything about Kristin now. "Not tonight. All I had in mind, I thought I'd drive for a little while."

"Maybe you were out casing a place. Is that what it's called?" Bending forward to pick up her glass, with the top of her robe falling all the way open. To Cully, seeing the robe and the white top of her bikini underneath, it was like he was looking at her bra. Sitting at the table, looking at her. If they were out in public and she was wearing a dress, a beautiful woman, she bends over and you can see the tops of her tits, you'd feel it in your balls. It didn't matter that he had just seen her without the robe. It was sexier this way. Her giving him a peek, talking about casing a place and showing Cully a little tit. Being cute.

He said, "Sure, but the thing is, you go out to case a place, just want to look it over, you don't want to do it in a nice car like a Caddy." He told her, "People see that, maybe somebody remembers. Or else they stop to take a look, admire the car."

She smiled at him. "See."

"What?"

"There're a lot of things. If I went out to do something like that, I would've done it wrong."

"Well, it takes practice, I guess." He waited a second and then said, joking with her, "It's something you're giving some thought to? Pull a robbery?"

She was quiet for a minute. Cully, sitting next to her, heard the music from the stereo coming from inside the house, with the light flickering in the trees, very aware of the woman next to him. Her husband was, where, up in Fayetteville? Three hundred miles away and not coming back until tomorrow. He took a drink, told himself to wait and see what happened.

She asked him, pulling her chair a little closer to the table, "When you used to do it, rob people, what did you think? Did you ever think maybe you'd live in a nice house? Make enough money to buy a place like this? Have your own swimming pool?"

He shook his head. "What I figured, maybe, if I was lucky, I'd be able to save some. But it never worked out."

"You never made enough?"

"It wasn't that. I made a fair amount. You hit the right place, you could walk off with twenty thousand dollars. Take you ten minutes." A mosquito landed on his forearm and he watched it for a couple of seconds and then flicked it off with his finger. "But what do you do, you make that kind of money?"

"Spend it."

He grinned.

"So then you're broke."

"Uh-huh."

"Go on out and do it again?"

He shrugged. "It was a living."

She turned on the chair until she was facing him, leaning forward in her robe and staring right at his face. She asked him, "Didn't you ever think, when you were robbing those little stores, those 7-Elevens and Piggly Wigglys. Didn't you ever think maybe you should go for something more?"

"I robbed a bank once."

"Did you?" Getting a funny look on her face. Cully thought maybe he'd caught her by surprise. Impressed her a little bit.

He laughed. "Eighteen thousand dollars. A little branch office of First Miami Savings. I went in a little bit before closing on a Thursday afternoon." Shaking his head, because the woman teller, he could still picture it, she'd been beautiful. He went in with his magnum and pointed it at her, trying to concentrate on what he was doing but having trouble with it, staring at her because she was so fucking pretty. She'd started to cry, shoveling the bills into the briefcase he had with him, with tears sliding down her cheeks. Not making any noise. But the whole time she couldn't stop crying. He wanted to tell her to forget it. Make a deal with him, he'd put the gun away if she'd go home with him. Looking at her, Jesus, but then at all that money going into the briefcase, telling himself to shut his mouth before he said something he'd regret. Eighteen grand and he's thinking about how good-looking some woman is.

He told her, "You know what it's like, robbing places? It's crazy. One day you go into a bank, you're talking eighteen grand. You go out the next week and everything goes wrong." He took a drink and then told her, "I went into a deli once, a little place that sold liquor and sandwiches. Nothing much, but it looked easy. I point my gun at a guy, it's eleven o'clock, nobody's around. I didn't even plan it. Go into a place to get a pack of cigarettes and all of a sudden you can see, it's right there in front of you. I figure, do it. I pull my gun out and this guy, I figure he's going for the cash register, you know, reaching towards it."

"What happened?"

"What happened is, his hand keeps going. I don't know, I'm watching him and I see it, he's not going for the register. But I don't do anything. Maybe I was tired. I stand there, nothing's happening except this guy, old guy, maybe he's in his sixties, something like that, he's reaching down and pulling a .38 out from under the register. I can't even blink and it's pointed at my nose."

"Jesus."

Cully laughed softly, thinking about it. "So what happens is, there we are, a standoff. I gotta figure this guy's serious about not wanting to be robbed. And I'm not looking to get shot. So I just start backing up. The whole time, this guy, he doesn't say a word. He'd'da wanted to shoot me he could've. I mean, maybe I would've shot him, too. But I don't know. I back out of there and go out to my car. Get the hell out of there."

Michelle laughed softly. "He never said a word?"

"The whole time."

She went inside and put some different music on. A little softer. Something with a country beat. When she came out and sat back down she told him, "I used to sing. I'd do clubs. Around town." Looking at him and saying, "We did a gig in a club, it was pretty big. Down in Savannah." Smiling and telling him, "The Royale, I think it was. I was all excited, thinking, maybe, you know, it was gonna be my big break."

"What happened?"

"Well, this place was kind of wild. Nothing like what I thought it would be. You'd be singing away, somebody would shove somebody and there'd be a fight. You're up there on stage, all this shit's going on and all you're trying to do is finish the song."

He told her, "You've got a good voice."

"You think so?"

"Sure." Looking at her and telling her, "Yesterday, in the car. I heard you."

She nodded. "That's right." She waited a second and then said, "My first husband, Benny, when we first met, you know what he told me?"

"What?"

"He said I was gonna be a country music star. I used to hear him say it, and I'd think about it, you know, what it would be like." She ran her hand through her hair, parting it with her fingers. Looking at Cully once again and saying, "He'd talk about it all the time.

116

Watch the Nashville Channel, 'Austin City Limits,' shows like that. See what the women looked like. How good they were."

"Yeah?"

"It'd get him mad. He'd be sitting there, listening to somebody sing, and he'd get all pissed off. Cursing at the TV and telling me I could do better than them."

Cully told her, "I don't know. Sometimes, you see somebody like that, they make it big, maybe they get themselves on television. They don't seem that good to me."

"You think he had a point?"

"Sure."

She nodded. "For a while I even believed him. He'd sit there, we'd be listening to a record. Or maybe out somewhere, at a show. And he'd tell me how good I was gonna be. All it was gonna take was one break." She shook her head slowly and looked at Cully. "I think, what it was, was Benny wanted it for himself. Wanted to be a big man in country music. All the time, that's all he'd talk about. I was going to be a star."

He didn't know what to say, listening to her. For the first time she seemed like somebody that had a nice side. But even as he watched her, he could see it, some kind of coldness coming back over her, like she was putting on a mask. She said, "What the fuck did he know?"

He was silent for a minute, looking out over the pool, aware that she was watching him. Not saying anything to him, but he could feel it, could tell that she had her eyes on him. Finally he said, "What about now?"

"What do you mean?"

He smiled at her. "You and I are having such a nice talk. You asking me about robberies and then telling me about your singing career. I'm trying to figure out, which one are you more interested in?"

She gave him a look. "Is it bothering you? Talking about it?"

"The robberies?"

She nodded.

Thinking about all her questions, maybe what he could do, he could ask her a couple. Saying, "No. I was wondering, does it bother

117

you? I talk about it, it's bringing up something, maybe some people might think it's something I want to forget. I was wondering, maybe you want to forget about it, too."

He saw her think about it. Saw it register and then she said, "Oohh," smiling at him, not taking offense, "you've been driving around town, out there tonight, and maybe somebody's been telling you things."

He shrugged. "I get a new job, the first day, I chase a guy off the property with a chain saw." Looking at her, leaning across the table and playing with her glass. Saying, "I'm wondering, am I getting into something, maybe I should back away?"

"Benny." Giving it a light touch. "Sometimes, if I think back on it, I can't believe it. I was married to him for, what, three years?"

He shrugged. "I guess a lot of people, they get married, I don't know, people change. Three years later, you look at them and you're thinking, who the hell is that?"

"It happens."

"Uh-huh."

She waited a moment, taking her time, playing with the ice bucket now, getting a few cubes and then reaching across the table to grab the bottle. Concentrating while she poured and then telling him, "Some people, I guess that's what happens."

He asked, "You?"

"I don't know. If Benny, if he hadn't of done what he did, would I still be with him?" Shaking her head. "I can't see it."

He looked around the pool, pointed back towards the house. "This is better?"

"What would you say?"

"I can see it. If I had kept all my money, from all the scores. Maybe, say, I invested it. Maybe not spend as much time in clubs, or at the track. I could do something like this." Thinking about what he wanted to ask her. Did he really want to get involved with it? Ask her what the fuck was she doing with Herb. The guy bringing other women home and not even bothering to hide it. Running around town, he wanted to shoot his pistol off, kill a couple of signs, he just went ahead and did it. Like a little kid. Spoiled. But what would she say? Maybe she was still loyal to Herb. You never knew with some

118

women. So all he said was, "I don't know, sometimes people, they want something, want to live the good life—whatever—they have to make a lot of compromises."

She was staring at him, holding her glass halfway to her mouth, and then telling him, "Like you did. You're trying to make money. Still, the only way you could think to do it, you had to go out and use a gun."

He shrugged. "It was the only thing that came to mind at the time."

She didn't say anything for a minute and then she stood up with her back towards him, with her drink in her hand, while he watched her. She lifted the glass, tilted her head back, and finished it. He could hear the ice cubes clink. And then she turned around, looked at him again, and then stepped up to the table. She put the glass down and stepped closer to him, reaching down and running the fingers of her right hand across his cheek. Moving closer, so that her leg touched the inside of his knee.

He stayed where he was, feeling the coldness in her fingertips from where she had held the glass. Looking up at her and hearing her say, "What you probably should have done, instead of dicking around, small-time stuff, you should have found one thing, one score, I guess. Something that would have set you up for life. What you should have done, maybe you should've been thinking about it differently. Maybe thinking big." Still looking at him, but not smiling now, and then stepping back. She said, "My husband told me the reason you got in trouble up here, you wanted money from a guy. You work for him for, what, four weeks, this guy doesn't pay you. What kind of person is it, they're gonna be happy working for free? And now this. How long are you gonna hang around here, taking shit from my husband?" She looked at him for another second and then turned away, walking back towards the open French doors, loosening the belt of her robe and letting it drop to the ground halfway there.

Cully sat there and watched her ass, seeing her disappear inside the house. Not really able to believe it, what she could do to him. Get him involved in a quiet little chat. They're sitting there, talking about her singing, his robberies, whatever. Having a nice time, being polite with each other, and the next thing he knows she makes some kind of shitty remark. Tells him how small-time he is. Jesus.

He sat at the table for a couple of seconds, not moving, wondering should he go back to his room. Or maybe get up off of the chair and follow her inside. Pretty sure that that was what she wanted. Hearing nothing but the cicadas all of a sudden because she turned the stereo off, and then not having to decide one way or another because he heard her voice, drifting out from inside the house, calling his name. Making him get up out of the chair and start walking towards the house without giving it any thought. Knowing if he thought about it for too long, he might not do it.

He walked inside—the living room, something like that. It looked the way Cully would picture a living room in a big house. A big open room, with a huge Oriental rug on the floor, a couple of big couches, and a baby grand piano in the corner next to a fireplace. With some oil paintings on the walls. Of old people mostly. Cully didn't know were they supposed to be of famous people or maybe they were relatives of Herb Dorrance. Wondering about it, but not really caring, because he was also looking at Michelle, standing there in the middle of the room. Without the bikini now. Naked. Looking at him and smiling. And then walking towards him, coming closer until she was right in front of him. Still smiling, while Cully looked at her tits, and down past them to the patch of blond hair between her thighs. Looking back up into her face while she concentrated, licking her lips and reaching over to unzip his pants, sliding her hand inside and touching him. Looking up into his eyes and grinning wider. Saying, "See, you're doing it already. Thinking big."

She walked over to the middle of the room, with Cully watching her, his fly unzipped, looking at her when she turned back to him and smiled. She stood there, staring at him, striking a pose, until he thought, Fuck it, knowing it was going to happen, knowing it since he came home and found her swimming laps out in the pool. He walked over and kissed her, getting excited, yeah, but feeling something more, picturing it, what it had been like the day before, driving her around town and listening to her shit, and hearing her make remarks out by the pool. He picked her up, jerked her up onto his hips, holding her with one arm and reaching down to undo his jeans, wriggling out of them and kicking them off of his feet. He could feel her pressing against him, moaning, saying yes softly and lifting her head up to kiss him as he lurched across the room towards the couch. He was still holding her, with his arm pretty tight, gripping her and not really caring was he hurting her or not.

He stubbed his toe on a chair and stepped back. Kicked it out of his way, heard it crash to the floor, sounding like maybe it broke. Cully, a wild man now, pushing the coffee table out of the way with his leg and swinging Michelle around, until her back was to the couch. He took two more steps, falling, landing on top of her, letting go of her for a second to look at her face. Grabbing one of her tits and squeezing it hard. Seeing the look she gave him, halfway there already, staring back up into his eyes for a second and then making a face, working her mouth into a circle and spitting at him, hitting him in the face with it.

He shook his head, wiped his face with the back of his hand, and picked her up off the couch with his other arm and slammed her down again. He put his hand on top of her head. Grabbed her hair and pulled it down towards the couch, twisting it, saying softly, "Is this it?" Seeing her nod, still staring at him, reaching down and grabbing his cock, guiding him, saying, JESUS YES, and moving under him like she was on fire.

He lost it then, still thinking a little bit about his anger, but not really caring because he was getting into it. Knowing it was what she wanted. But knowing it was what he wanted, too. Fucking her. Slamming into her until he could tell it hurt her. But feeling her lock her legs around him and start yelling, louder every time he slammed into her. He was holding her down, pinning her arms on the couch, swearing, with sweat popping up on his back. Wanting to hurt her. With her moving up to meet him every time he pulled back, telling him yes over and over again. Grabbing her own tits, pushing them up as far as they would go towards her face and leaning down to try to bite them. Both of them almost screaming, waking the fucking dead, until it was over and she pulled him down again and kissed him, looking at him like she hadn't seen him before, like he was somebody else. Staring at him in silence for a minute and then saying softly, *"Jesus, yes."*

• • •

Later, when she fell asleep, he got up and went back out to the pool. He poured a little Seagram's into a glass with some 7-Up and then walked back to the French doors. He stood there, sipping his drink and staring at the naked girl on the couch, wondering what the fuck was she up to?

CHAPTER

14

WHAT BENNY DID, after standing in the motel room, watching Michelle walk out to her Porsche, he followed her. It had put him in a good mood, fucking her. But it wasn't like he was gonna do the same thing all over again. She wanted to do it the right way—they get the diamonds and keep everything honest. That was all right. They could do that and then leave town. Maybe they *would* go down to Nashville, see if she could do it. Or else, open their own recording studio. He knew music. If somebody played him a song, he could tell you if it was talent. If anybody could do it, he could. Tell her what to do, what to wear, get her career started again. But differently this time. No more dicking around in small clubs. They'd start out right, with a record.

It would be all right, do something like that. If they went ahead and took the diamonds. Everything worked out and she was honest with him, he'd go along with it. But the thing was, if she had it in mind maybe she was thinking he was gonna let her lead him around by his cock, maybe it didn't matter to her if he wound up back at the penitentiary. If she wanted to do that, let her do it to the dude with the chain saw.

He waited until she started her car, giving it a half a minute and then walking out to his brother's Camaro, starting it up and following her down the road.

He stayed pretty far behind her, almost losing her on 21 out by the Marine Air Station, seeing the light turn yellow and having to punch it through the intersection. After that it was easy. He stayed a couple of hundred yards back, pretty sure she was on her way back home, neither one of them driving fast.

He could picture it, what was going through her head. Working the scam, if that was what she was doing. Lining everything up. Get Benny to do his part and then go back, work on Frank Cullen. He wondered about Cullen. What was he like? He was a con, yeah. But what did that tell you? Benny kept trying to picture it, had he ever met him or heard about him back at Raiford? He couldn't get a handle on it. There were all kinds of people down there. You'd meet some of them, the baddest people in the world. You take one look at them, they'd tell you, "I killed my mother." Man, it was something you'd believe. Have no trouble with. But you'd see others, maybe they'd be in there for murder, too, something like that. You'd look at them, maybe talk to them. And it would kill you, because they didn't belong there. They'd be sucking somebody's cock the day after they got there. Fucking prison eating them alive. So where did that leave Cully?

He saw Michelle turn into her driveway and went past slowly, turning around at the next intersection and coming back, pulling onto the shoulder of the road a hundred yards before her driveway and killing his engine. He could still see the driveway, tell if anyone came or left. He lit a cigarette and settled in to wait. Played with the radio for a bit, getting a country station, Garth Brooks, leaning back in the seat with his eyes on the driveway down the road.

He saw the Caddy maybe a half an hour later. Watched it slow down and pull into the driveway, pretty sure he knew who was driving but deciding what he wanted to do was make sure. He started the Camaro and moved along the shoulder until he was next to the driveway, getting out and starting to make his way through the field towards the house.

It made him smile, shake his head a little bit, seeing the two of them out by the pool. Sitting fifty feet back in the trees and watching Cully walk up to Michelle while she swam laps. Wondering did the man think it was a coincidence? He comes home, her husband's gone for the night, maybe she gave the cook the night off, and she just happens to be out for a midnight swim.

He watched Michelle get out of the pool and walk slowly over to the table, leaning over to shake out her hair, pointing her hips at Cully. Posing. Benny, standing in the trees, got a kick out of it. Smiling. Thinking she was good. She *should* have been an actress.

He watched the whole thing, hearing their voices but not able to tell what they were saying. Taking a chance and moving over to the house when Michelle went inside and Cully followed her a minute later. Moving across the side of the pool and going over to a window on the far side of the living room. Leaning against the house and seeing them fuck. Watching it, seeing Cully pick her up and throw her down on the couch. And all of a sudden it bothered him. Pissed him off.

It wasn't that they were fucking. That wasn't a big thing. Michelle, how else was she gonna do it? No, what pissed him off—standing in the dark, feeling like a fucking pervert all of a sudden—Cully, what he was doing, he was making her happy. Benny could tell, hearing Michelle start to yell and saying to himself, Ain't no act now. Seeing what was happening, Michelle, she was a fucking animal, something in heat. The thought of those diamonds maybe getting her horny, she couldn't get enough cock. Has to fuck Benny and then come home here and try it out with Cully. It didn't bother him, she was his ex-wife. That was all right. What Benny was thinking, she finds out maybe she likes things with Cully. Maybe if she had a choice, if it came down to that, she had to choose between the two of them? What if she chose Cully? Where did that leave him?

He left before Cully came back outside, working his way back to the road and getting in the Camaro, sitting there for a couple minutes, not sure what to do. Wheeling the car around finally, saying, Fuck it, still pissed off. Deciding what he could do, he could go on back into town, stop at a bar. Have a couple of drinks and see what happened.

Benny drove to Casey's and went inside, ordering a beer and a shot of whiskey. He looked around the place, thinking it hadn't changed much since he and Michelle used to go there. Except there used to be a little stage over in the one corner that was gone now. They'd have live bands every once in a while. Michelle sang there a couple of times. He could picture it, going back five years in his head, Michelle, up on stage, Jesus, she was even better looking back then, under the lights.

Benny used to tell her what to wear. He'd send away for different outfits from a place down in Nashville. Stuff with a lot of rhinestones. Make her sparkle up on that fucking stage. She'd tell him, I don't wanna wear that crap. He'd look at her, tell her, You think Dolly Parton looks stupid, the outfits she wears? Loretta Lynn, maybe she performs in blue jeans and a flannel shirt? Shake his head, because he knew he was right. He told Michelle, It's showbiz, hun-bun. And he'd get some outfits for himself, nice slacks, with a row of rhinestones running down each leg. And maybe a silk shirt and a bolo tie, one with a lot of turquoise in it. Sit there in the audience, Colonel Parker, at a table up front, while Michelle sang her heart out up there on the stage.

Drinking his beer, he wondered why they had gotten rid of the stage. Otherwise the place was pretty much the same. Still had the same dumb mural on the wall. Different waitresses, though. He watched the one, giving her a look and smiling when she looked his way. Being nice about it, dressed in his best jeans. He had on a wide belt, with a big silver buckle he thought went nicely with his lizard-skin boots, and a nice, button-down cotton shirt. Letting her see it, thinking, here I am, a country boy, giving her his Randy Travis look.

She kept walking back and forth, going from the tables to behind the bar, and Benny, after watching her do it for about the fifth time, smiled at her and said, "What's your name, hun-bun?" She gave him a look, tired maybe, or else just not up to it. Told him, "Jenny," but then moved away. Benny sitting there, still with his eye on her, because she had a nice ass, and even though it was stupid—dress the barmaids up in men's suits, who are they trying to fool—he liked the way she looked. Nice ass and a great set of titties.

When she came back, he asked her, "Hey, you ever see a pair of boots like this, lizard skin?" Holding his foot up in the air so she had to look at them. Asking her, "You want to know how I got them?"

She said, "I'm busy." Irritated now, he could see it.

He smiled, still being friendly, but thinking, Fuck her, leaning towards her and speaking softly. "Hey, I don't know, you're too busy, you don't care about my boots. You want to be rude about it. Maybe, instead, you want to come out to my car, make a hundred bucks. All you got to do is suck my dick." Watching her face, liking the way he saw it change, a whole different look coming over it. She was probably a nice girl. A guy, some cracker coming in here and spending five dollars a night on beer, he wanted to fuck her, or maybe just get a blow job, he was gonna have to take her out. Buy her dinner and work for it. Fuck that. Her whole face letting Benny know that nobody had ever asked her something like that, come right out and said it. Offered money.

He got a kick out of it, liked it when she turned to the bartender and said, "Tommy, I've got a problem here," Benny sitting there, sipping his beer and looking at Tommy. What the fuck was the skinny little bartender gonna do? Benny reached over and grabbed his change from the bar, looking at Tommy and saying, "Sport, you come around this bar, what'll happen is you're gonna get hurt." Still smiling, still being nice, because Tommy didn't want to come around the bar and they both knew it.

Benny looked at the money in his hands, took a five out and held it up, letting the girl see it. Smiling and saying, "See, it could have been twenty times this." Putting the bill down and shaking his head, a good old boy who just didn't understand it, a girl wanting to turn down easy money. Was rude about it. He didn't get it.

He left, feeling better, not worrying was Michelle gonna try to scam him. It didn't matter. She could give it a try, it wasn't something that he was going to let happen. Thinking about it, and deciding all he'd have to do was stay sharp. Running it over in his head and telling himself it was gonna work out. Thinking about the diamonds, and this time he was gonna do it right.

Benny saw the guy with the hat when he was leaving the bar. With a girl. The two of them holding hands, lovebirds. The girl all right looking. But Benny wasn't thinking about that. He was looking at the guy, at his head, and the big Stetson he had on top of it. Benny watched them getting closer, thinking, Hot dog, look at that hat. With a nice curve in the brim, you play with it, get it just right, it's like it was molded to your head. Still thinking about it, stepping towards the couple, clearing his throat and waiting for them to look at him.

Pointing and saying, "Man, that's some nice hat you got." Giving it a second and then asking, being polite about it, "What size is it, sport?"

CHAPTER

15

CULLY WOKE UP the next morning with the phone ringing right next to his head. He couldn't get it together at first, thinking he was back in the main house with Michelle. But then he remembered leaving the night before, Michelle asleep on the couch. That was her problem—he'd come on back to his apartment and fallen asleep.

He grabbed the phone, hearing a woman's voice, thinking at first that it was Michelle. Getting a little irritated, but then realizing it wasn't her, hearing Kristin's voice and trying to come fully awake, rubbing his eyes and sitting up in bed. Giving it a second and then saying, "Hi." Trying to sound pleasant.

What she had done, she'd given it a lot of thought. Should she call him or not? Waking up—it was Saturday morning—and wondering about it. What would he think? She put it off for a while. But then decided to do it. Get him on the phone, she could just say Hi, or else, if he sounded like he was glad to hear from her, she could ask him, What were you planning to do today? Let him know she was free.

She smoked a joint, feeling better, thinking about it. She'd known Cully for, what, a day or two? What was it about him she liked?

Maybe it was that he would sit there for an hour, just talking to her. Not try to get in her pants right away. She guessed that it would've been all right if he had tried, though. She'd seen him that first time, walking into the restaurant with Michelle, and she'd known she would have slept with him. Good-looking guy, he reminded her of Kevin Costner, the guy from *Robin Hood*. A guy that seemed pretty normal, a little quiet maybe. Not trying to be too flashy, but you could tell he was comfortable with himself.

She'd seen him, a couple of times, looking at her legs. Trying to be casual about it. Taking a peek every once in a while, back there in her kitchen, while she made coffee. She thought it was kind of cute, him trying to get a glimpse of her but not get caught, sitting at her table, with his James Dean expression. Serious, telling her, I just stopped by to see if your sister was here. But then not leaving for over an hour.

She lit another joint. If she was going to sit around and wait to call him she might as well enjoy it. She smoked half of it and then spent some time deciding if he wanted to see her, what should she wear? Something nice. Let him see her in something besides a long skirt or jeans for a change. Going through her closet she didn't come up with much that made her happy. She picked a denim skirt finally, a short one, telling herself it wasn't the same as wearing jeans. And then a tank top, nothing too outrageous, but still, if he saw a little bit of her shoulders, it wasn't like it was gonna do any harm. It had a bunch of cat hairs on it and she almost put it back, but then thought, the hell with it, and spent a few minutes getting them off.

Sitting there on her bed, with her outfit already picked out. Thinking, what she could do with her hair—she could mousse it, play with it, and then get a blow dryer out. See what he thought of that. Maybe wear a couple of bracelets on her arms. And some rings. Early punk. Or latter-day hippie. She wasn't sure. She didn't even know were they going to get together or not. Wondering why it was becoming such a big deal anyway.

She almost regretted it at first, when she finally did call him, because she could tell he'd been asleep, mumbling into the phone and calling her Michelle. But then he perked up. Told her he was sorry, saying, "I thought it was your sister, maybe she wanted to go somewhere."

She waited a second, taking a breath and then asking, "What are you doing?"

Hearing him pause and then ask her, "Today?"

"Yes."

He told her, "Nothing."

She couldn't think of how to say it. Feeling the pot all of a sudden and talking pretty quickly, because it always did that. Made her talk a lot. Saying, "I thought, if you weren't busy, if you didn't have anything planned, maybe you and I could do something. Get together. I don't know exactly what you had in mind for today, but I have most of the day off and I thought . . ."

But then she ran out of breath. Sitting there, with the phone in her hands, waiting to hear what he was going to say.

He gave it a second and then, sounding wide awake now, asked her, "What if we met somewhere for breakfast? How would that be?"

Cully couldn't believe it, sitting in Denny's, drinking orange juice and smoking a cigarette, seeing Kristin walk in. Staring at her as she walked over to him. He stood up, smiling, still staring because she looked so different, gorgeous, wearing a denim skirt that was a couple of inches above her knees and a nice tank top. She had big hoop earrings, made out of wood, with feathers on them—he thought they looked homemade—that bumped against her neck when she walked and a whole bunch of bracelets on her arm. Still wearing sandals.

She had done something to her hair. He didn't know what it was, spiked, kind of, like a *Vogue* model. With another flower in it. Making the other people in the restaurant turn and look. The Saturday morning customers, maybe on their way to the stores, the other women in the restaurant giving her a pissed-off look and then turning to their husbands, making sure they weren't staring. Walking in there, with Cully holding his juice glass halfway to his mouth.

131

He didn't know what she looked like, he couldn't have said was it any particular style or not. But still, it wasn't like he wanted to look away.

She smiled at him, sliding into the booth, nodding at the waitress and calling her by name. Giving it a minute, looking around the restaurant before swinging her face back to his, seeing that he was still looking at her and saying, "What?"

He didn't know what to say, shrugging and telling her finally, "You look nice."

She smiled. "Thank you." Looking at him for another second and then saying, "I gave it some thought." Picking up the menu and then asking him, "Did you order?"

He pointed at his juice. "I was thirsty." He was silent for a minute and then told her, "I'm glad you called."

"You are?" Smiling.

Already he could feel it, like the night before. They were pretty comfortable with each other. He told her, "Nobody ever said so, but I was thinking, Saturday's probably my day off. I didn't have much of an idea what to do." Not even wanting to think what it would have been like back at the house. When Michelle woke up, it was still just going to be the two of them there. He was pretty sure he didn't want to be around for that. Not until he'd had some time to get used to what had happened.

For a second he thought she had read his mind. She said, "Michelle didn't need you?"

He shrugged. "I don't think so. I left before she got up anyway." Thinking about what he'd said and adding, "I didn't see her around at least." Wondering, did it sound bad, saying it like that? Seeing the look she gave him, not saying anything, but giving a little nod, picking up her menu and opening it up.

After they had eaten and were sitting there drinking coffee she asked him, "What do you like to do? On your days off, what do you usually do?"

"I just started the job."

She smiled, leaning forward. "But before that? What did you do, if you had a whole day to yourself?"

He shrugged, thinking maybe he should tell her. Thinking it over and finally saying, "For a while I didn't have a choice."

"What do you mean?"

He drank some of his coffee, looking around trying to figure out how to say it. Not make a big deal out of it. "I was in prison." Hearing the words and looking at her. Waiting to see how she was gonna take it.

"Prison?" She was staring at him, not taking her eyes off of him. But he didn't see anything in her face that made him think she was gonna get mad, get up and walk out. She didn't seem mad.

He nodded.

She asked him, "For how long?"

Cully said, "Five years." Waiting and then telling her, "I held people up." Keeping it simple because it wasn't something he wanted to go into now. She kept staring at him, playing with her coffee cup and looking at him with those beautiful brown eyes. Making him uncomfortable so that he finally had to ask, "Is that something that bothers you?"

She shook her head, smiling all of a sudden. "I don't think so."

Later, they were walking on the beach, out at the state park on Hunting Island. Cully had asked her did she want to go anywhere special, and at first she couldn't decide, telling him, "Wherever you want." He thought about it, came up with a couple of places he might suggest, but before he could tell her she smiled and said, "Wait." Asking him, "What about the beach?" He said, "What about it?" Being dumb at first but then realizing—feeling a little foolish and telling her, "I've been here for, what, six weeks now. I've never been out there."

They drove out to the state park, leaving the car by the lighthouse and walking across the dunes to the sand. He held her arm while she bent down and took her sandals off, the wind bringing a little hint of the perfume she was wearing. And then he took his own shoes off, following her pretty far down the slope of the sand to get to the water because it was low tide.

It was windy out, not cold, but they had to shout to hear themselves if they got more than ten or twelve feet away from each other. Cully didn't have a lot to say, he wasn't feeling too sure of how things were going ever since he'd told her about being in jail. She'd said it didn't bother her, but he wasn't certain. He'd see her, every once in a while, if they weren't talking, he'd be looking at something else, maybe the water, or a gull, something like that, and then he'd turn around and she'd be staring at him. With a look on her face like she was thinking about something. He couldn't tell, was she having a good time or not? Not sure how to act because she was different than most of the women he had ever known. Different than her sister, too. With Michelle it was one thing, you knew why she was there. Knew what it was you wanted from her. With Kristin he couldn't figure it out. Because what was happening, he was having a good time just being with her.

They came to a place about a mile down from the lighthouse, where there were a lot of dead palmetto trees half buried in the surf. There was no way to get past them so they walked up to the dunes and found a place to sit. Cully, making room for her and then sitting himself, dug in his pockets for a cigarette.

She waited for a minute and then told him, "You come out here in the summer, July or August, there's no way you could come up here to the dunes. The bugs would eat you alive."

"Pick you up and carry you away, huh?"

She smiled. "Sometimes you wonder."

He didn't say anything. He was starting to feel a little comfortable again, because she was still smiling, and it didn't seem to be bothering her, spending the morning with him. He was still thinking about it, wondering should he bring the subject up again when she reached over and took his hand, looking at his face and smiling at him. Like she was reading his mind. She said, "I would've thought, if somebody had asked me, told me you just got out of prison, I would've thought you'd be different."

"Different how?"

She shook her head. "I don't know. More like Benny or something. When I see Benny, even before he got sent to prison, I'd always end up thinking he was dangerous. Like if you said some-

134

thing that made him mad he'd hurt you. Or maybe even hurt you just for the fun of it."

Cully was very aware of the warmth of her hand in his. Looking at her, seeing a thoughtful expression on her face. He thought she looked beautiful. It crossed his mind that he could never remember being alone with a woman this good-looking when he hadn't tried to get in her pants. But it was all right. Sitting here like this, he was feeling pretty good about just talking to her. He said, "Well, you meet a lot of people like that. In prison and out. Some people, it's like they go out of their way to be nasty."

She nodded. "How come you're not like that?"

He smiled, tried to make a joke out of it because he didn't know what to say. Telling her, "How do you know I'm not?"

But she didn't smile back. She pinned him with her eyes, staring at him for a couple of seconds and then saying, seriously, "I just do."

They were walking back to the car when he finally kissed her. Feeling like he was back in junior high school because it was awkward as hell. They were walking along the edge of the water, not talking, when she suddenly stopped and looked at him. When he moved towards her they almost bumped heads because she went to the same side as he did. It didn't last long, the kiss. Maybe ten seconds. He could feel her tremble a little in his arms and then she pulled away. But she was smiling, giving him a look that made Cully think she was the sweetest thing in the world.

After that he felt more comfortable with her. It didn't matter he was an ex-con. It didn't matter that maybe they hadn't slept together yet. It was like the kiss, that was the important thing. Everything else would happen when it was supposed to. It was something he'd never felt before. A whole new way of thinking.

They held hands the whole way back to the car. She kept saying things that didn't make a whole lot of sense to Cully. She'd pick up a shell, throw it out into the water, and then turn to Cully and say something like, Did you see that? Like it was important. He couldn't quite get a handle on it, the way she was acting.

When they got back to the car she stood there, with her hair blowing a little bit in the breeze. Staring at him. And smiling.

She said, "I had fun."

He nodded. "It was different." Then saying, "Nice." Looking at her, feeling closer to her, like he was starting to figure out what made her tick. He could picture her, remember when he was younger, he'd seen a photograph in *Life* magazine, people at Woodstock. You take away her spiked hair and she would have fit perfectly.

She asked him, "Did you really rob people?"

He looked at her, nodding. Telling her, "It was a while ago. Something I did in the past."

She told him, "The other night, at my house, when you came by looking for Michelle?"

"Yeah?"

She shrugged. "I had a feeling. From the way you talked. About Benny. Like it was something you were pretty familiar with."

He nodded. "It's not something I go out of my way to tell people."

Kristin said, "Yeah, but on the other hand, you do something, it's in the past. What's done is done."

He laughed. "Everybody doesn't think like that."

"They should." She waited for a moment and then said, "Do you think you'd ever do it again?"

"I don't know." He thought back to when he was in Raiford, talking to his cellmate, Bobo. Bobo telling him, Things get bad, man, what are you gonna do, pick up a gun? He said, "It's not something I can picture doing."

She was quiet for a second and then asked him, speaking softly for a change, "Do you believe in astrology?" He didn't know what she was talking about. Coming up with something like that, out of the blue.

He shook his head. "Like, what sign are you? That kind of thing?"

She nodded. "Yes." Serious about it, like she really wanted to know what he thought.

He told her, "No."

She shook her head. "Me neither."

"Jesus." Looking at her and saying, "If you don't believe in it, it's not something you agree with, why are you asking me about it?"

She ignored him. "I believe that there are things, though, I don't know what you'd call them. Something. Things that make it all right for two people to do whatever they want."

Cully figured he'd give it a try. He said, "You mean us?"

She nodded. "Two people want to do something, they should just do it."

He said, "I guess so."

She nodded. "Of course they should." Stepping up to him and touching his chest, letting her head lie there for a couple of seconds and then looking up into his face. With the same look in her eyes that she'd had when they were back at her house the other night. When she'd been talking about Benny, and how he had fucked up. With a look on her face like she'd been running it over in her mind.

She stepped back from him and said, like she was talking about the weather, "I want to rob a bank with you."

He told her, "It's not something you even want to kid about." Trying to be nice because he was starting to like her a lot. Telling her, "I know a couple of hundred guys, some of them are psychos, I'll give you that. But a lot of them, you see them in the street, you'd think they were normal. They're all sitting in cells back at Raiford."

He asked her, "You know what they all have in common?" She shook her head, "What?" He said, "They all thought, at one time or another, something just like that. Let's rob a bank."

He touched her cheek. "It's not something—you don't play around with it, think it's a game."

She looked at him. "I can see it. Dumb broad. That's what you're thinking."

He grinned. "Maybe. But listen, if you were a guy, I'd be thinking, dumb guy."

She walked a couple of feet away from him, digging her toes into the sand and then turning back to face him. "Let me ask you something. You making a killing, driving my sister around town?"

"That's not the point." Saying it and seeing the look she was giving him. Walking towards her and lifting her head in his hand.

She told him, "That place I try to run. The Shrimp Boat. You know how much money I owe on that?" Looking at him and saying, "This isn't Michelle talking, somebody, if she gets in a jam all she has to do is run to her husband, give him a sweet look."

He said, "Look, I had fun. It was nice—the beach, all of it." Waiting and then saying, "But you start talking about banks"—he shrugged—"you don't know what you're saying."

"Yeah," she said, "maybe I don't. I never did anything like that." Staring at him, doing something to him with her eyes, because he couldn't seem to look away. Telling him, "But you have." She waited a second and told him, "I've been thinking about it, off and on, for, what, four years?"

He looked away from her finally, turning towards the ocean to look at the waves and then glancing up to the parking lot, seeing the car parked there. Thinking this woman scared the shit out of him. One minute she wants to kiss on the beach, act like a couple of teenagers. You give her a few seconds and she's talking about grand theft. Armed fucking robbery. Looking back at her finally and saying, "Jesus, you're serious."

Seeing her nod, with a little smile on her face. Telling him, "Nothing gets past you for too long."

Cully had a beer in his hand when Benny walked in. He was sitting at Casey's, talking to Jenny, holding a bottle of Budweiser. There was a plate of boiled shrimp in front of him. Fresh. Cully couldn't get over it, how good they were. Jenny told him, "What'd you expect, they came out of the ocean about an hour ago." He'd take a sip of his beer and then eat a shrimp. Dip it in the sauce and pop the whole thing in his mouth.

Jenny would wait on somebody, get them a drink or else something to eat, and then she'd come on back and sit on the bar stool next to him. Talk to him about what her day had been like. Cully was having a good time. It felt fine talking to Jenny and not having to think about it much. Not have every word running through his head like when he talked to Kristin or Michelle.

He'd taken Kristin home. Dropped her off and then come on over here. He could still see it, her standing in her doorway after he had kissed her again. She had looked at him and said, "You think it's dumb, don't you?"

He said, "The bank?"

She nodded.

He told her, "Yeah, to be honest with you, I'd have to say it's not a good idea. I don't know, maybe you think it would be fun. Do it for kicks."

She looked at him, surprised. "You dummy, who said anything about fun?"

"I thought that was what you had in mind."

She told him, "I guess, you do it right," touching his arm, "and with the right person, it could be fun. Exciting." She took a step back and said, "But see, the real reason, I need the money."

He said, "Everybody needs money."

"Uh-huh." She let the silence hang there for a second and then told him, "When Benny robbed that bank, he took John Lewis, the guy I was living with at the time, with him. And nobody ever saw John again. I'm sitting there all by myself, people got nothing to say to me that isn't pretty nasty. Telling me that John ran off with the money when what I think is Benny killed him, left him to rot in some salt marsh or else at the bottom of the ocean." She was looking right at his face. "You know what kind of life I had with John? Always, he was hanging around with Benny. Neither of them ever worked. I'd give John money, and then I'd still have to buy the groceries, the beer. Whatever. Hell, half the time I'd give him cash, I think he gave some of it to Benny." She put her hands on her hips and said, "You know what I think?"

He said, "What?"

"I think those two screwed it up. The robbery. I think I could have done it better."

He didn't know what to say, thinking about it carefully because he didn't want to make her mad. He told her, "Here's the thing, if I do

139

rob a bank, if that's something I decide I want to get involved in, we can do it together. How would that be?" Grinning when he said it. But she didn't smile. She looked at him for a second like he was retarded. Saying, "Uh-huh," and then nodding slowly, walking into her house and closing the door.

CHAPTER

16

N O W   H E   W A S drinking a beer, watching while Jenny served food to a group of people, and then turning towards the door when he heard it open. Seeing Benny walk in, Jesus, he looked like somebody off of "Hee Haw." Wearing a ten-gallon hat and a pale blue suit, stepping inside the door and shooting his cuffs. His sleeves had ruffles on them. Cully, sitting there, waited to see was Benny gonna do anything, maybe start something because of the other day. Looking at the man's outfit—big silver buckle on his belt, shiny new cowboy boots, and a lump of turquoise on a string tie around his neck—and getting ready for it if he was gonna cause trouble.

Benny saw Cully right away. He grinned, gave it a big effort and came on over, bending down when he was a couple of feet away and pretending to look underneath Cully's bar stool. Saying, "Hey, sport, you don't mind, maybe if I look hard enough, I'll find a chain saw." Looking at Cully and grinning again. "Or did you forget to bring it?"

Cully smiled. "It's not the kind of thing I walk around with."

"Too big?"

Cully nodded. "Yeah." He looked at the man for another second and then said, "Nice hat."

Benny smiled. "You like it? I just got it last night." He took it off

and showed it to Cully. "Hey, this here is a gen-u-ine Stetson."
Holding it up in the air and telling Cully, "It ain't like they grow on trees."

Cully nodded. "I got to tell you something." Smiling and saying, "It goes pretty well with the rest of your outfit."

Benny leaned forward. Cully couldn't tell, was he being serious or not? "You think so?"

Cully nodded. "I see you walk in here, I know you. But I was thinking if I didn't, say I just met you, I don't know. I might think maybe you were somebody. A star, something like that."

Benny whooped. "You mean it? Son of a bitch." Then he lowered his voice and said, "What I believe, I don't believe it matters, are you a star or not. But"—he winked at Cully—"if you can get people wondering, keep 'em off balance . . ."

Cully nodded, wondering was the guy nuts or was he putting him on? Not worried any longer was Benny gonna do something, try to get back for the other day with the saw. If it was gonna happen it would have already taken place. He was getting a feeling about Benny. Thinking that if he was mad at you, he'd do something. But only if he was pretty sure things were gonna work out in his direction.

He realized Jenny had come back and was standing near them, looking from Cully to Benny.

Benny saw her and took off his hat again. "Hey, sugar, maybe I could get a beer?"

She looked at Cully. "You know him?"

Cully shrugged. But Benny smiled and sat down next to Cully, looking at Jenny and saying, loudly enough for everybody nearby to hear, "Hell yes, sugar, Cully and I go way back." Talking like a jig. Saying, "We graduates of the same *institution*." Looking at Cully now and saying, "Aren't we, sport? Raiford State." Slapping his knee and telling Jenny, "That's our alma mater."

Cully had been looking at Jenny. Seeing something in her face when she looked at Benny, like she had already met him and didn't like what she saw. He wasn't really paying attention to what Benny was saying. But when he heard the word Raiford, he turned around and looked at him, seeing the smirk the man was giving him and then hearing Benny say quietly, "That's right, sport. I walked out of that place four days ago."

Cully was trying to place the face, looking at Benny and wondering had he ever seen it in the yard. Not coming up with anything, but deciding, hell, he'd been too busy trying to mind his own business down there. He asked Benny, "You were at Raiford?" Acting interested, but not giving it too much.

Benny nodded, smiling and saying, "That's right. Maybe a little different time than you. You got out, what, a couple of months ago?" He waited while Cully nodded and then said, "Hey, for a guy, he just got out of jail, you're doing all right."

Cully looked at him, seeing Jenny walk back to a table—it was just Benny and him now. He said, "See, I know you're trying to surprise me, be mysterious, whatever. You want me to guess what that means."

Benny grinned. "You don't even have to guess. I'm gonna tell you."

Cully said, "Yeah?"

Benny nodded. "I see a guy, he's out of jail for, what, a couple of months? Next thing you know, he's banging his boss's wife." Benny taking a quick drink of his beer and then saying, "Not only that, the very next day, he's out on the beach, spending the morning with his boss's wife's sister." Grinning and saying, "It gets kinda complicated."

Cully didn't say anything for a second. Thinking what Benny might be expecting was for him to get mad. Maybe stand up and start something, make everybody in the bar think it was his fault. He looked at Benny and said, "You've been following me?"

Benny nodded and said, "See, I told myself you were pretty sharp."

Cully said, "Uh-huh." He picked up another shrimp and ran it through the sauce. Looking at Benny carefully and then taking a bite of the shrimp. "You making sure I'm okay? Following me around just in case, what, one of those ladies decides to get violent? Maybe I could get hurt?"

Benny chuckled. "Hell, from what I saw last night, you and Mrs. Herb Dorrance, my pretty little ex-wife, you could've gotten yourself hurt. Pulled a muscle or something."

"Uh-huh."

Benny said, "That's right, sport. Thing is, you look like the kind of guy I should keep an eye on. Maybe, I don't know, maybe I might learn something from watching you."

Cully nodded. "Uh-huh. Guy like you, you don't seem to have anything to do except follow me around, see what I'm up to."

"Sure." Taking a sip of his beer and then looking at Cully. "Thing is, I'm wondering, big guy like you, you're knocking the ladies dead, but how long is it gonna be before you get tired of it? Before you get sick of listening to that son of a bitch tell you how to live your life."

"Herb?"

Benny nodded. "Yeah, Herb. Sounds like a fag name, don't it?"

Cully shrugged and Benny snapped his fingers, smiling, and said, "Hey, wait a minute, maybe I got it wrong. Maybe what you're gonna do, you're gonna make it a family affair. Maybe you and old Herb, you two're gonna start getting it on." Nodding his head like it was important and telling Cully, "You want to be careful. You do a thing like that, try to satisfy all three of them, you're liable to wear yourself out." He took a sip of his drink and then pointed at Cully. "You want to know something?"

Cully shrugged and Benny told him, "I think old Herb, I think what he wants, he wants to see me dead."

"What gives you that idea?"

Benny smiled. "Cause I got a feeling about him. He and I, we aren't that different. He ain't ever gonna forget that I was once married to his wife."

"People get divorced all the time."

Benny nodded. "Yeah, but it'd be something personal to Herb. Something he'd feel he had to do something about."

"And maybe it'd have something to do with you robbing that bank. Something more than just you used to fuck his wife."

Benny stared at Cully for a few seconds and then burst out laughing. "Jesus, boy, I knew you was sharp." He leaned forward, with his elbows on the table, and said, "Thing is, you don't want to

144

get too sharp. You start making too many remarks like that one, it'll get you in trouble."

Cully picked up his Budweiser and took a drink. He held it to his mouth, finishing it and putting the bottle on the bar. He stood up and looked at Benny. "Now I remember you. Back at Raiford. You were the one, somebody wanted a good blow job, you were the one they went to." Walking past him without saying anything else and heading for the door. Hearing Benny behind him, in his country boy voice saying, "Hey, sport, what'd I say?" Acting hurt.

Cully didn't look back.

Benny drove from Casey's straight to Dave Ross's garage, pulling into the lot and honking the horn of the Camaro. He waited for his brother to come out, thinking about Frank Cullen. The guy was pretty smooth, Benny had to give him that. Benny tells him he's been following him around, watching him bang broads, and Cullen just gives him a look. Comes out with a crack about blow jobs without losing his cool.

Benny had pretty much decided that what he'd do, he'd sit back and see if Michelle could talk Cully into doing what they wanted. If she could, that'd be fine. He'd go along with it and maybe, the first opportunity he got, after they had the stones, he'd take them all for himself. Put a bullet in Frank Cullen, wave good-bye to Michelle, and he'd be out of there. Fuck everybody.

Meanwhile, what he had to do was get ready. Make sure he was prepared for anything. He shook his head, because it was gonna be a lot of work, watching Cully and keeping an eye on Michelle, seeing that she didn't try to screw him. But it was gonna be worth it.

Earl came walking up to the car and Benny rolled the window down. Earl with a big grin on his face like he was glad to see Benny, and Benny, he didn't even say hi. Just looked at Earl and said, "I need a gun."

Earl stopped walking a couple of feet away from the car. He ran a hand through his hair and said, "Jesus, what do you need it for?"

Benny shook his head, acting like he was talking to a retarded person. Telling Earl, "I don't remember telling you it was okay you wanna know my business." Giving him a cold look, staring right at him until Earl nodded and said, "Okay."

Benny said, "A pistol. Something nice."

Earl nodded again. "Back home, in my drawer. In my bedroom, next to the bed. A .38."

Benny nodded. He put the car in gear and started to pull away. Earl took a step towards him and called out, "Benny . . ."

Benny stopped the car and looked at his brother. "What?" Giving him that look again, impatient because he wanted to get going. Get the piece and see what was gonna happen next.

Earl just stood there, like he was afraid to say anything else. Staring at Benny, the man using the car, taking it away from him. Benny could see that was what Earl was thinking. And then coming to him for a gun. Earl, a fucking washout, a drunk, he didn't have the fucking nerve to stand up to Benny if his life depended on it. Benny smiling now and saying, "Why don't you do this. Why don't you head on back into that garage, get your pint bottle, whatever, suck on that for a while. Make yourself feel better." Seeing the look on Earl's face before he drove away.

Dave Ross, standing in the office of the garage and watching Earl talk to Benny, waited for about thirty seconds after Benny left and then, seeing Earl still standing out there, walked on over. He stood next to Earl for a couple of seconds, rubbing his hands on a rag and looking down the street to where the Camaro had disappeared, clearing his throat finally and saying, "What'd he want?"

Earl shook his head like he was coming out of a trance and turned to Ross. "He wanted to borrow something."

Ross asked, "What?"

Earl looked back out into the street. "Nothing."

Ross snorted. "Jesus." Turning to Earl, getting in front of him and saying, "The man's your brother, I'll give you that. But he doesn't give a rat's ass about you."

Earl gave it a second and then nodded slowly. Looked at Ross and said, "He wanted to borrow a gun."

"Shit." Putting his hands on his hips and saying, "What for?"

Earl said, "He didn't say."

Ross reached up and touched Earl on the shoulder, turning him and beginning to lead him back towards the garage. Saying, "Why don't we find out." Walking next to Earl and nodding his head, like he had thought it over and decided it was a good idea. Telling Earl again, "Why don't we find out what the son of a bitch is up to."

Earl stopped walking and looked at his boss. He looked like somebody had kicked him in the balls. Maybe he was going to start crying, Ross wasn't sure. Earl shook his head again, hard, like he was trying to clear it, get the cobwebs out. Looking at Ross and then at the garage. Saying, "I need a drink."

Ross gave it a second and then nodded. "Sure you do. What we'll do, we'll close up early. Maybe go down to Casey's, get a couple of beers." Seeing Earl start to nod again and saying, "What we'll do, we'll have a beer. Maybe a couple of shots. And talk this thing out." Leading Earl back into the office again and saying, "Figure out what we want to do."

Cully was tired when he got back to Herb Dorrance's place. There was no sign of either Herb or Michelle so he parked the Caddy and made his way up the stairs, thinking that he'd sack out for a while. Maybe later he'd get up the nerve to go up to the main house and say hello to Herb. Act like nothing had happened. Like he hadn't fucked the man's wife on the living room couch the night before. He was pulling his shoes off, sitting on the bed, when he heard footsteps on the stairs outside his room.

Herb Dorrance was in a good mood. It was something Cully could see right off. Coming to the door of Cully's little room and knocking even though it was open and he could see Cully sitting there.

Cully nodded at him and Herb came in, looking around the room and asking, "You comfortable up here? Everything okay?"

He looked at the man, wondering should he say something like, I was thinking of having your wife move in, make it easier for her and me to fuck. He said, "I'm fine." Waiting a second and then asking, "How'd it go, up in Fayetteville? You get the tractors?"

Dorrance shook his head. "Too much money for what they are. I told him, the guy that's selling them, he wants to deal with me, come down in price a little, maybe we could work something out." Herb made an expression like he couldn't believe how dumb people could get. He said, "The guy with the tractors, I guess he thought I didn't know what I was doing, like I'm a fucking novice, don't know my ass from a hole in the ground. I could see it, he wanted me to buy those tractors, thought maybe I'd go for his price." He looked at Cully. "You watch, he'll call me by the end of the week. Meet my price."

Cully nodded. "That's the way it is sometimes."

"Yeah, well, you got to show these people who's boss." He changed the subject, telling Cully, "My wife tells me it was pretty quiet last night."

Cully looked out the window, and then made himself look at Dorrance, saying, "Yeah, it was."

Dorrance stood up, starting towards the door but then turning back, clearing his throat and telling Cully, "See, maybe you got all worked up for nothing. About the gun." Saying, "You let your temper get in the way when all I was doing was asking you to do your job. If I hadn't given you the job, what would you be doing now?" He looked at Cully for another couple of seconds, nodding, and then he turned to leave.

CHAPTER

17

MICHELLE WAS THINKING it was time to get it going. She spent the whole morning, from eleven o'clock on, when Herb got home, following him around making sure he was having a good time. Spending the day waiting on him, for Christ's sake. Making sure he still knew what a great wife he had.

The whole time, what she was thinking was, she'd better get things moving, pull Cully into this thing before Benny got too impatient. Before he did something stupid.

When she woke up, she'd thought at first that Cully was still in the house. Maybe he'd gone into the kitchen to get something to eat. But she couldn't find him anywhere and when she went outside the Caddy was gone. She stood there looking at the Porsche, all by itself in the garage, wondering where was it Cully had to go, he gets up early in the morning and takes off? Wondering about it, because she realized that she might have wanted him to be there. Spend a little time with him, just the two of them, without any of the pressure. Maybe just have fun with him. It amazed her that she felt like that. Like she actually enjoyed being with him. After a bit she put it out of her mind. Talked herself into being a little mad at him for leaving.

She met Herb out in the driveway. All morning long she'd had her eyes peeled. Wanted to be there when he got home. Hurrying out to see him, saying hello to Billy Eagle, and then hugging Herb. Giving him a kiss. Showing him, Hey, I'm just a poor little southern girl can't make it without her man. Jesus.

She made him lunch because Amelia wasn't there, and he sat at the kitchen table talking to her. Saying, "I've got to run into town for a little while." She acted like she was disappointed, giving him a look and saying, "You just got home." He told her to mind her own business, which didn't bother her a bit because the whole time she'd been wondering how could she get him out of her hair for a little while.

She asked him, making it sound like she didn't really care, "Have you seen Cully?" Being casual about it.

He told her, "I just saw him, in his room. I think he's taking it easy." Leaning forward in his chair and smiling, saying, "I think he's hung over. He looked a little washed out." Looking at her and saying, "I don't know, guy like that, basically he's a lowlife, maybe he's a drunk, too." With Michelle going along with it, joining her husband in a little gossip about the chauffeur and listening to him ramble on about how there were two types of people and Cully was at the bottom end.

She asked him, "You think so?" He gave her a look, nasty, not moving for a couple of seconds, and then asked her, "You're pretty interested in this guy? You like trash like him, reminds you of your ex-husband? Dumb bitch like you doesn't know the difference." She shook her head, trying to sound nice, saying, "Herb, honey, come on. I was only making conversation." He told her, "Yeah?" Laughing at her and then reaching over and grabbing her cheeks in his hand. Squeezing them hard and smiling into her face. "You're so interested in him, why don't you go on over, see if you can make his hangover go away."

She pulled away from him and said, letting a little of her anger show, "I don't think I'll do that." Wanting to tell him, maybe he's just tired from fucking your wife last night.

She waited until Herb left, giving it ten minutes in case he forgot something, and then walked over to the garage. She made her way up the stairs quietly, walking into Cully's room without knocking and seeing him there, sound asleep, in his undershorts, with his clothes piled in a heap and the bedcovers kicked all over the place.

She thought what she might do, maybe she could slip her clothes off. Slide into the bed with him and surprise him. Get him going and then tell him what she had in mind. She was trying to decide was that a good idea when he opened his eyes and said, "Back in Raiford, I don't know, I got to the point where I was never quite asleep. At least it never felt like it. You get so paranoid in a place like that. You feel like you've got to be aware all the time."

She pulled the chair over to the bed and sat down. Laughing and saying, "I make you paranoid?"

He sat up in the bed and said, "No, it's not that. I think it's just a state of mind. Something you develop over a period of time."

"Yeah?"

He nodded. "Which brings me to something I want to ask. Your husband, Herb—he around?"

"Is he gonna come barging in here any minute?"

"Something like that. He comes in here, next thing you know I'm out of a job. Maybe even more than that."

"And what would you do then? Is that it?"

"It's something to think about." He gave it a minute and then said, "The thing is, I can't help it, I'm wondering, maybe what your husband's doing, he's setting me up. Get you in here, all of a sudden he comes up those stairs. It'd be kinda uncomfortable."

"You think I'd do something like that?"

"Well, he and I—the subject came up."

She nodded. "Somebody like you, in your position, that could be a bad thing."

He said, "Uh-huh." Leaning down to look at her legs. Smiling and saying, "Hey, you want to know something, I think you forgot to put on underwear this morning."

"I might have."

"I think you did."

"What I could do, I could get in that bed, let you find out for sure."

He shook his head. "No, I don't think so."

"Last night, it was too much for you?"

He looked at her. "Last night was . . . I don't know."

"Interesting."

He laughed. "I wouldn't have said that."

She pulled the chair closer to the bed. "Last night, what I would have said . . ." Stopping and then leaning forward so that her face was only a foot away from Cully's. Saying, "You want to know what it feels like when I sleep with Herb? We're talking maybe once every two or three weeks. I have to work at it—it's like a job—do exactly what he wants every time. He's got these things, ways that he wants it to happen. You want to know what that's like, how it compares to last night?"

"I'm getting a good review."

She smiled. "Maybe."

He got up off the bed and picked up his jeans. Pulled them on and then picked his shirt up off the floor, digging in the pocket for his cigarettes. Lighting one and then turning to her. Sitting back on the bed and saying, "I'm not sure where we're going with this. Did I have fun last night? Maybe I could say no. You could call me a liar."

"Except you're not going to say no."

He shook his head. "Neither one of us would believe it."

She got up out of the chair and walked to the window, staring outside for a minute while he watched her. And then turned back to him and said, "I want to tell you something. I want you just to listen to me."

She came back to the bed and took one of his cigarettes, lighting it and walking back to the window. Asking him, "All right? Just listen?"

He nodded.

She said, "I'm going to leave my husband. I can't take it. Looking at him, listening to him talk about his goddamn farm. Putting up with his shit. You see what he does. Bringing women home. You want to ask me what he's doing, bringing whores home. You think they fuck *him*?" She shook her head. "I can't *do* it anymore."

He said, "And you and I, we ride off into the blue?"

She got mad for a second, let a look cross her face, but then got rid of it. She said, "Let me finish."

"Okay."

She told him, "I know it seems like I've got all the money in the world. You look at this place, the house. With the pool and everything. I'm rich, right?"

"Doing better than a lot of people."

She nodded. "Yeah, it would seem that way." She was quiet for a second and then said, "You have to understand. None of it, and I mean none, is mine. I want to buy something, maybe it's a couple of hundred dollars, or even a thousand. That's not a big deal. I got to work for it, though, do what he says. But if I do, and I go to Herb, maybe smile at him . . ."

Cully said, "Maybe do more than smile." But grinning, being nice about it.

"Yeah, whatever it takes. I need that kind of money, it's not a problem." She took a drag of her cigarette and then pointed it at him. "But that's it. That's all I can get."

"What'd you do, sign an agreement?"

She nodded. "At the time I thought it was all right. I thought I could get him to change his mind."

Cully said, "Herb, that son of a gun, he turned out to be pretty stubborn."

She gave him a look. "Shit. I even bring the subject up, he looks at me and asks, 'What would you want to change things for?' Like I'm being foolish. But getting a kick out of it. The power of it, you know?"

Cully got up off the bed and walked over to the window. He touched her shoulder and said, "Okay, I'm getting the picture. You're stuck here."

"That's right."

"So why don't you do this, why don't you get to the point?"

She nodded. Walked to the far side of the room to where there was an ashtray and said, "Maybe I'm getting tired of you, you ever think about that? You spend a lot of time acting like you don't like me. Why's that?" She didn't wait for an answer. She put her smoke out in the ashtray and then looked back at Cully. "The point is, I *am* going to leave him."

Cully nodded. "Okay. Do it."

She shook her head. "Not like that. Not poor. Shit, I've done that before. On my own. Without a fucking dime. Why do you think I married Herb?" Shaking her head again and saying, "Never again. I told myself that it would never happen again."

"So what are you gonna do?"

She walked back to him. Stood there, a couple of feet away from him, looking him right in the eye and said, "I'm going to take his goddamn money is what I'm gonna do."

Cully couldn't believe it, looking at Michelle and thinking, what was it, a conspiracy? The two sisters, they see Cully and they figure, let's turn to crime, get him to do it? Looking at her, maybe what he should do, he should tell her, Hey, your sister might want to get involved in this. But he decided he wasn't going to bring up Kristin now.

He took a step back from Michelle and said, "What, you figured, get the ex-convict to help you?"

She seemed surprised, asking him, "Is that what you think?"

He didn't answer. She shook her head and told him, "I wanted to get an ex-convict to help me? If that's all I wanted, why wouldn't I get my ex-husband to help me." She shook her head. "I'm going to do it. I could use some help. I'm not going to tell you I couldn't use it. I think you and I, if we did it, it would work out nicely."

Cully held up his hands. He said, "Forget it. You want to leave your husband. That's fine. Take his money, too. I don't care. Hell, maybe you've even earned it. But don't tell me about it."

She stared at him, neither one of them saying anything.

Cully was thinking he should get out of there. Leave the whole fucking town behind. A little pissed off because all he'd tried to do, since he got out of Raiford, was keep a low profile. Not get involved with a lot of things that he knew would get him in trouble. The reason he left Miami, came up here, was he knew if he had stayed down there he would've ended up doing armed robberies again. Get involved with people he knew from before and next thing he knew he'd be out on the streets again. Sticking a gun in people's faces.

He shook his head. "No way. I don't even want to hear about it."

Feeling good that he was saying it. Not caring was he maybe being nasty to her. Thinking about it, he hadn't wanted to hurt Kristin. But he didn't give a damn about Michelle.

She gave it another couple of seconds, nodding finally and walking towards the door. Pausing when she got there, looking at him again and saying, "In a way, it's a shame. I thought maybe you'd at least be curious. Besides, the way he treats you like shit, I thought maybe you'd want to be involved in something like this."

He shook his head. "When I was into that, armed robbery, it wasn't anything personal. I didn't have anything against anyone. I just wanted their money."

"It's not personal, a guy like Herb, a fucking psycho, he gets off on making your life miserable?"

"What do you think I'm gonna do? I'm gonna stick it out. I can get through a place like Raiford, I can deal with Herb's shit. I make a little money and I'm gone."

She smiled. "Well, see, we're not talking a little money here. We're talking a lot of money."

"No." Putting something into it because he didn't even want to hear about it anymore. He didn't trust her. Didn't trust himself either. You start talking about a thing, he knew this from experience, and before you knew it you *were* interested. It had crossed his mind a couple of times. Go back to it, pull a couple of scores maybe, and then get the fuck outta town. He'd told himself not to do it, though. Stick it out. It had been getting bad enough, maybe it had to get better. He said it again. "No."

"You don't want to even hear any of it."

"No." He was getting mad again because he could tell, he was a little curious.

She smiled and said, "Okay." Looking at him and nodding. Saying, "No hard feelings?"

He looked at her. "No hard feelings."

"Good." She gave it another couple of seconds and then turned towards the door, walking a couple of steps into the hallway, while he watched her. But then turning back and stepping into the room. Grinning now, having fun with it, he could tell, waiting for her big moment. All of a sudden he could see, she'd been building up to it all the time. Waiting to get to this point. Standing there, just inside the doorway, with her hip cocked a little bit toward him and looking at him with a half grin on her face. And Cully, sitting on the bed, watching the way her skirt clung to her hips and knowing that she wasn't wearing anything under it, thinking about it without wanting to. Hearing her say, "Because we're talking about some serious money." Acting like she had to think about it, come up with a figure. While Cully tried to say something, tell her to get out. But, all of a sudden, he had to know. He waited for her to say something else, looking at her while she gazed at the ceiling and then looked back at him and said, "Last time I counted, we were looking at something, I think it was over four hundred thousand dollars. Just sitting there."

He tried not to say it, thinking about it. Four hundred thousand dollars, Jesus, and he was trying not to say something stupid. Something he'd regret. Opening his mouth to tell her he still wasn't interested. Thinking the words out in his head and then surprising the shit out of himself by telling her, "Why didn't you say so?"

He sat there feeling dumb, wanting to kick himself as he watched her come back into the room and sit down. Saw her tuck her skirt under her legs and smile at him. Telling him, "You forgot to ask."

CHAPTER

18

CULLY WAS DRIVING on 21, wheeling the big car past a semi loaded with logs and then heading through town. Going out over the bridge, leaving Beaufort behind. Cruising now, the needle on a steady sixty-five as he drove towards the Shrimp Boat. Slowing down when he got to Frogmore because of the speed zone, but then punching it again, making the last three miles in about two and a half minutes.

He'd had, what, twenty-four hours, maybe a little longer, to think about it? He'd listened to Michelle lay it out for him the day before. The whole thing. Jesus, Cully had been thinking she was gonna get him to walk in there and rob the whole bank. She'd looked at him and said, "No, forget about the bank. All we want is the one box." Smiling at him and saying, "The beauty of it is, you do it right, nobody even knows what's going on except the one guy you get to open the box."

He told her, "See, that's what a lot of people do."

"What?"

"They keep looking at it from the wrong angle. They tell themselves nothing's going to go wrong."

She nodded. "Well, nothing should go wrong."

"Uh-huh. And then, when the shit hits the fan, something does go

157

wrong. Which it probably will. You've spent all this time telling yourself how perfect it's going to be, you don't know what to do."

She'd smiled at him and said, "Think positively."

He looked at her for a minute and then told her, "The thing is, we'd be better off, in better shape, if what we did, we thought realistically instead."

He'd gotten maybe two hours of sleep the night before, running the thing over in his head up in his little apartment. Deciding, okay, he could do it. Take Herb Dorrance's money, did that bother him? Herb Dorrance, all the time he pulled little shit to remind Cully who was boss. Like he had to have people around, on the surface maybe they didn't measure up, so that he felt better about himself. Could he take the man's money? Yeah, it wouldn't be a problem. He'd enjoy it. And it was four hundred large, maybe more, something he'd never even dreamed about before. The other thing was, did he think he was going to be able to go in there, get the diamonds, and everything would be okay? Lying on his bed the night before, he had to shake his head because there was no way that was gonna happen. He was supposed to believe, what, maybe Michelle, she takes one look at him and decides he's the guy she wants to do this with? Maybe they get the diamonds, cash them in, and spend the rest of their lives on some tropical island? Just the two of them? Cully had to smile, even thinking about it. Seeing Benny in this somehow, waiting on the sidelines to come in and take Cully out once the score was over. Or else, maybe Benny was thinking he'd take everything for himself. Leave Cully *and* Michelle behind. It gave Cully a headache thinking about it. All the possibilities.

When he got to the Shrimp Boat he pulled into the lot. He didn't even get out of his car. He hit the horn and then didn't have to wait at all because Kristin, maybe she saw him coming, she was out the front door of the restaurant in about twenty seconds.

He told her, rolling the window down and sticking his head out, "I want to go for a ride." Not telling her anything else except when she started to say she couldn't go, he said, "It's important. And it won't take all day." Waiting a second and then telling her, "I'm not fooling here."

She nodded and ran back inside. Came out a minute later without her apron and got in the other side of the car, looking at him but not saying a thing.

Cully took his time about it, not coming right out and saying anything about the diamonds. He drove back on 21 into Beaufort, going slowly while she sat quietly next to him or pointed something out if they were going by a nice house or something. She made him take a left off of Carteret onto Prince Street and then make the dog-leg onto Hancock. She said, "Drive down to the end."

He pulled the Caddy down to where the road dead-ended at the bay and stopped. She pointed at the house across the street from the car and said, "Well?"

He looked at it. "I'm supposed to say something, I don't know. It looks like a nice house."

She just kept looking at him.

He said, "I'm still not getting it."

"Haven't you seen that house before?"

He shook his head.

"In the movies." Waiting a few seconds and saying, "Come on. *The Big Chill*."

"I didn't see it."

"Damn." Looking disappointed but then saying, "Wait, they made another one there. I can't remember it, it had"—snapping her fingers and then saying—"I know, Robert Duvall. Where he's a Marine pilot. Did you see that one?"

He shook his head. "I haven't seen many movies lately."

"I can't remember the name."

He put the car in gear and started to turn around, saying, "It'll come to you."

"Maybe." She was quiet for a minute. He could tell it was bugging her, not being able to remember the name and then suddenly she said, "Wait. I got it. *Great Santini*. With Robert Duvall and some-body else. I can't remember. Like Jill Clayburgh. Only it wasn't her. But some actress, I always get her confused with Jill Clayburgh."

Cully looked at her for a second, driving down Prince Street now, coming to the stop sign where it met Carteret. He said, "I'm pretty sure I didn't see it."

"Well, when they filmed it and *The Big Chill,* it was pretty neat. Everybody got all excited."

"I can imagine. Hollywood in your own back yard."

"Yeah." She waited until he pulled back onto Carteret and said, "I guess it would be kind of nice. Be an actress."

"You think so?"

She shrugged. "If you were good. I mean, if it were up to you what parts you got. That kind of thing."

"Lotta work, though."

She nodded after a second. "Yeah, I guess so."

Going down Carteret to the Plaza by the Winn-Dixie and the movie theater she finally asked him, "What're we doing?"

"Working."

She nodded. "Uh-huh. Is it something you want to tell me about?"

He took his eyes off the road for a second. Glanced at her and said, "Tell me the truth, how well do you get along with your sister?"

She shrugged. "We live near each other. If she gets drunk, she usually comes out to see me. Other than that, I see her maybe every couple of months. Maybe a little longer."

He said, "Uh-huh." Slowing down because the traffic was backing up. "You think, the two of you, you're the kind of sisters, one of them gets something, they're gonna share it with the other?"

"I don't know what you mean."

"Say Michelle makes a lot of money. Is she gonna call you up, tell you, Hey, come on over and get your share?"

Kristin smiled. "I can't see her doing that."

Cully shook his head. "It's what I would've said."

She leaned over in her seat and touched his shoulder. "You want to tell me why all these questions?"

He smiled. "Sure." Reaching in his pocket for a smoke. Taking his time about it. Lighting it and then glancing at her. Saying, "Michelle, she's got this wild idea she's gonna steal her husband's money. Diamonds. A lot of them."

160

Kristin said, "Jesus. Is this for real?"

"I don't think she's kidding around about it. If that's what you mean."

"And she wants you to help?"

"Uh-huh." He took a drag of his smoke and said, "Listen, I can't see it. I help her do this, she and I, say we do get all those diamonds. Where does that leave us?"

"You don't trust her."

He laughed. "You want to tell me I should?"

She thought about it. "No."

"I see Benny out there somewhere. Hanging back, waiting to see if I'm gonna do it."

"You think they're going to use you. As a . . . patsy."

"Patsy . . . yeah, that's what you'd call it."

"So what are you going to do?"

"Well . . . ," he shrugged. "I think I'm gonna do it."

"But you just said . . ."

"The thing is, I'm gonna do it before they do."

"Oh."

He smiled. "Yeah, oh." He waited a second and then asked her, "Is that something that bothers you, taking your brother-in-law's money?"

"I don't think so."

"Don't forget, if I take it, it means I'm taking it from your sister, too."

"I know."

"What do you think?"

"I don't know." She looked out the window and ran her hand through her hair before she said, "I mean, it's like you asked me. If she did it, it's not like she was going to give some to me."

"There's that."

She was quiet for a minute and then said, "Why are you telling me all this?"

He looked at her again, driving past the Toyota dealership. Telling her, "What I was thinking, if this is something I decide to do—go ahead with it—well . . . you're gonna help me."

He told her, "Look at me." Waiting at a traffic light and then not saying anything else until she was staring at him. "I'm thirty-six years old. I know how to do, what, fix cars a little bit?" He let off the brake and moved through the intersection, telling her, "I get out of jail and I keep telling myself, you can do it. Get a job and earn an honest living." He asked her, "You know what your brother-in-law is paying me? We're talking two bills a week."

He waited to see if she was going to say anything and then told her, "What I am is a thief. I was thinking about it. It's like—I don't know—I guess it's like, say you're an alcoholic, something like that, all you can think about is booze. Maybe you're all right if you can keep away from it. But if somebody puts a bottle in front of you—say it's Jack Daniel's, maybe that's your favorite drink, whatever—and then they leave you alone with it—tell you, I'm gonna go and you're on your own—" He looked at Kristin again and asked, "What are you gonna do?"

She said, "You feel that way about the diamonds?"

He was starting to get used to it, talking to her about maybe they were gonna steal something and it was beginning to feel natural. He said, "Yeah, it's there, I can feel it. Before, talking to your sister, it was just something—I don't know—I was listening to her talk and it was like I wasn't really paying attention at first."

"What about now?"

"Now I've had a little time to think about it. It's different."

She was quiet for a minute and then asked him, "What about me?"

He could see, out of the corner of his eye, she was leaning against the car door, staring at him. He heard something in her voice, it wasn't something that'd been there before. It took a moment but then he got it. She was nervous.

He asked her, "What do you mean?"

"I mean, a day ago you were almost laughing at me. Or else you were mad. I couldn't tell. I tell you I might be interested in doing something like this, you look at me like I'm crazy. But then, when Michelle tells you about some diamonds, you think about it." She took a deep breath and asked him, "What do you see when you look at me? People tell me, they're at my restaurant and they tell me, You're so nice. What does that mean? I'm not a bitch? Maybe. But

162

the other thing, the other side of it is, maybe I'm tired of working all day long—where am I going with it? And now you tell me you want to do something like that. My sister gives you an idea and you come to me with it."

He told her, "There's a difference."

"What?"

He shook his head. "I don't know. I think"—telling himself to go ahead and say it—"I think, it's that I trust you."

She said, surprised, "You do?"

He shrugged. "I guess so." He was being careful to not look away from the windshield, not take his eyes off the road because maybe then he might glance at her, have to say it while he was looking into her face. He told her, "I decided, do one more. Don't hurt anybody. Just do this one thing, a last score, and, if it works, I'll be set."

He took a breath and said, "I get out of jail, what happens? There's all kinds of people out here, they'll fuck you over worse than the people inside prison almost. Your sister, she's married to a guy, even she says he's a psycho, she can't wait to get away from him. I got a feeling I hang around there any longer either I'm gonna kill him or he's gonna kill me. So something comes up, this score. Maybe it's too good to be true. But what am I looking at—what kind of choices do I have? The bottom line—and this is if you get away from all the bullshit—the bottom line is, ain't nobody gonna do anything for me. I got to go out there and do it for myself." He still wasn't looking at her. "Look at it from my position. I look around, who do I want to do it with? Maybe I can go along with your sister, see where that leaves me. Or I can do it with you. Somebody I got a feeling about."

She scared the shit out of him because she threw herself across the seat and wrapped her arms around his neck. She gave him a kiss and then looked at his face from about six inches away, with her one hand still on his shoulder. Staring at him for a long time and then saying, "I knew there was something about us. I saw you, that first time, I knew it would be good."

He glanced at her. "Yeah?"

She nodded.

He told her, "Here's the thing, which I want you to listen to. We got a thing going, we like each other. It's nice. But see, you've got to

163

realize—the thing that's important is, you and I, if we do this thing, you're gonna have to do everything I say. I tell you, this is what we do, I don't want to have to argue about it. Okay?"

"Okay." She was quiet for a second, sitting in the seat next to him with her hand still on his shoulder, her index finger tracing little circles on his neck. With a serious look on her face until all of a sudden she perked up. Giving him a big grin and asking him, "Do I get a gun?"

He looked at her, shaking his head and saying, "Jesus."

They drove to the bank, First Carolina Federal. A one-story building right next to a place that sold live bait and T-shirts. The building was red brick, with a big double-glass-door entrance and a drive-through window on the far side. It had a wooden sign out on the front lawn between two palmettos, like a thermometer. It was halfway filled in with red ink that showed how much money had been pledged to the United Way since the beginning of summer.

Cully parked the car and turned around in the seat to get a better view of the building. Beside him, Kristin turned also, leaning her shoulder against his and asking him, "Is this it?"

He nodded.

She said, "What are we gonna do?" Getting excited all of a sudden and saying, "Are we going to do it now?"

He turned and looked at her. "Jesus. You think, what, we just walk in there and point our fingers at them? Say, stick 'em up?"

She shook her head, smiling, and said, "I guess not."

Cully looked at the bank and then at Kristin. "What we do . . ." Stopping after he said it and shaking his head. "What *I* do is, I go in there, when we're ready, and I ask them, would they mind giving me Mr. Dorrance's diamonds. Be polite about it. And then I come out here, to where you're waiting in the car."

He reached over and touched her chin, turning her face towards his and saying, "Is that something you think you can do? Sit here in the car while I go inside and take care of the thing?"

She nodded. And then smiled, leaning forward to kiss him. She settled back in her seat, still giving him a smile—bright-eyed—and told him, "Of course I can. I told you, this is what I want."

They went inside after about ten minutes, Cully taking her by the hand and leading her into the building, a man and his wife maybe, looking to open an account. There was a counter along the left side of the bank, with three tellers behind it, one of them working the drive-through window while the other two waited on customers lined up inside the bank itself. In front of Cully and Kristin was a table, with deposit and withdrawal slips in little slots and a couple of pens chained to it. Behind the table was a big blackboard with white letters on it, giving all the CD rates that the bank offered.

Cully took Kristin by the hand again and walked over to the table. He pulled a deposit slip out and started to write on it, looking towards the other side of the bank while he did, seeing two men in suits, each at his own desk, and behind them, in the far corner, the room where the safety deposit boxes were. He watched while a man came in and spoke to one of the men at the desks. A minute later they got up and went to the back room. The bank man took a set of keys out of his pocket and unlocked the door. It gave Cully a funny feeling, standing there, pretending to fill out a form, and seeing all those boxes. Knowing that he was that close to four hundred thousand dollars' worth of diamonds. Jesus, it was something you could almost taste.

He turned to Kristin after a couple of minutes and said, "Okay, let's go."

She looked at him. "What do you mean?"

"I've seen enough."

"You have?"

He nodded and took her arm. "Let's go."

He didn't say anything else, walking out to the car, thinking it over, the way the bank was set up. He could picture it—walk in there, talk to one of the guys in the suits. All he had to do was keep a low profile, act like it was okay for him to be taking the guy into the safety deposit room. Like he had a box there himself.

He got in the car and leaned over to open Kristin's door for her. Waiting until she slid in and then looking at her. Telling her, "You know, your sister, she's got this big plan. Probably the same one she tried four years ago with Benny."

Kristin turned in her seat until she was looking at him. She said, "Yeah?"

Cully smiled. "The thing is, it could work."

That night, as soon as Herb was asleep, Michelle called Benny. Drumming her fingers on the kitchen counter and humming while she waited for Benny to pick up the phone.

When he said hello she told him, "It's me."

"Hun-bun, you're calling me to see, maybe you should come on over and climb in bed with me. Is that it?"

She told him, "Benny, I'm calling to tell you that he's gonna do it."

It took Benny a moment but then he said, "Cully?"

Michelle said, "Yes. I told him about it."

"What'd he say?"

"He acted like he wasn't gonna touch it. Like he wasn't interested. Until I told him how much money was involved."

Benny laughed. "Let me guess, he had a change of heart. He finds out we're talking four hundred large and all of a sudden he's a thief again."

"Something like that."

Benny said, "And he just jumped at the idea then?"

"Uh-huh." Michelle could hear Benny breathing on the line. Could picture him thinking it over. Now that she had told Cully, they were committed to it. It wasn't like they could tell Frank Cullen, Hey we were only kidding.

After a couple of seconds Benny said, "You got any kind of a plan, an idea maybe, on how to keep this guy, Cully—all of a sudden he's a thief again—how're we gonna keep him on our side? Keep him honest."

She had known he was going to say that. She told him, "Leave that up to me."

"Uh-huh," Benny said. "And how are you gonna make sure our friend doesn't do something we don't like?"

Michelle sighed. "Benny, we get him to do this thing, we keep an eye on him the whole time. When it's over, we'll be right there."

Benny said, "Okay, hun-bun. Meantime, what I'm gonna do, I'm gonna hang around with our friend Cully. Make sure he doesn't have ideas of his own."

Michelle said into the phone, "You do that." Waiting for an answer from Benny but hearing only the buzz of the dial tone because he had already hung up.

She put the phone down and stood there, thinking about Cully. And Benny. She was, what, supposed to keep an eye on Cully? Did that mean she was supposed to *trust* Benny? It almost made her laugh, standing in her kitchen late at night, with the hum from the refrigerator the only noise she could hear. You do a thing like that, trust somebody like Benny, and where was it gonna get you? It was gonna get you in trouble was what it was gonna do.

The next morning Cully drove Herb and Michelle into town. It made him a little nervous, driving the two of them together. He could hear them in the back, chatting away. He'd glance in the mirror and Michelle would be turned towards Herb, with a smile on her face, listening to her husband and nodding. Cully watching it and thinking, was it possible that she had been doing this, leading a double life, for a long time? Wondering, was there ever a time, maybe when they first met, Herb and Michelle, that she liked the guy? Or was it always like this? In front of her husband Michelle put on an act. Dutiful wife, putting up with his shit. And inside, the whole time, she's scheming, trying to figure out how to separate him from his money. Cully had met guys back at Raiford, mean sons of bitches, con men, that didn't give it as much effort as she did.

When they got to town Herb leaned forward and tapped Cully on the shoulder. He said, "You can drop me at the Island Club. My wife wants to do a little shopping." He looked at his watch. "Pick me up in two hours."

Cully nodded, going across the bridge and then turning into the big marina, letting Herb off at the entrance to the club and waiting while he walked across the lot and entered the big building where the bar and restaurant were.

He looked in the mirror, saw Michelle grinning at him and asked her, "Where do you want to go?"

She laughed. "I thought maybe we'd get a drink. That sound good to you?"

Cully shrugged. "Where?"

She was still smiling. "Why don't you surprise me?" Leaning back in the seat and humming a song while Cully turned the car around and headed back into town.

He thought about it, where should he go, and decided on Casey's because he didn't want to go to the Ramada Inn and he didn't really know anywhere else. When he got there he parked the car and walked around to open the door for Michelle.

She got out and looked at the bar. "This is cute. Brings me down memory lane." She squinted up at Cully. "Did you know I used to sing here?"

He shook his head. "No."

She gave him a look like she didn't believe him but then shrugged and started to walk towards the building.

CHAPTER

19

CULLY ORDERED A beer and Michelle, after thinking about it, told the bartender she'd have a vodka tonic, smiling about it and saying to Cully, "See, you were probably thinking, she's going to order a Manhattan, like before." Sipping her drink and asking him, "Am I right?"

Cully shrugged. He didn't really care what she drank. But he told her, "Yeah, I figured, after the other day, it was what you drank if you were gonna drink during the day." She looked at him over her glass and asked, "You think I drink too much?" He shook his head. "I don't know. I guess it would be up to you to decide. Is it something you look forward to a lot? That kind of thing." He watched her think about it. Finally she said, "I guess it could be a problem, if I let it get out of hand."

She lit a cigarette and told him, "I'll tell you one thing . . ."

"What?"

"If it works out, if we get those diamonds, then it's something I'd have to be careful about. Make sure I didn't turn into a rich alcoholic."

"Have all that free time on your hands. Maybe you'd get bored?"

She nodded. Took a sip of her drink and then looked around the bar for a couple of seconds. When she swung her gaze back to him she said, "You're going to do it, aren't you?"

"Am I gonna back out, maybe I've had second thoughts?"

"Yes."

He looked her right in the eyes. "I'm gonna do it. It's something you can believe in." And then he told her, knowing it would sound funny if he didn't, "But I'll tell you one thing, I'm gonna be watching my ass. Making sure I don't get set up for something. Something comes in from left field, Benny, something like that. It wouldn't be smart for you to think I'm not gonna be ready for it."

She gave him a look, surprised, and said, "Jesus, you think something like that. *Benny?*" Giving the word a lot of emphasis, like it had never crossed her mind.

Cully felt like laughing, not really sure what was it she had in mind. Maybe she was gonna bring Benny into it. She probably already had. But he had to admit, sitting there with her, watching her face, the expression on it—like she was completely startled—that she was pretty damn good.

He told her, "I'd be stupid if it hadn't crossed my mind."

There were a couple of seconds when neither of them spoke and then she said, "I guess you would." Giving it a minute and then saying, "I guess, if I were in your shoes, I'd be thinking the same thing."

"Yeah, well, there it is."

"You think I might be setting you up?"

He told her, "That's not the point. You might be. Or maybe you're not. The thing is, if you are, I'm letting you know that you should maybe think about being careful."

She raised her eyebrows. "Oooohhhh . . . ," letting the word out slowly, ". . . you're threatening me." But smiling a little bit, like she was teasing him.

He didn't let it bother him. He wanted to keep on acting a little paranoid. The big-time crook letting his partner know that he was thinking about things. Let her know he was doing what would be natural if he intended to go along with her idea. He told her, "No threats. I just want us to understand one another."

She finished her drink and waved to the bartender for another. Cully asked for another beer and when their drinks came she said, "What would you say if I told you something—without laughing or saying anything snotty—if I told you I could really see it."

"See what?"

"You and I, we do this, get out of town. What would stop us from staying together?"

Cully acted like he had to think about it. Finally he said, "Travel around, spend some of that money."

"We could have a great time."

He shrugged. "Why don't we do this—see if it works out, make sure we don't end up in jail. Or worse. Then, if you want, we can talk about other things."

She smiled at him and said, "See, that's what I like about you. You never give an inch. It's always, Why don't we think realistically or Let's see how it works out. You don't spend any time bullshitting, or bragging about what you're gonna do."

"Well, that way, you don't end up disappointing people as often."

She nodded. "Yeah. It makes sense."

He asked her, "What are you going to do about Herb?"

"What do you mean?"

"Well, it's not something, if you go through with this—if everything works out—you can't stick around here."

"Do you think I would?"

He shook his head. "No, I can't see it. I picture you someplace else. Someplace with a beach maybe. Where it's warm all the time."

"With somebody to wait on me hand and foot."

He smiled. "Yeah, I can't see you doing your own laundry if you're all of a sudden rich."

"No."

"So you're gonna leave."

"Uh-huh."

Cully looked at his watch and said, "We gotta go soon. Herb'll be expecting us."

She said, "One more drink."

"You don't want to do anything that'll make him upset."

She was signalling for the bartender, and then turning back to Cully and asking him, "Like what, be a little late to pick him up at his club?"

Cully smiled. "Everything should be low-key at this point."

She gave him a look, a little drunk now and pissed off. "Fuck low-key." Giving it a second and then saying, "Fuck Herb."

But he shook his head, waved the bartender off, and took her by the arm, helping her to her feet and whispering in her ear, "Yeah, fuck Herb. But not now. Later. Later we fuck Herb."

She looked up into his face, giggling a little, not mad any longer, and said, "Yeah, later we fuck Herb."

Michelle made a fuss when they got in the car. Cully wanted to go directly across the river but she told him, "I want to see the bank." He asked her, "What do you mean, you want to see it?" She said, "I want to drive by the bank, take a look at it so I can think about it. All that money in there, I want to be near it." He could see her, in the back, pouting like a teenager. He told her, "Look, it's there, it's not going anywhere." She said, "I don't care. Take me by it. Let me look at the building. That's all I want. After that, I don't care what we do, we can go get Herb." Cully looked at his watch and said, "I'll drive by. How would that be?" He could see her smiling, sitting in the back and nodding. Saying, "I just want to see it."

He took a shortcut, getting to the bank in about five minutes and parking across the street at the dry cleaner's. He sat there, with the engine running, while Michelle looked across at the bank. Finally she looked at him and said, "When are you going to do it?" He told her, acting like he wasn't quite sure, "I was thinking towards the end of the week. Thursday or Friday, something like that." She got a sly grin on her face and said, "You're not thinking about doing this on your own, are you?" He shook his head, looking right at her and saying, "No, if I did that, I know you'd do something. Turn me in, something like that." She nodded her head, "You got that right." She told him, "When you go in, I want to be right here, watching." He looked in the mirror, seeing her looking back, and he told her, "That'd be all right. That way we avoid any confusion." She winked at him, saying, "That way we avoid a lot of things." Leaning back in the seat and looking content as he turned the Caddy around and headed back towards the Island Club.

Monday evening Earl Marsh drove up to his brother's motel room. He wasn't drunk, not really. Somebody seeing him drive down the road wouldn't think, Uh-oh, that car's all over the place. But he had a pretty good buzz on. He'd been sipping Wild Turkey ever since he quit work, getting a mellow feeling going and keeping it there. Sitting in his house and thinking things over, deciding maybe he'd drive on out to his brother's motel and have a chat with him.

What he'd been thinking, in between sips of bourbon, was maybe it was time to stop taking shit from Benny. Let Benny see that Earl was okay, he could do whatever anyone else could do. Maybe he'd never spent time in jail, anything like that, but still, he and Benny were brothers. It had to mean something.

Benny was staying at the Econolodge in town. Earl couldn't understand it. Why didn't Benny find somewhere else to live? Rent a mobile home or something. He had to ask what room Benny was in, and then he wandered around back, walking all the way around the motel and then up to the second floor to Benny's room, knocking on the door and waiting.

Benny had the pistol in his hand when he opened the door. Earl didn't see it at first. He was looking at Benny's face and he took a step toward the door to go in but Benny put the hand with the gun in it on Earl's chest and said, "What do you want?"

Earl wasn't sure what to say. He'd had it all ready—driving here and running it over in his head—what it was he wanted to tell Benny. But now he was confused.

Finally he said, "I thought I'd come on over and we could shoot the shit."

Benny gave him a look. For a minute Earl thought he was going to tell him to get lost. But then Benny smiled. He took a step back and waved Earl into the room. Saying, "Yeah, why not? I got nothing I've got to be doing."

The TV was going — "Wheel of Fortune," which Earl liked a lot. He sat down on the bed while Benny went into the bathroom to pee, staring at Vanna White and trying to guess what the phrase was. He heard Benny flush the toilet and looked up when his brother came into the room.

He still had the pint of Wild Turkey and he showed it to Benny. Asking him, "Hey, you want a drink?"

Benny looked at him like he was gonna say something nasty, make a comment about Earl's drinking, but then he just nodded and said, "There're glasses over there," pointing towards the little alcove next to the bathroom and then sitting down on the chair near the door.

Benny was giving it some thought, watching Earl pour the drinks. He wasn't sure why he had let his brother in. His first thought, when he opened the door and saw his ding brother standing there halfway lit as usual, was to slam the door in his face. But it occurred to him maybe he should talk to Earl. Be nice to him. He wasn't sure why, but he thought, for now at least, he should be nice to Earl. Keep him happy, in case, for some reason, he needed him later on.

Earl came on back to the bed and handed Benny a glass. Benny watched him take a drink and then Earl turned to look at the television. Benny kept his eye on him, seeing the look of concentration on his face as Earl watched Vanna turn the numbers. Jesus.

He said, "Turn it off."

Earl looked at him. "The TV?"

"Yeah, turn it off."

Earl shrugged. He stood up and leaned over to the TV. When it was off he swung around and looked at Benny. "Okay?"

Benny nodded. He said, "What are you doing?"

Earl looked confused. "You mean tonight?"

"Yeah."

Earl shrugged. "Same as always. Driving around. I stopped for a drink. At Casey's. I don't know, maybe later I'll go back. See who's there."

Benny said, "Uh-huh." He looked at Earl. He didn't feel anything towards him one way or the other. Like they weren't even related. He asked him, "You got a girl?"

"What do you mean?"

"Jesus. What do you think I mean?"

Earl looked at the door of the motel room. "No."

Benny said, "Why not?"

"I don't know, I don't meet many people."

"Uh-huh." He waited a minute because he had suddenly thought of it, why he was willing to let Earl in, and he wanted to think it over—run it through his head and get it straight. Earl, what he was was a drunk. Nothing more. You see him any time of the day or night and chances were he'd be smashed. You could talk to him, get him to do just about anything when he was like that. Benny was thinking, why not use Earl as a last resort? A diversion, whatever you wanted to call it. Earl would do anything he told him, like a fucking puppy that would lie in its own piss to please its owner.

Benny leaned forward and touched Earl on the knee. He said, "I'm glad you came over."

He could see it. Earl, hearing the words and getting all excited. Happy, starting to smile already just because Benny was talking to him. Telling Benny, "Yeah, see, I thought we should spend some time together."

Benny, making himself smile, said, "Well, I've had some things to take care of."

Earl nodded. "Well, that makes sense," slurring his words a little bit. Taking a big gulp of his bourbon and then saying, "I mean, you get out of prison, I would think there's some things that you got to attend to."

Benny leaned forward again and said, "I still do."

Benny couldn't believe it, it was like they were reading a script, with Earl saying all the right lines. He watched his brother, saw Earl lean forward also and when he spoke it was barely more than a whisper. He asked Benny, "Is it something, I mean, do you need help?"

Benny almost laughed, thinking, Bingo, and saying, "Yeah, I could use it." Smiling at Earl—he had to fight down the urge to wink at him—and then telling him, "I got some people, I think they're trying to set me up, make it look like I did something that I didn't. You know, broke the law."

Earl asked, "Who?"

"Frank Cullen."

Earl shook his head, swearing and starting to stand up, saying, "That son of a bitch."

Benny pushed him back onto the bed. He said, "Take it easy. It's not something . . . we don't want to do anything about it now."

"When?"

Benny shrugged. "I'll let you know. Just go to work like usual. I'll call you." He looked at his brother. "Can you do that?"

Earl said, "Jesus. Of course I can." He stood up, saying, "Just call me, I'll do whatever you want."

Benny gave it a second, trying to work his face into something that might look like relief. He told Earl, "Thanks."

Earl was grinning. Benny could see it, proud as a peacock. Standing there, weaving back and forth a little bit and then saying, "What are brothers for?"

And Benny told him, "Yeah."

CHAPTER

20

AFTER HE HUSTLED Earl out of the room Benny drove to the Shrimp Boat, deciding, what he'd do, he'd pay a call on Kristin. She was getting pretty friendly with Frank Cullen. So Benny decided what he should do, he should let her know that he was keeping an eye on things.

She had a big smile on her face when she opened the door. Staring at Benny, she lost the smile. He figured maybe she'd been thinking it was going to be Cully banging on her door. She got a scared look on her face for a second but then got rid of that, too. She started to close the door but Benny put his foot in it and then pushed past her.

He took his hat off and walked down the hallway, with her following, telling him, "Hey . . . ," but not saying anything else because it took her by surprise, Benny walking in like he lived there.

He kept on going until he got to the kitchen. He couldn't believe it, how many cats there were—all over the place. He picked one off the kitchen chair and held it up to his face and said, "Hey, puss. Good little puss." And then turned to her and smiled, saying, "Hunbun, I think you've gone around the bend a little with the cats."

She had caught up to him and was leaning on the doorway, watching him. She said, "What in the world are you doing out here?" Acting calmer now, Benny could see it. Like she wasn't gonna let on that it bothered her, him being there.

He said, "Hey, hun-bun. I'm sitting back at my motel room, thinking about things and all of a sudden I start to feel guilty. I'm saying to myself, all the people I've seen since I got out, and I haven't even come on over to say hello to you."

She moved away from the door and walked across to the sink. She leaned against the counter and looked at Benny. "Jesus, Benny. I can picture it, you'll be eighty-five years old, walking up to people and saying, Hey, hun-bun, or How's it going, sport."

He spread his arms wide, innocent, and said, "What do you mean? I'm being nice, is all."

She shook her head. "Benny, you can't be nice. You can sweet-talk people. That's different."

He started to say, "Hun-bun . . ."

But she cut him off. "I've got an idea. Why don't you leave. I'll pretend you were never here. That way I won't have to scrub the place."

He shook his head, made his face look like she had hurt him. Saying, "Hey, what is this? What'd I ever do to you?"

"Jesus, I can't figure out—are you serious, or is this an act?"

He smiled, nodding at her and saying, "Well, partly it's an act." He stood up and took a step towards where she was standing. "You remember back when you and John lived here? And we used to come out here, have a few beers?"

He waited for her to answer, not saying anything else until she nodded slightly. Then he said, "See, I used to watch you. John would be in the other room maybe, and I'd watch you. Take a look at you when you didn't know it. I used to think, why was I with Michelle? Sitting there, looking at you, you were all the time quiet. Not saying much." Benny whistled. "But, Jesus, you were looking good." He reached over and touched her shoulder. Squeezed it and said, "I always wondered, you and I, why didn't we ever do it? I'd sit there, talking to your goofy boyfriend, and think about it." He smiled and said, "The thought ever cross your mind, hun-bun?"

"Jesus, you never quit." She shook her head and said, "Yeah, you and John. Best buddies. What ever happened to John, Benny?"

"Far as I know he took off for who knows where."

"Uh-huh."

"Hey, believe me, I'd like to know where he is, too."

"Benny, what is this crap?"

He ignored her and said, "You were always different."

She shook her head in frustration and straightened up from the sink. "I want you to leave."

He was motionless for a couple of seconds but then he sighed. "Hey, I can understand that. Maybe you aren't too happy, I just show up at your door." He nodded and said, "I'll go if you want." He started to turn away and then looked back at her, smiling and snapping his fingers. "I almost forgot, the reason I came out"—looking relieved that he'd thought of it before he left—"I wanted to tell you, cause I couldn't help but notice, you and that fellow—what's his name, Cully?—I just wanted to save you any heartbreak. Because I got a feeling, just from watching things. I got a feeling him and your sister, Michelle, they got something pretty strong going on."

He looked at her to see if she was going to show anything. He had to admit it wasn't much, the look that crossed her face. It was gone in an instant, leaving behind a disgusted expression. She said, "Jesus, Benny. Is that why you came out here?"

He shrugged. "I just thought I should let you know. I mean in case you had an idea about Frank Cullen. Maybe you and him were planning on doing something. Make a move together."

"I don't know what you're talking about."

He grinned. "Yeah, maybe I'm way off base." He started to move towards the door, leaning down to pet another cat, saying, "Hey, puss." Picking the cat up by the scruff of the neck while Kristin started to say something. Telling him, "Put it down." He held the cat in the air and said, "Puss, maybe I'll take you with me, take you out to the beach and see how you like the water." Looking at Kristin for a few seconds while she reached for the cat. Laughing and telling her, "Hey, sugar, I'm kidding around here. You got to have a sense of humor."

He handed the cat to her and then moved into the hallway. Looking back and saying, "Yeah, it's probably none of my business.

Michelle wants to get herself involved with Frank Cullen, maybe they're planning to do something stupid. It's not my worry." Smiling now and letting her follow him to the door. Putting on his hat and looking at her one more time. Smiling and saying, "Well, hun-bun, I had fun."

He knew she was looking at him as he walked to his car. He heard the door close as he slid into the Camaro and started it up. He sat there for a moment, looking at the house and saying to himself, That's what you do, just throw a lot of shit at everybody, get 'em all excited and see what happens.

It made her think, that's what really bothered her. The fact that Benny—she knew what a sleaze he was—he could still get her a little upset. Says those things about Cully and Michelle and she couldn't help herself, she starts to wonder was she being foolish, getting involved with a guy she didn't know anything about.

She ran it over in her head, what it was like to be with Cully. She could picture him, smiling, with his hair blowing in the breeze when they were driving in the car or else when they had gone to the beach. See him the way he had looked after he'd kissed her the first time. Like he cared.

She could look at him sometimes—if he wasn't watching—and she'd see him like he was on television. Or maybe in the movies. Like he was an actor and he was pretty good at it. Had all his lines down and all he had to do was say them and they'd come out all right. Even when he was nervous, or a little shy, which she'd noticed a couple of times. Like when she walked into Denny's and he'd stopped with his orange juice halfway to his mouth. Like he couldn't believe she had shown up. She could picture somebody, Al Pacino maybe, using that same look.

Thinking about it and then almost jumping out of her chair because the phone next to her started to ring. She picked it up slowly—wary—because she thought it might turn out to be Benny, calling her up to say something else. Saying hello and then feeling relieved, because it was Cully. But then feeling tense again because it came back to her, what she had been thinking. She listened to his

180

voice, trying to picture him, decide who she was talking to, the nice Cully, or the one that was a crook.

He asked her, "What are you doing?" Sounding pleasant, like they were just a guy and a girl and he was maybe calling her up for a date or to say good night to her before he went to bed.

She told him, "I'm sitting here, getting a few things done before I go to sleep. Maybe I'll watch some TV."

"Yeah?" Waiting a second and then asking, "How are the cats?"

"Fine."

There was a pause when neither one of them spoke and then Cully asked her, "Everything all right?"

"Fine. I'm happy."

"Yeah?"

She made herself sound perky. "Really."

"Okay." She could hear him take a breath. He told her, "Your sister wants me to do it this week."

"She does?"

"Yeah. So what I thought . . . I thought we'd do it tomorrow."

She couldn't believe it, what it sounded like, actually hearing him say it—do it tomorrow. Like it was really going to happen. She said, "What time?"

"Around two o'clock." He sounded so businesslike about it. It reminded her that it wasn't a game. It was something he'd done before. How he made his living. She couldn't think of what to say.

He asked her, "You all right?"

"Sure."

Suddenly there was a different sound to his voice, almost nervous, or tense. He said, "You sure? Cause it doesn't sound like you're too happy."

"No, I'm fine. Excited."

He waited a few seconds before he said, "Okay." And then told her, "All you got to do is exactly what I say. It'll be fine. Okay?"

"Uh-huh."

He told her, "I drive Herb's Cadillac into town, drop it at Dave Ross's garage for service, walk a block down the street, and you pick me up." She said, "What time?" He told her, "One thirty." He said, "We do the bank and then you drop me off back at the garage."

She asked him, "But what about the cops, won't they be looking for you?" He said, "Let me worry about that." And then he said, speaking slowly, "Do you know what you have to do?" She ran it through in her head and said, "Yes."

Cully said, "It'll be fine."

"You're sure?"

"Trust me."

She was waiting for him to say something else when she heard the phone being hung up. She wanted to ask him more, wanted him to tell her what was going to happen afterwards, what were they going to do. She wanted him to tell her something more than where to be at one o'clock the next afternoon. Thinking about it and saying his name into the phone—"Cully." Not even sounding like herself. More like a scared teenager. And then saying, "Damn," because the line was empty.

CHAPTER

21

WHEN SHE GOT out of bed the next morning—waking up and sipping a cup of coffee and then smoking a joint so that it wouldn't be too bad, her having to wait until one to go get Cully— she was wondering, what do you wear to a bank robbery? Making herself forget about the phone call from Cully the night before, how he'd sounded. She went through her closet and pulled clothes out. She'd hold up an outfit, a pair of slacks maybe, with a blouse, shake her head and then maybe try a skirt with a different blouse.

It popped into her head, a movie she'd seen. One of her favorites. *Bonnie and Clyde.* She remembered the scene, Warren Beatty and Faye Dunaway in an old car, speeding across some dust-covered hillside in Oklahoma, with carloads of cops after them. She'd loved it. There was banjo music in the background and Faye Dunaway had looked great in a white dress that came down to her ankles. A little dusty maybe, but still there was something about her, hanging on for dear life as the car rocketed across the field, with one hand holding a hat to her head.

She kept thinking about it, picturing Cully instead of Warren Beatty. Lighting another joint and going back to her closet. Looking for a hat.

. . .

At eleven o'clock in the morning Cully told Herb, "I made an appointment to get the car serviced."

Herb looked at him. His eyes were a little bloodshot and he didn't look too happy to be up and around, like maybe after he'd come home the day before from having a few drinks at the club he'd had a few more before going to bed. He asked Cully, "What's the matter with the car?"

Cully shook his head. "I'm not sure, it's not running well. I thought I'd take it into town. Get somebody to tune it up."

Herb waited a couple of seconds and then said, "Where're you taking it? Dave Ross's?"

Cully nodded.

Herb managed a smile, giving Cully a snotty look and saying, "You wouldn't be thinking maybe you'd go in there, take another shot at getting your money from Dave Ross, would you?"

Cully thought about it, looking at Herb, standing in front of him—pretty hung over and stinking of day-old gin. He thought, no more of this shit. One more day and no matter what happened, he was gonna get out of this man's sight. He said, "Herb, the money you pay me, you think I got to go looking for it anywhere else?" Waiting a second and then adding, "Hell, on my salary I'm gonna be a fucking rich man. Be able to retire in a couple of months." He wasn't sure why he said it, it wasn't the smartest thing to do, get sarcastic with Herb on the day he intended to rob the man. But he decided, walking away from Herb, it wasn't something he was gonna worry about.

He called Kristin before he left, telling her, "I'm on my way." And then saying, "All you have to do is pick me up at the corner at one thirty."

And then he was in the Caddy. Backing it out of the garage and wheeling it down the driveway. He was gonna do it. One way or the other, he was gonna get in that bank and take the man's money. At least, wasn't anybody gonna stop him from trying.

. . .

He did a little shopping, spent an hour driving around to a couple of stores, getting some things together that he knew he'd need. Some clothes that he thought he'd use for the robbery, smiling about it, because it was gonna be a disguise.

He pulled into Dave Ross's garage at a quarter to one, parking the Caddy in front of the service bays and walking slowly towards the front office. He could see Earl, Benny's brother, working on a car inside the building, the man bigger than Cully remembered. Leaning over the car with a wrench in his hand but looking up when Cully slammed the door of the Caddy. Earl took a couple of steps away from the car he was working on and stared at Cully. Still holding on to his wrench and looking like he didn't know, was Cully here to finish what he'd started in the bar the other night?

Cully nodded at Earl, acted like nothing had happened, and even gave the other man a smile, nodding his head and saying, "Hey." Grinning a little bit and then opening the door to the office and walking in. Dave Ross was sitting behind a desk, going over some papers. He didn't look up right away but when he did he got a look on his face just like Earl had. Cully nodded at him and, before Ross could say anything, he threw the keys on the desk and said, "That's Herb Dorrance's car. It's running like shit. He wanted me to bring it down."

Cully stood there, waiting for Ross to say something and finally the other man nodded. Barely looking at him, like he was scared if he did, Cully might decide to break his nose again.

Ross said, "I'll get Earl to take a look at it."

Cully nodded and said, "I'll be back in something like four, five hours." He turned and walked out the door, walked over to the Caddy and got his shopping bag out of it and then started to walk down Carteret Street, whistling, because now he was one step closer. Starting to get a little nervous.

Dave Ross watched him walk across the lot and then disappear around the corner of the Rite Aid next door. Staring at Cully's back until he could no longer see it and then opening the door that

185

separated the office from the garage itself and yelling for Earl to come on over.

When Earl got there, Ross asked him, looking at Earl and wondering was the man going to be able to keep it together, if what Dave thought was happening was really happening? He asked Earl, "Tell me what your brother said again."

Earl looked unhappy. Ross knew what he was thinking; talking about Benny bothered Earl. Like he was breaking some kind of goddamned pact with his brother. Jesus. He still couldn't see it. Earl, he could be on fire and Benny wouldn't cross the street to piss on him.

Ross said it again. "Come on, tell me what he said."

Finally Earl spoke. He told Ross, "Benny said that he might need my help. Said that they were planning to get him in trouble."

"And he said it was Cully?"

Earl nodded. "Yeah. That's the only person he said by name."

"But he did say that Cully, and maybe somebody else, were gonna do something illegal? Make it look like Benny had done it?"

"Yeah."

Ross thought about it. He told Earl, "Call your brother. Tell him . . . tell him you're not sure, but you think Cully might be up to something. Say that Cully came in here and was acting real funny."

Earl asked, "Was he?"

Ross looked at him and shook his head. He said, "No. But it doesn't matter. Just tell your brother what I said." He looked out of the window again, to where Cully had walked down the street, and said, almost to himself, "I got a feeling."

CHAPTER

22

CULLY COULDN'T BELIEVE it. Opening the door to Kristin's car and scrambling into the seat, not really seeing her until he was already inside, and then so startled he didn't know what to say. She looked like somebody out of a B movie. Wearing some kind of dress, he couldn't see the whole thing, but it looked like it was out of the twenties or something. And her hair, it twirled around her head and then was pinned to the top, with a wide-brimmed hat above it. She was wearing a lot of makeup, too. Tons of mascara and enough rouge—it made her look like she had some kind of fever.

Cully caught his breath and said, "Jesus." Still staring at her and then asking, "You mind if I say something?"

She didn't answer so he said, "What the fuck're you doing? We're going to rob a bank, you come out dressed like it's Halloween."

He could see it was the wrong thing to say. See her face start to change because, he figured all of a sudden, she'd probably put a lot of thought into it, deciding what should she put on to rob a bank. It bothered him, because, thinking about it, it wasn't something she should've been worrying about. All she should have on her mind was she was gonna drive the car. He had a couple of things in his shopping bag, things he'd bought to wear. But that was different. There was a reason for that.

The last thing he wanted to do, though, was get her upset. Say something snotty about her outfit and maybe she'd throw a fit. Wouldn't drive the car. He'd known, going into it, he was dealing with an amateur. What he had to do now was calm her down. Not act mad at her. For just long enough to get it over with.

He said, "Hey. I'm sorry. You want to get dressed up, make yourself feel comfortable with it. That's okay." Touching her on the shoulder and saying, "Come on, start the car up and let's go." But being nice about it, talking to her softly because he had to keep her mind on what they were going to do.

She started the car and pulled out on the road. Cully dug into the shopping bag and said, "Hey, I got an outfit to wear, too." Grinning, trying to loosen her up. Reaching into the bag and pulling a big ten-gallon hat out. Putting it on his head and grinning at her. Saying, "Hey, hun-bun, who do I remind you of?"

She wouldn't look at him at first. Just kept driving towards the bank until he told her, "Hey, we're both a little nervous here, sport." Poking her in the ribs and saying, "I knew Kenny Rogers. I ever tell you that, sugar?"

He kept looking at her, waiting for her to say something. Thinking if she didn't lighten up pretty soon he was gonna have to call it off. And thinking if they didn't do it today, right now, she probably wasn't gonna get up the nerve to try ever again.

But she came through, looking over at him finally and nodding, getting a little smile on her face and asking, "Is that what you're gonna do? Go in as Benny?"

He nodded. "I was thinking. Four years ago the bank gets robbed and now, just after Benny gets out of jail, it gets robbed again. They're gonna be dying to pin it on him."

She nodded and said, "You walk in there with that hat and all they see is what's on top of your head."

He nodded. "Except, see, I got more than that." Reaching into the bag and pulling out a pair of cowboy boots. Saying, "I couldn't find the kind with the skin on them. But these should do." Pulling out a shirt, a pair of pants, and a sport coat. Taking his own shoes off as Kristin drove down the road. Pulling the boots on after he put on the slacks and then undoing his shirt. Thinking about it. It might

188

work. He goes in there with the hat pulled low, calls everybody sport, maybe they'd think it was Benny.

The thing was, and he wasn't gonna say anything to Kristin about it: Maybe they wouldn't.

Benny, getting the call from Earl and then hopping in the Camaro, got there in time to see Cully get into the car with Kristin. He hung back a couple of hundred yards as they drove down Carteret, keeping Kristin's Toyota in sight but not pushing it. He didn't know was this it or was it gonna be something as simple as Cully taking Kristin somewhere to bang her? But he started to get a feeling as they passed Route 281, giving the Camaro a little gas because he was starting to sense it, what they were gonna do, and he didn't want to lose them now.

When they pulled into the parking lot at the bank he pulled over a hundred yards behind them. He could see the two of them, Kristin and Cully, moving around a little bit in the car, and then the passenger door opened and Cully stepped out wearing a cowboy hat. It took Benny a couple of seconds to get it but then he understood, sitting in his car and saying, Son of a bitch, because Cully, what he was gonna do, he was gonna make it look like Benny was robbing the bank.

Benny watched Cully lean down and say something to Kristin and then straighten up again and take a look around. Benny was too far away for Cully to recognize but still, he couldn't help it, when Cully looked his way he turned around and hid his face. He waited until Cully had started to walk towards the bank and then he climbed out of the car, standing there, looking for a pay phone and seeing one finally, maybe fifty feet away. He walked on over and picked up the phone.

When Michelle came on the line he didn't give her a chance to speak. He said, "You know who this is, right?" Not waiting for an answer. Saying, "I want you to go to the Econolodge over on Route 21. Do it now. Get a room. Not in your name. It doesn't matter how big. Just get the room and be watching for me."

Michelle started to say something but he interrupted her. He said, "Look, nothing else matters. Just get the room and be looking out the window for me. I'm gonna be in a hurry. So when you see me, come on out, so I'll know what room you're in."

He hung up and walked back to his car, looking up the street at Kristin's Toyota. Seeing her but not Cully. Knowing he was already in the bank. Benny climbed in his car and said to himself, Come on, sport. Do it. Bring those things out of there. Bring them to Benny. Smiling, because it was gonna be easy.

Kristin felt like lighting a joint. She wanted to real bad because she was pretty nervous, sitting in plain sight, waiting while Cully went inside the bank and committed a felony. She'd even brought one with her, a big joint she'd rolled that morning—already high and thinking they were going out to rob a bank, it wasn't like they had to worry about getting busted for smoking a little weed. But she wasn't gonna light it now, not sitting in the car while they robbed a bank.

She was still a little upset over what Cully had said. The way he'd looked at her when he'd seen what she was wearing. Like he couldn't believe she was that dumb. It bothered her, made her feel a little foolish, because she was getting the feeling, ever since they decided to rob the bank, that he was different. Like he didn't really care about her, all he was interested in was the diamonds.

It had been on her mind all of last night and this morning. What was gonna happen when they were finished with it? Was Cully gonna take off, maybe leave town with all the diamonds? Or else did he really have something going with Michelle? They had maybe planned the whole thing and were using her as, what was it again . . . a patsy? Yeah. Maybe what Kristin thought Cully and she were doing to Michelle . . . maybe that's what was happening to her.

She started to squirm, sitting there in the front seat, thinking it over and deciding—all of a sudden—if she was gonna go through with it, she needed to hear something from Cully. Now. Not later, when things might be all screwed up. She needed to hear something from him right this minute.

She nodded her head once, comfortable with the idea. And then she got out of the car and started to walk towards the bank.

Cully started to get a bad feeling about the whole thing when he saw Mr. Hendershot look past him at something over Cully's shoulder. Until then, Cully and Hendershot had been having a nice conversation—Cully asking questions, like he was new in town, and Hendershot, a VP with the bank or something, answering them politely. What Cully was doing, he was checking things out, making sure there wasn't anybody there to cause problems before he showed the man his gun.

He was getting ready for it. Feeling good. Satisfied, because it seemed okay. He could show Hendershot the .38, let him see it in the waistband of his pants—right there—where it would be easy to get to if he needed it. And then he could walk Hendershot over to the room with the safety deposit boxes. Get him to open Herb's and the whole thing would be done.

But Hendershot stopped looking at Cully all of a sudden, staring past his shoulder and starting to smile politely. Saying, "Yes, ma'am." Cully, starting to turn, too, with his hand actually touching the pistol in his belt—he was that close to starting the thing—feeling all of a sudden like somebody had kicked him in the stomach because he could hear, even before he could see her, Kristin's voice.

She smiled at him when he looked at her and then said to Mr. Hendershot, "I'm sorry, I just need to see my husband for a second." She looked at Cully and smiled again, saying, "I'm sorry, Benny." Making Cully wonder, did she think that was gonna make things okay, calling him Benny? She told him, "I just need to ask you something." And then she walked away, over to the front doors of the bank, like she didn't even have to check to see if he was gonna follow.

It was in Cully's head to ignore her. Just go ahead and pull Herb Dorrance's gun out and shove it in the face of the asshole sitting across the desk from him. Walk him back to the security room and take the diamonds. And then walk right past Kristin like he barely knew her. Wait until the last minute to ask her, Are you coming or what? But he didn't do it. He couldn't, because he didn't know what was in Kristin's head. What was she doing, coming into the bank in the middle of the fucking score?

He made himself smile at Hendershot and then stood up. Told the man, "I'll just be a minute," and then walked over to Kristin.

He asked her, hissing the words because he was so mad that she'd do something like this, "What the fuck're you doing?"

She shook her head. "I'm not going to do it."

He couldn't believe it. "What are you talking about?" Still whispering. Wanting to shout, maybe give her a rap on the head, she was pissing him off that much. He said, "There's no 'not going to do it.'" He told her, "We *are* doing it. Right now." Leaning down to look her in the face from maybe five inches away. "It's already happening."

She moved away from his face and shook her head. He could see what were maybe tears in her eyes, just beginning to form. He couldn't believe it, staring at her and then glancing back at Hendershot, the man either busy with some papers or pretending to be—being polite because maybe he could tell they were fighting.

Cully turned back to Kristin and said, "Pull yourself together."

She looked at him, staring at him for a couple of seconds, and then said quietly, "You're using me. You're gonna screw me over just like Benny screwed over John Lewis four years ago."

He couldn't believe it. He had thought she was scared, losing her nerve, that was all. Figured he should have known better than to use a fucking amateur, even somebody he thought he could trust. She walks into the bank and tells him she can't go through with it and right away, he figures it's because she lost her nerve. Then hearing her speak and getting a different feeling about what was in her head all of a sudden. She was in love with him. That was what it was. Jesus. He couldn't believe it.

He shook his head, smiling at her and saying, "I'm gonna tell you one thing. And then I'm gonna go back there and do what we came for." Looking at her and then reaching over and touching her face. Not caring that maybe anybody in the bank could see. Maybe it would even help. People, they see something like this, a man and a wife, looking like they were fighting—it got embarrassing so people tended to look away.

He told Kristin, "I'm only going to say it once. But you got to

192

believe me. Cause I don't have time to convince you." He touched her again, lifted her head up, and smiled. "Okay?"

She nodded and he said, "It's gonna be fine. You go out in the car and wait. Everything's gonna be fine." Looking at her and then giving her a little push to get her started back towards the door. She turned to look at him for a second and he said, "I promise you." Waiting for what seemed like minutes but then feeling a surge of relief because she nodded and then smiled at him.

He waited for her to go outside and then walked back to the desk where Hendershot sat waiting for him. The man looked at Cully and smiled, saying, "Everything all right with the wife?"

Cully nodded, smiling back at him, and then thought, Fuck it, what else could go wrong? Thinking about it, and deciding in a split second to go through with it. Hoping Kristin was gonna be there when he came out. He took one more quick look around the building. Saw everybody going about their business and turned back to Hendershot.

Cully said to the man, "What I'd like to do is go on back there." Pointing towards the security room and smiling.

Hendershot looked confused. He said, "I thought you wanted to open a new account. . . ." Looking at Cully and saying, "I didn't realize . . . do you have a box with us?"

Cully, feeling it now, relaxed because he was in the middle of it and he could feel himself growing cold in his gut. Looking at Hendershot and saying, "No, but I got the next best thing." Leaning back in the chair and letting the man see the .38 in his waistband. Smiling like he was talking nicely to the bank man. Telling him, "Look here, sport, you do this right, you can maybe live to tell your wife about it."

CHAPTER

23

BENNY COULDN'T FIGURE it out, sitting in his car
and watching Kristin walk into the bank. Wondering, what the fuck
was going on? Thinking maybe he'd been wrong about the whole
thing but then relaxing when he saw her walk back out a couple of
minutes later. She got in her car and started it up but didn't go
anywhere. Benny, nodding now, because maybe he didn't know all
the details, but he could recognize a heist when he saw one.

He gave it another minute and then got out of his car. He threw
his hat back in, almost laughing because, what with Cully wearing
his, it wasn't gonna be too smart to be seen on the streets looking
like John Wayne.

He began to walk slowly towards the bank, not hurrying—
a guy, maybe he's out for a nice stroll, doing a little window-
shopping. Not even looking at Kristin or the Toyota until he was
about ten feet away and then walking towards it quickly. Popping
open the rear door and sliding in. Scaring the hell out of Kristin.
Hearing her yell and then leaning over the seat and squeezing her
shoulder. Smiling at her and showing her the stainless steel pistol he
had in his hand. Saying, "Imagine seeing you here." Giving her a
country boy look—stupid—like he had no idea what was going on.
Saying, "You waiting for your boyfriend? Maybe he's around here

somewhere." Looking towards the bank and saying, "Maybe, what I'll do, I'll wait with you."

It took Cully about twenty seconds of talking to get Hendershot to calm down. He told him, "See, the important thing here, sport, is you and I walk back there like everything is okay. We're buddies and you're taking me back there to the boxes." He looked at the man across the desk. "Whatta you think, you and me, we can do that?"

Hendershot managed to nod his head. Cully grinned at him and told him, "Listen to me, I know banks. And one thing I know is you got a list. A piece of paper that'll tell you what boxes belong to who." Cully, still smiling, glancing around the bank and seeing everything looked normal, and then turning back to Hendershot. Asking, "Am I right?"

He waited for Hendershot to nod and then told him, "What you do is, you get the list, and you and I, we go on back there to that room." Waiting for Hendershot to go through his desk and come out with a computer printout. Cully nodded and said, "See, so far it's going okay." He took the list from Hendershot and gave it a quick look and then handed it back.

Cully smiled again. "Okay. Now all we need is the keys."

Hendershot started to speak but then stopped. Cully looked at him for a second and then started to shake his head. He said, "Wait, you're gonna tell me that you don't have the keys. That only the owners of the boxes have them. Am I right?"

Hendershot nodded.

Cully looked at him for another couple of seconds and then said, "Hey, you and I both know that's bullshit. You got the keys. Somebody loses their keys, I know how it works, that's what you tell them. Make 'em pay a service charge to get into their box. But the truth is, you got a set of master keys. You got to be able to get into a box if something comes up." Cully stared at Hendershot with a serious look on his face, letting the man know he wasn't fucking around. Waiting while the man glanced around the bank and then telling him, "Look at me. Don't worry is anybody going to come on over to help you out." Telling Hendershot again, "Look at *me.*"

Finally the man went back into the desk again, pulling a set of keys out and starting to hand them to Cully. Cully shook his head and said, "Un-uh. Do it like you always would. Just take the keys and the list, and you and I will walk on over."

Cully stood up. He could feel himself start to sweat a little bit, drops of it rolling down his back and in his armpits. But he told himself, Don't even think about it. Just keep Hendershot under control, smile at everybody, and it'll be over in maybe ten minutes. Tops.

He walked with the bank man over to the security room and had to tell him, "Go on," because at first Hendershot just stood there. Cully could see it, the man was close to panicking. He spoke softly to him, being polite, saying, "Open the door," in a nice voice, looking once more around the bank itself and seeing nothing out of the ordinary. Hendershot opened the door and Cully reached over and gave him a gentle push, following him inside the room.

He couldn't believe it, standing there in the room, with a couple of hundred safety deposit boxes and as far as he could tell, everything going pretty smoothly.

He looked at Hendershot and said, "Herb Dorrance. Which box is his?" And then shook his head because Hendershot, all he did was give Cully a stupid look and say, "I don't know."

Cully told him, looking at the man like he was a half-wit, "See, that's why we brought the list in with us." Giving it a second and then, when the man still didn't seem to get it, telling him, "Look it up, dummy."

He forced himself to stay calm while Hendershot ran his finger down the list and then said, "Thirty-three. Herb Dorrance's box is number thirty-three."

Cully started to look at all the boxes, running his eyes along them until he found it. He looked at Hendershot, standing there like an idiot, not doing anything, and finally it got Cully a little mad. He was thinking, it was hard enough, coming into a bank like this, he was doing the whole thing by himself, he could've used a little cooperation. He reached over and grabbed the other man by his coat, pulling him closer and taking the .38, Herb Dorrance's gun, out of his pants. Holding it against Hendershot's head and saying, "What, to you this is a fucking joke? I got to tell you every time I want something? I got to practically beg you for it?" Seeing the man's eyes start to bug out of his head. Cully was holding him, pulling Hendershot's face close, with the .38 almost touching the man's nose. Hendershot, what he was doing, he was looking from the pistol to Cully, straining his eyes to look down past his nose to where the .38 was and then staring up into Cully's eyes.

Cully told him, "I could use a little help here." Hissing at the man and saying, "Is that something you could do? Help me out?"

Hendershot started to nod. Cully could see maybe the man was finally starting to get the message. When Cully let go of him he reached into his pocket for the keys and tried to open Herb's box. But his hands were shaking so bad that Cully had to help him, sticking the gun back in his pants and taking the keys from him. He put both keys into the box and turned them, feeling a rush because he was a couple of seconds away from being rich. He almost forgot about Hendershot but then he turned and told him, pointing towards the far end of the room, "Just stand there. Stand there and keep telling yourself, This is going to be over in a couple of minutes."

Cully watched him walk to the other side of the room and then he went back to the box, pulling it out and taking it over to the table in the center of the room. He looked out into the bank one more time, telling himself everything looked okay, and then pulled the box open. It was like something you'd see on TV. The whole thing slowing down, like an instant replay in a football game. CBS clicker. Cully getting almost schizophrenic for a couple of seconds as the sounds from the bank started to fade and his own movements seemed to slow down. Like he was watching somebody else do it. Feeling a rush, something almost sexual because here it was, a last score, and it was almost over. Almost a half a million fucking dollars in diamonds. Pulling the lid of the box open and staring inside the container.

Everything came rushing back—Jesus—the noises, the sound of people chatting from the next room. Even the sound of Hendershot's heavy breathing—the man maybe going to have a heart attack right there. Cully seeing things clearly again, at full speed.

Looking down into the box, unable to believe his eyes because the thing was—all this shit to get there—and the fucking box, what it was . . .

It was empty.

He looked at Hendershot, thinking for a minute that what he'd do, he'd shoot the motherfucker right there for playing games with him. Feeling like doing it—pulling the fucking trigger—he'd never felt that way before, doing his armed robberies down in Miami; it had never crossed his mind. Put a bullet in the man's brain and then go on back out into the next room and get somebody else in here. Keep shooting them, if that's what they wanted, until somebody played straight with him. He actually started to pull the pistol out, thinking all he had to do was pull that hammer back, look over the barrel until he saw Hendershot's face, and then pull the trigger. Easy.

He had to talk himself out of it. Make himself count to five while he told himself to calm down. He looked at Hendershot. Seeing the man in the corner, kind of pasty, not looking too good, and not even looking at Cully. Like he was too scared.

Cully said, "Come here." At first Hendershot didn't respond but when Cully said it again, telling the man, "Come here, sport," still making himself act like he was Benny, Hendershot looked up and then shuffled over to the table.

Cully asked him, "What's your name?"

Hendershot told him, "Robert."

Cully nodded and said, "Bobby, we've got a little problem. I don't know, maybe you're nervous. Maybe you made a mistake. What I'm gonna do, I'm gonna give you another try. You take a look at the list and then tell me, which box is Herb Dorrance's?"

Hendershot looked confused. He looked at the box and then back at Cully. Finally he said, "That's it."

Cully said, "What?"

Hendershot started to shake. His face scrunched up and he told Cully, "I swear to God, that's Mr. Dorrance's box."

Cully shook his head. "You're making a mistake." He pointed at the list, "Look it up again."

Hendershot started to look at the list but his hands were shaking so bad Cully could tell he wasn't reading it. Cully grabbed the list and ran his finger down it until he saw Herb's name, seeing the number thirty-three next to it. He looked at Hendershot and said, "What the fuck is going on? He have another box?"

Hendershot shook his head. He said, "That's it. That's the right one." Nodding now, trying to please Cully. Saying, "I know it is. I'm sure of it. He comes in here all the time."

Cully didn't know what was happening. Was this some kind of big joke? He turned towards the next room, looking out past the bars, expecting to see a hundred cops coming in the front door. But everything still looked normal. But it was there, right in front of him. Somebody was setting him up. He didn't know why but he did know what he'd better do, he'd better get the fuck out of the bank and see what was going on.

He turned to Hendershot and told him, "What I'm gonna do, I'm gonna lock you in here and I'm gonna leave." He pointed out into the other room and said, "I got a buddy out there, waiting in line. You don't know who he is, but he knows you. You come out of here before five minutes is up and he's gonna pop you." Looking at Hendershot and saying, "You understand." Waiting for the man to nod and then stepping through the door.

He forced himself to be calm. Walking across the carpet, the whole time he kept expecting somebody to start yelling. He even smiled at a couple of people, let them see him, all he was doing was going about his business. And then he was outside, making himself stroll over to the car, wanting to run but being calm about it.

He opened the door and slid in, seeing Kristin sitting there, with her hands on the wheel, and saying, "Let's go, let's get out of here."

But she didn't do it. She just sat there, with the car running and her hands still on the wheel. But not moving, not reaching down to shift the car into drive. He couldn't believe it. He reached across and touched her. Saying, "Come on, for Christ's sake. Get us out of here." Seeing out of the corner of his eye a movement in the backseat and hearing Benny's voice as he was turning. Seeing the

.38 in Benny's hand, his own gun useless in his pants. Hearing Benny give a little laugh and say, "I got to admit, sugar, the man's got a point. I think we should get out of here." Laughing again as Kristin finally moved, not looking at Cully yet. Putting the car in gear and starting to pull out of the lot.

CHAPTER

24

B E N N Y T O L D K R I S T I N where to go. He made Cully give him his pistol and then told Kristin to head back towards town. Sitting in the backseat with the .38 in his hand and telling Kristin when to turn. Not saying where they were going at first, just telling her, "Turn here" and then finally, when they got to the Econolodge, pointing into the parking lot and saying, "Go on around back. Drive slowly and stop when I tell you.

They had to make the circuit twice, moving slowly in Kristin's Toyota. Finally, Michelle stepped out of one of the rooms and waved at them. Benny told Kristin to park the car and then he waited while she shut it off.

He looked at Cully, still smiling. Cully could see he was enjoying himself, saying, "Sport, the three of us are gonna walk over to that room. Nice and easy. I don't know, you're maybe thinking, Try something on the way. Don't even consider it." He looked at Kristin and asked her, "What do you say, sugar, your boyfriend gonna behave himself?"

Kristin looked from Benny to Cully. She told Cully, "I never even saw him."

Cully nodded. He was trying to control his breathing. Still feeling the shock of not finding the diamonds and then running out to find

Benny in the car. He wanted a couple of minutes to think. He told Kristin, "It's all right." And then he glanced at Michelle, still standing by the door of the motel room, and then back at Benny. "You want us to walk over there. It's all right. We'll do it. Nice and easy." Keeping his eyes on Benny while he said it.

Benny nodded, still staring at Cully. Smiling finally and saying, "The thing is, sport, you should probably keep it in mind"—he held the pistol closer to Cully's face—"I'm looking for a reason."

Cully nodded and slid out of the car. He walked around the front while Benny got out with Kristin. When he got to them he put his arm around Kristin's shoulders. He could feel her shaking, scared to death, and he kept his arm there, hearing Benny say, laughing, "This is cute. I like this," while he walked behind them to the room.

Michelle was pacing. Smoking a cigarette and walking back and forth while Benny told everybody to sit down. Looking at Cully and saying, "Except you, sport. You I want to empty your pockets. Give me the diamonds and everything'll be fine."

Cully thought it over, what he could say, knowing there was no way Benny was gonna believe him, but starting to get a little bit of an idea. Maybe a way out. It wasn't like he had a choice.

He looked at Michelle and said, "You wanna tell him?"

She stopped pacing and stared at Cully. "What the fuck are you talking about?"

He kept his voice calm. "I don't know. You wanna tell me how come I go to all this trouble, go into the bank when you tell me. The right day and everything. *And there aren't any fucking diamonds there?*" Letting his voice sound mad, like it was him that had been double-crossed. Asking her, "You wanna tell me how come he's here?" Pointing at Benny.

He could see Benny, in the middle of the room, looking from him to Michelle. And Kristin, on the bed, staring at him with a funny look on her face.

He looked at Benny. "I'll tell you, I'm new in this town. But somebody's pulling my chain. Maybe yours, too."

Benny said, "What are you talking about, sport?"

Cully shook his head. "I don't know. I was supposed to go in there, get the diamonds, and it would be done." He looked at Michelle. "She didn't say anything about you." Smiling and saying, "All she did was give me the key to the box and tell me to go get them."

Benny looked at Michelle. "You gave him the key?"

Michelle took a step towards Cully, looking at Benny and yelling, "He's lying. I didn't give him any goddamn key."

Benny moved closer to Cully. He held his pistol up to Cully's face and said, "Fuck this shit. Give me the diamonds."

Cully, looking at the pistol, the barrel enormous from this close, shook his head and leaned back on the bed. He looked at Michelle and said, "What's going on?" Trying to sound as calm as possible. Making it sound like all it was, was a misunderstanding, maybe something that Michelle could explain. But putting it on her. Making it something she had to explain. She wanted to put Cully in a spot like this—fuck her—he could do it right back.

He could see it, Benny's face starting to change. Getting a look of confusion on it and starting to turn towards Michelle. Cully thinking Benny didn't know what to do and then deciding to make him wonder even more.

He turned to Benny and said, "We've been set up, man. I don't know how. But it's what's been done."

Michelle yelled at Benny, "He's full of shit. He's got them. I know he does."

Cully shook his head. He looked directly at Benny and said, "I don't know, maybe this isn't news to you. Maybe you know all about it. She tells me to go into the bank—sets the whole thing up—and the whole time maybe she knows there aren't any stones."

"Bullshit." She was yelling at Cully now. "You're a goddamn liar." She turned to Benny. "Give me the gun. I'll make him tell us where they are."

Benny shook his head, giving her a look, smiling, but Cully could tell he wasn't happy. "Hun-bun, I think it's fine, me having the gun. I think it's the right way to do it."

Cully glanced at Kristin, sitting wide-eyed and quiet next to him. She still had the car keys in her hand and he reached over and touched her arm. "Are you all right?" Saying it calmly, because he wanted to reassure her and he also wanted Benny to hear it in his voice, let the man know he wasn't worried. He saw Kristin nod and then ran his hand down her arm until he touched her hand, squeezing it and then closing his hand on the car keys, taking them out of her hand and looking back at Benny.

He told Benny, "What they're doing, it could be one of a couple of things." Looking at Michelle and then back at Benny. "Maybe, what she and Herb got in mind, they're gonna let me go through with this, and then, when we get caught, they collect on the insurance. Something like that."

Benny kept staring at Cully, not saying anything now. But with a look on his face like he was willing to listen.

Michelle shook her head and took a step towards Benny. "Benny, he's lying. It's not true."

Benny, not even turning in her direction, told her, "Why'n't you shut the fuck up." Not smiling anymore, with something in his face, maybe in his eyes, that flat look Cully had seen before. Benny, getting ready to make up his mind, maybe getting ready to kill somebody.

Cully told Benny, "What it also could be, maybe it's as simple as Herb wanting you to take another fall. Maybe he just wants you back in jail. Maybe he's pissed off that at one point you were married to his wife." He shrugged his shoulders. "Or maybe it's just Herb, he wants to fuck us all. Somehow he found out about it and he wants us all to get screwed."

Benny walked to the front window of the motel and swept aside the curtain. Cully waited until he was looking outside and then dropped the keys down on the floor and kicked them under the bed. When Benny turned around, Michelle was glaring at Cully. Benny said, "Okay. Who the fuck knows what happened." He looked at Cully. "Maybe you got them. Maybe not. Maybe they weren't there." He thought about it for another couple of seconds and then nodded. "Take off your clothes."

Cully didn't say anything. What was he gonna do, act modest all of a sudden? If Benny wanted him to strip, it was because he was starting to believe him. He nodded and stood up. He started to take his shirt off and Benny said, "You too, sugar." Pointing the pistol at Kristin and saying, "Hurry up."

Kristin looked at Cully, who said, "It's all right. Do it." She looked at him for another couple of seconds and then stood up also.

Michelle was quiet while they stripped. If it bothered her to be in the same room with her sister, while Benny made them take their clothes off, she didn't show it. Benny looked nervous. He kept looking out the window and then back into the room, snapping his fingers every once in a while and saying, "Come on, come on."

When they were naked Benny came back to the middle of the room. He looked at Cully for a second and then told Michelle, "Go through his clothes."

While she was doing that, he stepped up to Kristin and said, "Jesus, honey. You always wear them funky clothes. You shouldn't, it hides your body." He turned to Michelle and said, almost laughing, taunting her, "Hey, hun-bun, I think her tits are nicer than yours." Not saying anything else until Michelle told him, "There's nothing here."

Benny stood in the middle of the room for almost half a minute. Cully, standing there naked, wanted to crouch down and put his hands over his crotch, protect himself because he felt so defenseless, getting cold and feeling his pecker start to shrivel up. Feeling stupid, because with all this shit going on he was aware that Kristin was standing naked next to him. He wanted to reach over to her and wrap his arms around her. Tell her it was gonna be okay. But he knew it would be the wrong thing to do. Show fear in front of Benny and the man would be all over you. Like back at Raiford, you'd get guys in for the first time, maybe a con would do them a favor, give them a couple of cigarettes. And the new guy would be so happy, making a friend in the joint on the first day in general population. Until the friend came back later for payback. Cully, what he had to do, was stand there like it didn't bother him a bit.

He kept his eyes on Benny, thinking he could tell what was going through the man's mind. Maybe Benny, what he was thinking, he could kill the two of them. Maybe even Michelle, too. Then he'd be free to go on out to Dorrance's place. See if the man did have the diamonds.

Cully cleared his throat. Benny looked at him and said, "What the fuck do you want?"

Cully shrugged and made a guess. "It's worth a try."

Benny stepped up to him and said, "What the fuck're you talking about, sport?"

"You leave us here, take her," pointing at Michelle, "and go on out. Maybe you'll get lucky."

Michelle said, "What's he talking about, Benny?"

Benny didn't answer her. He was looking at Cully and starting to grin. He said, "It's what you'd do, huh?"

Cully shrugged and said, "We've all of us been to a lot of trouble."

Benny nodded and said, "Uh-huh. And what, I leave you here, maybe you walk out of here and call the cops."

Cully held his hands up and said, "What am I gonna tell them? They see me, maybe take me back to the bank. That guy ain't gonna forget my face in a half an hour."

"Except you walked in there trying to look like me."

Cully shrugged and said, "They see me now, take me back to the guy that gave me Herb's box. I don't think he's gonna have much trouble."

Benny nodded finally. He looked at Michelle and said, "Get their clothes."

She said, "What?"

He raised his voice, almost yelling, telling her, "Goddamn it, get their clothes."

She picked up the pile of clothes and stood looking at Benny. Cully had never seen her like this. But he'd seen it happen before. A person, they're used to doing things a certain way and things go wrong. All of a sudden the rules change. Or there are no more rules.

Michelle, the rich woman, she could be a bitch to anyone she wanted. And now she wasn't even there anymore. What he was seeing was somebody, all of a sudden she was scared to death because she'd come too close maybe. Fucked with Benny. He was probably a lot meaner than when she'd done it four years before. She was starting to see it, she was face to face with something she couldn't even begin to control.

Benny asked her, "Where's your car?"

"On the side of the building."

He nodded. "Go get it, put their clothes in there. Bring it back and honk the horn when you're outside." Turning away from her before she'd even moved, like he knew she would go do it and then come on back.

When she had gone Benny looked at Cully and smiled. He said, "Here's my problem, you got the woman's sister with you. Nice tits and all. I kill you—that means I got to kill her, too."

He pointed towards the motel door and said, "I think my girlfriend out there might not go for it. Maybe she'd lose it, go running to the cops."

Cully nodded, feeling relieved, like he'd taken a piss or something. Maybe Benny wasn't gonna shoot them.

Benny kept smiling, stepping up to Kristin and touching her on the face, saying "Maybe, if I had more time, I'd try some of this." Running his hand down her chin and onto her chest, cupping one of her tits in his hand and smiling at her. Saying, "I never would have guessed it but I think you have a better body than your sister." Kristin was starting to shake again. Cully could see she was terrified.

He told Benny, "Don't even think about it. You got a thing going, maybe you can save it. You start fucking around now and it'll go up in smoke."

Benny stepped away from Cully. Outside they could hear a car horn. Benny glanced towards the door and then back at Cully. He said, "Sport, ever since I met you, all you've been doing is getting in my face. Comin' after me with a chain saw and hassling me every time I see you." He took a step towards the door and then turned back quickly, bringing the hand with the .38 in it up into Cully's face, catching Cully on the cheek and raking the barrel of the gun across his nose. Cully felt his face explode and fell backwards over the bed. He heard Kristin scream and then Benny said, "Sport, you been a pain in my ass."

Cully stayed where he was, thinking maybe his cheekbone was broken. Working his mouth back and forth slowly, not trying to get up until he felt Kristin kneeling next to him and heard her say, "They're gone."

He sat up on the bed, with his head killing him, feeling the blood running down his chin and waiting while Kristin went to the bathroom and got a towel. He got back down on the floor, with the towel pressed to his face, and fished around with his hand until he found the car keys.

She watched him do it and then asked, "What are you doing?"

He didn't answer her, walking instead over to the mirror and looking at his face. It had a gash in it that was gonna look even worse in the next day or so. Maybe it needed a couple of stitches in the cheek and one or two on his nose. But it wasn't as bad as he'd first thought. He could move his mouth without feeling anything grinding inside. A couple of his back teeth were loose but if he left them alone they'd be all right. He saw Kristin in the mirror, coming up to him and touching him on the shoulder. She asked him again, "What are you going to do?"

He looked at her. "I'm gonna go out there. Maybe try to put a stop to this thing."

She said, "You can't."

He told her, "Look, Benny's got your sister with him. He's on his way out to Herb's house. He ain't gonna stop until he has those diamonds."

"All you want is the diamonds."

He shook his head. "All I want now is to come out of this alive. And out of jail."

She gave him a look. "And you're gonna be able to do that?"

He thought about it. "The only way I can see getting out of this thing, I got to go out there and stop him."

She started to laugh. He could tell, looking at her, she was near panic, with a sound in her voice, standing there and laughing, like maybe she wasn't going to be able to stop.

He grabbed her and shook her gently. She stopped laughing and looked at him, trembling and saying, "Jesus Christ, we're naked, your face is split open, and you're telling me we got to go out there and stop Benny." Waiting a second and then saying, "He's got your gun, for Christ's sake."

Cully nodded. "I know." Looking at her. Touching her face and saying, "The thing is, what else are we gonna do?"

CHAPTER

25

EARL ASKED DAVE Ross the same thing, sitting in the parking lot of the Pancake House across the street from the Econolodge and seeing Benny and Michelle pull out onto the street, and then saying, "What are we gonna do?"

Dave watched Benny until he was almost out of sight, looking at the Econolodge and then at Earl. He said, "We follow them. See where they're going and what they're up to." He kept staring at Earl until the other man looked away. He told him, "It's all right, Earl. All we're doing is making sure Benny's all right."

Earl looked at his boss and said, "That's it?"

Dave Ross nodded. He reached into the glove compartment and pulled out a pint bottle of Jack Daniel's. He took a swig and handed the bottle to Earl, watching him drink and then saying, "We make sure your brother's okay. And then what we do, maybe we ask him for a cut of whatever they got going. Just for helping him out. Right?"

He waited for Earl to nod. Saw the other man tilt the bottle to his lips again and then Ross pulled out onto the street and started to follow Benny.

. . .

Benny, driving towards Herb Dorrance's house, with the gun in his hands, looked at Michelle and said, "I get out there, you'd better hope that your husband's got the diamonds."

Michelle said, "Benny, how can I know that?"

Benny smiled at her. He leaned over in his seat and pinched her hard on the cheek, hearing her give a yell, and told her, "Just hope he does, hun-bun."

He gave the car a little more gas, on the outskirts of Beaufort now, traveling a little bit over the speed limit. Not even worried was a cop gonna spot him and maybe pull him over for speeding.

He'd had a little time to think about it. Maybe it was true. Herb Dorrance, maybe he *had* figured out that they were gonna hit his safety deposit box. He wanted to get smart, take the diamonds out before anybody else had a chance to? That was fine with Benny. Driving the car down Route 21 and starting to smile. Because what Herb Dorrance probably didn't figure on was Benny coming out the house to take the fucking things.

Yeah, it was gonna work out fine. Cully and maybe the bitch next to Benny now—Michelle—maybe they figured they could pull a fast one. But it was like Benny had figured all along. Wasn't anybody gonna be able to stop him if he stayed on top of things.

It almost made Cully laugh, running out to the car naked. What would happen if a cop was driving by? Cully, he robbed a bank today and he ends up getting busted for indecent exposure.

He made it to the car, and pulled it around to the room and honked the horn. Kristin came out, wrapped in a sheet, swearing while she ran barefoot to the car. Cully pulled the car over to the very end of the lot and then reached into the backseat where the bag with his other clothes was. He pulled them out and gave his shirt to Kristin.

"You put this on. I gotta wear the pants and the shoes cause I'm gonna need them." He pulled the pants on and then his work boots, waiting while Kristin pulled his shirt over her shoulders and tucked it under her ass. He reached out and touched her shoulder, smiling at her and trying to lighten things up for a second. Saying, "It looks good, like a miniskirt."

She managed to smile back at him and then, with her voice a little shaky, she asked him, "Is it going to be all right?"

He kept smiling, nodding his head and saying, "It'll work out." Wondering, what the fuck did he know?

They were pulling into the driveway and Michelle asked Benny, "What if they're waiting for us?"

He laughed. "If they're waiting for us, then we'll deal with that when it happens."

She grabbed his arm and said, "Benny, listen to me, we don't have to do this. We can turn around now. Get out of this town." Saying, "It's over. Herb knows what we did. He must."

He laughed, enjoying himself, because he was getting the feeling that this was what it was all about. It was something that he was supposed to be doing, following this thing to the end. Still driving the car slowly up the driveway he said, "Those fucking things are mine. Two times I tried to score. Spent four fucking years in jail. I'm not gonna walk away from it now. I don't care what I got to do."

"Listen, Pete, I appreciate your letting me know," Herb Dorrance said, pacing in his den, with Billy Eagle on the leather sofa across the room, watching him as Herb held the phone to his ear. Talking to the sheriff, Pete Williams and saying, "I don't think it's necessary, I got Billy here. Anything happens, we'll be all right."

Herb held the phone for another couple of minutes, listening, and then said, "I'll let you know if they do show up." Nodding to himself and winking at Billy. And then saying good-bye. Hanging up and looking out into the room for a couple of seconds.

Herb said finally, "They fucking did it. Pete Williams got the call an hour ago. He's at the bank now." Herb walked over to a little bar in the corner of the room and lifted a bottle of scotch, holding it for a second without undoing the top, like he was stuck there, thinking about things. He grabbed a glass finally and poured an inch of scotch into the bottom.

He took a drink and told Billy, "From what the guy said, Henderson or something—the guy that got held up at the bank—from his description Williams thinks it was Benny."

Billy nodded. "We couldda told him that." Waiting and asking, "What about Cully?"

Herb shrugged and said, "Nobody's seen him."

Billy said, "He's got to be around somewhere."

"Yeah." Herb took another drink and said, "Williams said there was a woman, too. No good description of her." When Billy didn't say anything Herb said, "I guess we know who that was, too."

Billy shrugged his shoulders. "There's no way to tell."

Herb looked at him and said, "Hey, I don't pay you to talk shit. You know damn well who was with him."

He walked to the window and looked out. When he spoke it was as if he was talking to himself. "What that woman is, is a whore. I should've seen it. Give her everything and she pulls this shit." He turned back to Billy and asked him, sounding like he really didn't understand, "What kind of a place is it, a bank, somebody can walk right in and take the money? Get into the safety deposit boxes, which are supposed to be secure, and take whatever's in them?"

Billy said, "I don't know." He got up off the sofa and stood there, looking at his boss, seeing the man standing behind the desk excited. Jesus, rubbing his crotch and grinning. Billy looked away. Coming to the conclusion that Herb had been waiting for this all along. Finally he asked him, "What are you gonna do?"

Herb smiled. "Well, what Williams wants me to do, he wants to send some people out here, in case, I don't know, he figures they might come on out. I told him, No way."

"You tell him the box was empty?"

Herb shook his head. "He doesn't have to know what was in the box. It's none of his business."

He walked back to the desk, finishing the scotch and then sitting down. He opened the top drawer of the desk and pulled out a pistol, an automatic, sliding the lock back and then looking at it. A little piece of blued steel sitting in his hands. He put the pistol down on the top of the desk and picked up a small velvet bag, bouncing it in his hand. Looking at Billy and smiling. Saying, "I knew it. Benny, that fuck, he gets out of jail and what does he do? Basically, he does the same dumb thing that put him there in the first place. He thinks I'm gonna leave these stones in the bank so he can walk in there and try to take them like he took the money. Jesus." He laughed and said, "I'll tell you something else. That whore—her and her boyfriend—they want to come out here . . . maybe they still want to try to get these." He lifted the bag in one hand and picked up the gun with his other, winking at Billy again. "Big-time Benny, he's got a hard-on ever since he got out of jail—he wants to come out to my place. Maybe take my stones. I've been waiting for it. I'll kill the son of a bitch myself. They wanna come out here—give it a try—we're gonna have some fun."

Billy, thinking about it and remembering Benny—what he was like—wanted to say something. Maybe tell Herb that they could use some help. Could use a couple of sheriff's deputies out here. But seeing his boss, the man prancing around with a big grin on his face, what he decided, he decided that Herb knew what he was doing.

By the time Benny got out of the car he had worked himself into a rage, thinking about it. Herb Dorrance—peckerwood son of a bitch—had everything. Benny, what he had to do, he had to work his ass off for every little piece of shit he wanted. People like Herb, they were born to it. Grow up on a nice place like this and it was all just given to them.

He was thinking, too, what he should have done, he should have wasted Cully back there in the motel room, instead of giving the guy a break. It didn't make sense to leave any loose ends lying around. Benny figured he was either gonna get the diamonds, convert them to cash real quick and get the fuck out of the country, or it was all gonna fall apart.

He slammed the door of the Camaro, walking quickly around the car and grabbing Michelle by the arm—half dragging her and half pushing her towards the front door of the house.

Going up the front steps, he told her, pulling the gun from his belt and hissing in her ear, "Do what I tell you. I swear to God, hun-bun, you get in my way, fuck with me, and I'll gun you down." Stopping at the top step and shaking her, seeing the fear in her eyes and asking, "You hear me?"

She nodded and he pushed her toward the door and tried the knob. It turned and he kicked the door open, pushing her in and following after her. He was holding the gun in his hand. Relaxed. Feeling good all of a sudden. Because it was almost fun, exciting, doing shit like this, barging into a man's house—you're there to fuck him over, take his shit—and what was he gonna do about it? Like back at Raiford, you saw somebody and you just fucked with them, took their space away and abused them until they were yours. It gave Benny a good feeling, owning people.

He dragged Michelle further into the house and started to call Herb's name. Yelling it, "Herb, you got company." Keeping it up until he heard somebody laughing, turning to Michelle and asking, "Where's it coming from?"

She said, "The den."

He looked at her and then had to shake her, saying, "Where the fuck is the den?" And then shaking his head in disgust because she took a little bit of time to answer.

She finally pointed and he dragged her down another hall to the room where Herb and Billy Eagle sat. Benny pushed Michelle into the room, seeing the two men, Billy—over on the sofa—and Herb—sitting like a goddamn pharaoh or something—with his arms crossed over his chest and a silly-assed grin on his face. Benny gave Michelle another push. Saw her sprawl on the floor and looked back at Herb and Billy Eagle. Billy looked unarmed but Benny could see—on the desk near Herb's right hand—a pistol. He took one more look at Billy, heard Michelle start to yell on the floor, the bitch screaming to her husband—saying, "He made me do it, Herb"—and then Benny pointed the pistol at Billy Eagle and said, "Whatta you think this is, sport, fucking television?" and shot him between the eyes.

He turned, the sound still slamming back at him from the walls—with Billy's body not even hitting the floor yet—and pointed the pistol at Herb. Benny grinning now, because the smile was gone from Herb's face. The man staring at Benny, saying, "Wait a god-damn minute." With a look on his face like, Hey, you can't do that. Benny grinning at him because what it was, Herb was like a lot of people. Trash. They think they watch enough TV, maybe read about killing in the paper, they get the idea they can go up against somebody that'd been there before.

He told Herb, "I gotta tell you"—pointing at the velvet bag on the desk next to Herb—"if that ain't what I came for, you're a dead man."

Herb was starting to shake. Benny, standing there, with the .38 pointed at Herb's chest, was watching something go out of the other man. Seeing Herb looking older by the second. Not even sitting up straight anymore, slumping down in his seat, looking from the gun in Benny's hand to Billy Eagle, dead on the carpet ten feet away. Benny didn't know, maybe did Herb already piss his pants?

Benny said, "Well, you gonna show me?" Pointing at the velvet bag.

Herb looked confused. He stared at the bag and then looked at Benny, saying, "What?"

Benny swore. "Goddammit sport, it's been a long fucking day. Show me the fucking stones."

Herb nodded slowly, dazed now, looking at the bag for a long time and then picking it up and saying, "They're really quite pretty." Like he was a school kid at show-and-tell. Spaced out from watching Billy Eagle die. He undid the string around the top of the bag and then turned it upside down on the desk.

Benny, standing six feet away, couldn't believe it, what they looked like, falling onto the desk. If somebody had asked him how much space did he think four hundred grand worth of diamonds would take up, he would have said Maybe a coffee can full. Something like that. But it wasn't nearly as much as that. It was maybe seventy-five stones, none of them bigger than a pea. Not even as sparkling as Benny would have thought. Maybe they weren't cut. Benny couldn't tell.

But still, looking at them sitting on the desk, and knowing what they were, it did something to him. Made him feel almost high. Like his whole life, what he'd been doing, he'd been leading up to this point. Get the fucking things and get out of town. It was right there in front of him.

When he tried to talk he had to clear his throat. But then he told Herb, "Put them away."

"What?"

"Put the fucking things away. Back in the bag." He waited, while Herb put the diamonds back in the little velvet bag, nodding and telling Herb, "Get them all." Looking once, for a second, at Michelle. Seeing her, still on the floor, staring at the diamonds, too.

When Herb was done, Benny nodded. He said, "Put the bag on the edge of the desk." And then, smiling, he told Herb, "What I'm gonna do, I'm such a nice guy, I'm gonna give you a chance." He pointed at the gun on the desk and said, "That's your chance." Laughing now, and telling Herb, "You think—you son of a bitch— you think you can get to it in time? Give it a try."

Michelle started to move on the floor. She started to stand up, taking her time—still staring at the bag but beginning to swing her head towards Benny.

She said, "Benny, Jesus, don't. Let's just get out of here. Take the things and go."

Benny looked at her and said, "Shut up." He looked back at Herb and said, "Well?"

Herb started to shake his head, looking from Michelle to Benny and saying, "I can't." He was drooling, a little ribbon of spit running down from the corner of his mouth, shaking his head continuously now. Looking at Benny with wide eyes and starting to sob. "I can't."

Benny roared at him, "Motherfucker. Do it. You got three seconds. They put me in a fucking jail cell and now you're gonna cry about *this*." Benny, he could've told it. Dorrance, arrogant son of a bitch. Pissing on people his whole life. But now, when it came down to it, the cocksucker starts to cry. Benny was getting a little hard thinking about it. Like back in jail, you make somebody do something, turn them into a punk, so they'd take care of you in the showers. Half of it, the exciting part, was making them do it. Thinking about it, he realized that he missed it. Jail. Maybe not the part where they locked you up. But the part of it where it was you against anyone else. Where it was up to how strong and how fucking vicious you could be. He missed it.

It made him hate Herb even more. Seeing him sitting at the desk, crying his eyes out now, begging, and Benny, disgusted, raising the pistol and saying softly, "Do it." Giving Herb two more seconds and then pulling the trigger. Seeing the man's head snap back, then come slamming forward onto the desk, like John Kennedy, the same way he was in that home movie film.

Michelle started to scream, and Benny, taking his eyes off of Herb now that he was dead, stared at her. Looking at her and seeing her for what seemed like the first time, hysterical, with all her makeup running down her face. Wondering, like it was a revelation, what the fuck had he ever seen in her? Raising the gun again. Fuck it, he wasn't gonna leave anyone around to bother him. He was gonna start all over. Pulling the hammer back and getting ready to pull the trigger. Seeing her start to swing her head back from where she'd been staring at Herb. His arm tensed up now, ready for the recoil, ready to see her head snap back—seeing the whole thing in his head but then hearing a sound from the front of the house and turning. Taking two steps towards Michelle and wrapping his arm around her throat. Holding the .38 to her head and turning towards the door of the den.

CHAPTER

26

WHEN EARL CAME through the door Benny almost shot him. The shock of seeing his own brother, the last person he would have expected, come running into the room was almost enough to make Benny point the pistol at him and fire. He lowered the gun finally, still holding on to Michelle, and looked at Earl. Saw Dave Ross come in the room behind his brother and heard Ross say, "Jesus Christ." Ross was carrying a long-barreled pistol, something big, a .44 or something, Benny didn't know. But he could see from where he stood with his arm around Michelle's throat, the gun in Dave Ross's hand looked like a cannon, the kind of thing, somebody shot you with it, it would tear half your head off.

He looked at the two men, neither one saying anything because they were too busy looking at the two dead men.

Ross said it again, "Jesus Christ." And then he looked at Benny.

Benny had thoughts whipping through his head, seeing the two men and realizing that they had followed him, maybe for the whole day. It wasn't something Earl would have thought of. But Benny could see it. Ross, what he would've done, he would have fed Earl some kind of line, told him a story so that Earl would do what he said.

He made himself smile, looking at his brother like he was glad to see him. Saying, "Earl, I think maybe you forgot to tell me what you had in mind. Showing up . . . well . . . it's a surprise." Benny took a step away from the desk and looked at Ross. Telling Earl, "Bringing your friend with you, too." He shook his head, still moving a little bit to his right with Michelle. Getting himself in a better position. To where he could see both men at once.

Earl found his voice. "Benny, Jesus, what happened?"

"Well, old Herb and me—we had an argument." He saw Ross move a little bit. Not much, but the man took a step to his left, away from Earl, and Benny shook his head and said, "No, I think, what I want you to do, Ross, is just stay still."

Ross looked at Benny but he stopped moving. The pistol was still at his side, hanging kind of loosely from his hand.

Benny looked at it and then said to Earl, "Earl, you wanna do me a favor?" Waiting until Earl was looking at him and then saying, "What we got is a tricky situation." He looked around the room but then swung back to his brother. "You got a couple of people, they're already dead." Giving his brother a long look and then telling him, "The thing we don't want to do is kill anybody else." He smiled and asked Earl, "Am I right?"

Earl nodded and Benny said, "Good." Looking at Dave Ross and saying, "Earl, why don't you do me a favor. Take that cannon from your buddy there. Just take it, hold on to it. I don't care what you do. But we don't want anybody doing anything they'd regret." He nodded to his brother and said, "I'd feel better if you had it."

Earl said, "What are you gonna do with her?" Pointing at Michelle and not making a move to get Dave Ross's pistol.

Benny reached up with his gun hand and stroked Michelle's head. He said, "Man, she and I were just playacting. Make it look like I was gonna hold her hostage cause we didn't know who was comin' in the house." Still stroking Michelle's hair and saying, "Ain't that right, hun-bun? We thought you-all might be the cops."

He looked back at his brother and told him, "Now we know who you are, we can get everything straightened out. All right?"

Earl looked at him for a full minute and then said, "Okay."

Benny nodded. "That's fine then." He pointed at Ross and said, "Take his gun and we'll get out of here."

Earl took a step towards Dave Ross but the man backed away. Earl stopped. He looked at Benny and then back to Ross. "Hey, Dave, it's all right. All he wants is, I carry the gun." He looked at Benny and said, "It ain't like he's saying to give it to him."

Benny said, "That's right. I'd just feel more comfortable if you had it."

Earl nodded and told Ross, "See, it's all right. I get the gun, that's all. Then we can get this mess cleared up."

Ross shook his head. "Ain't no way I'm giving you this pistol."

Benny acted like he was starting to get a little mad. "Now listen, Dave. Ain't nobody gonna do anything. We can set this thing up, make it look like Billy Eagle and Herb had an argument. We just leave quietly. Ain't no reason for any more trouble." He looked at Earl. "Am I right?"

Earl nodded, looking like he was eager to please Benny. He said, "Come on, Dave. Give it to me."

It took Ross a while, maybe forty-five whole seconds, staring from one brother to the next, seeing the look Earl was giving him, and the calm expression on Benny's face. And saying, "All right," finally and handing the pistol to Earl.

Earl beamed and said, "That's all right then." He looked at Benny and said, "What do we do now?"

Benny smiled, shaking his head like he couldn't believe it, seeing his own brother standing there, with the big pistol in his hands, looking like the village dummy. Asking, What do we do? Jesus, like it was a grade school Christmas play and Benny had the script.

Benny shook his head again and said, "I'll tell you what we do." He pushed Michelle away from him, gave her a shove. Watched her land on the floor—deciding he liked it, seeing her down there again—it was where she belonged.

He told Earl, "The first thing we do, we get rid of the baggage."

"What are you talking about?"

Benny smiled. "I'll show you." He raised his pistol and pointed it at Michelle.

Earl said, "Benny, don't." There was a note to his voice, uncertain, like he didn't know, was Benny kidding around or not? He said, "Benny, stop it. Leave her alone."

Benny looked at him. Dave Ross was next to Earl, both men staring at the gun in Benny's hand. Benny said, "Jesus, you drunk son of a bitch. You ain't never gonna learn." He pulled the hammer back and looked down at Michelle.

Earl yelled, "Benny, don't fucking do it. She ain't never done nothin'."

Benny only shook his head. He was looking at Michelle now, concentrating, ready to fire and then turn to Earl and Ross, seeing it in his head—take Michelle out and then be pretty quick because Ross was probably gonna go for the gun in Earl's hands. He could hear Earl start to say something, his brother's voice getting louder, until Earl was screaming. But he tuned it out and pulled the trigger of the .38, getting a sweet feeling in his bones because the last thing he saw of Michelle was a look on her face like it wasn't fair. Feeling the pistol kick in his hands and seeing the look on her face disappear—replaced by a bright red volcano, blooming where her nose had been. It seemed almost like it had come from within her. The face: one second it looked pretty normal, and the next, it was like some creature had erupted from underneath the skin, said, Fuck it, and popped out bringing bones and blood with it. Benny, standing there, was fascinated with it, staring at her face as her body slammed back down on the floor.

He could hear Earl, still yelling, the sound starting to penetrate his brain again. Sounded like Earl was mad, maybe crying a little. And yelling, Benny could hear it now. Earl, furious. Saying, "Goddammit, Goddammit," over and over.

Benny turned toward him, still grinning a little bit, because there was no stopping him now. He ignored Earl, seeing the man standing there, a fucking pussy, eyes brimming over with tears. Still yelling, but Benny, he wasn't even paying any attention. He was gonna put one in Dave Ross, put a slug in his chest maybe. He liked the way it sounded—in the chest—like it was a medical term. And then what he'd do, he'd swing the .38 back at Earl. Put one in him, too. But be nice about it, though—a head shot. Quick.

He was lining up on Dave, seeing the man—scared—trying to back away but with nowhere left to go. Aiming but then getting a signal from his brain. Something wrong, running the scene over in his head—it took a split second to do it. Replaying it and then getting it. What was wrong. Picturing it as he had swung his gaze past his brother—the man crying, but doing something else. Raising that cannon he had in his hand and pointing it at Benny. Benny looked away from Dave Ross and at his brother again. Seeing that he had been right. Earl had the .44 lined up on Benny's face.

It almost made Benny laugh. But he was too mad. Seeing his brother and thinking, what the fuck did Earl think he was doing? Pointing a loaded gun at somebody. Being rude. Maybe Benny, maybe what he'd do, he'd make it a little hard on his brother. Put one in his gut, make him sweat it out for a while.

He opened his mouth, looking at Earl like he was retarded and said, "Earl, what the fuck you think you're doing?" Waiting for a reply but not hearing one because all of a sudden a bomb exploded, and Benny, all he could see was a huge spout of flame coming from where Earl stood and then something picked him up and slammed him across the room. Benny, in maybe a second, wondered what it was, cause he sure as hell never felt anything like it before. Seeing the floor, looking right at it and deciding that there was something wrong with it. Knowing it was a game, you go outside the room and somebody changes something. And you got to come on back in and figure out what it was that was different with the room. Walk around and listen to them laugh and tell you whether you were hot or cold. He almost had it, wanted to say, Wait, don't tell me, because he was that close to figuring it out. Yeah, because he had it now and it was pretty good. What they'd done, they'd switched the whole thing. He wasn't looking at the floor. They'd turned the whole fucking room upside down and he was staring at the ceiling. He wanted to stand up and shout at them. Say, Hey, I got it. But it wasn't worth it. He figured, what he'd do, he'd tell them later. Thinking, Fuck it, and closing his eyes.

Cully almost lost control of Kristin's car, wheeling it around the bend in 21 right past the Whale Branch River. Coming over the bridge, doing maybe ninety-three miles an hour and taking the last turn too wide. Feeling the tires start to slide on the gravel off to the side of the road. Seeing Kristin, next to him, put her hands on the dashboard and start to tense up.

He made himself slow down. Told himself it wasn't gonna do anybody any good if they got themselves killed in an automobile wreck. Easing off on the gas and then starting to slow down because he was almost there anyway. Seeing Herb Dorrance's driveway ahead—maybe a quarter of a mile away—and a car, he didn't recognize it at first, flying down the driveway and not even stopping. Pulling onto the road and leaving tire tracks on the macadam behind it. The driver, whoever it was, flooring it and hurtling towards Kristin's Toyota.

It wasn't until the car had whipped by them that he realized who it was. Dave Ross, and somebody next to him in the passenger seat. Looked like it might be Earl. Cully wasn't sure but he thought so.

He kept on going, making the left into Dorrance's place. Wondering about it. What were Earl and Dave Ross doing here?

When he got to the house he could see Benny's Camaro parked in front. He got out of the car and then leaned down to Kristin. He said, "I'm gonna go in there." Looking at her, her face wide with fear, and telling her, "I want you to stay here. I don't come out, or you hear anything—gunshots, something like that—I want you to get the hell out of here. Go to the cops. It doesn't matter. Just get out of here."

He kept looking at her. She didn't say anything and he had to ask her, "All right?"

She nodded finally and he stood up. His face was killing him now and he had to make himself not think about it as he walked towards the house. Behind him he heard Kristin call his name once, the sound floating over to him. Heard her say it again, but he made himself keep going without looking back.

He could smell it. At first he didn't know what it was. Like something had been left on the stove too long. Not like it was burned, more like it had been overcooked. You take a pot of coffee, something like that, and you leave it on the burner for too long and it gets that kind of metallic taste. That was it. Like overheated metal. With something else to it, something more meaty smelling.

He figured it out by the time he found the bodies. Knew where it was that he'd smelled it before—going through Chicago one time, near the slaughterhouses, and smelling that same thing. Thinking, Jesus, what had happened? Because the whole time he'd been inside the house—maybe five minutes—he hadn't heard a thing and he was starting to get an idea of what he was gonna find.

But it surprised him, seeing them *all* like that. Herb, and Billy Eagle. Maybe he was ready for that. But the other two—Benny and Michelle. He couldn't believe it. Like what had happened was everybody had counted to ten and then shot each other. The smell in there was unbelievable. Blood. And gunpowder.

He stood there for a couple of minutes. Staring. Seeing the bodies and the walls splattered with the mess of it. Walking over to Michelle finally and kneeling down. Looking at her, with her face all fucked up. Not even really able to think of her as a person because she barely looked human. Surprised because it made him feel terrible, seeing her like that and knowing what she had been like. A bitch maybe, but still she'd been alive. Somebody, they spent their whole life playing a game. But they hadn't ought to have ended up like that.

He heard a sound, somebody calling his name, and whirled around. Trying to get to the door in time to stop Kristin from coming in. Because that's what she was doing, coming into the room slowly, like she was in a trance. Not even looking at him. Still saying his name, like it was a chant, "Cully," over and over again, softly. But stepping right by him and walking past him to Michelle's body. Kneeling down and looking at her sister. Not speaking now. Just staring at Michelle.

He walked over to her and tried to get her to stand up, saying, "Let's get out of here."

But she shook her head. He looked at her for a couple of seconds and then decided, let her be, because what he had to do, he had to figure a way out of the whole thing. Thinking, it was right there in front of him. All he had to do was convince her it was the right thing to do. He looked at her, wondering, could he leave her alone for a minute. But she didn't seem to know he was even there.

He walked out the door of the study, back to the front door, checking to see if he had done anything when he had first come in. Left any sign of himself. Going from door to door, rubbing the door handles. Not wiping them clean, because that would look like somebody had done it on purpose. What he did, he smudged them, so that there wouldn't be any useful prints.

And then he made his way back to the study. He walked in and saw Kristin. She had moved and was standing over by the desk, looking down at Herb Dorrance. He went up to her and touched her shoulder, putting his arm around her and leading her from the room.

He walked her out to the car. Looking around, out towards 21 and then back at the fields behind Herb Dorrance's house. Making sure that nobody else was around and then helping Kristin into the passenger seat of the Toyota.

He spent most of the drive to Kristin's house thinking about it, what he was gonna do and the story he was gonna use. She didn't say a thing the entire time and he let her sit there with whatever thoughts were going through her head.

When they got to the Shrimp Boat he pulled the car past the lot and back behind it to where her house was. He sat there, looking at her for a minute and then told her, "I'm gonna have to use your car."

She looked up at him finally, and he was glad to see that she wasn't crying. It was a good sign. And when she spoke her voice was pretty steady. Not dazed, like she was in shock. But almost normal, like she was upset but she realized that it wasn't over yet. They still had a ways to go if they were gonna get out from under it. She said, "What are we gonna do?"

He smiled slightly and said, "It's simple. We do nothing. I go back there, like I spent the afternoon with you. I'm borrowing your car—you're lending it to me so I can get back." He paused, getting it straight in his head, and said, "When I get there, I'll act like I don't know anything. Wait a little bit and then I'll make the discovery. Find them all. And then I call the cops."

"You think they'll believe it?"

He shrugged. "I don't know."

It was quiet for a minute. He had a lot of things he wanted to tell her. Let her know that maybe it was gonna be all right. But he didn't know, maybe it would be the wrong thing to do. Finally he started the car again and said, "I got to get back."

She looked at him and then opened the door and slid out. She leaned back in the window and said his name, "Cully . . ." Like she wanted to tell him something.

But he was thinking he had to get moving. Not being able to stand it almost, knowing what he had to do and wanting to get it over with.

He smiled at her and said, "I've got to go." Telling her, "It'll be all right. You'll see." Not even waiting for a reply, just putting the car in gear and backing away. Looking once in the rearview mirror and seeing her, still with nothing but his shirt on, her legs looking nice, just staring at him as he pulled back onto the road.

He put a shirt on. That was the first thing. Made himself wait while he looked in the mirror—checked his appearance—and then he walked on over to the main house. When he got there he put his hand on his face and rubbed his nose and cheek until they started to bleed again. Then he wiped his hand on the stone pillar by the front door. Let the cops find it and he'd say that's where it happened, running down the steps after finding the bodies and he panicked. Slipped and cut his face on the pillar.

And then he went inside and made the phone call.

CHAPTER

27

IT WAS THE same cell as before—like they'd kept it open for him. They made him sit there for a day and a half. Barely talking to him. It almost killed him. Sitting there, he wanted to shout at them, ask them did they believe him or what? But he kept silent. Made himself wait it out. Not saying anything when the guard finally came to take him downstairs.

It was the same room, too, with Cully getting a sense of déjà vu because the sheriff was sitting there. By himself this time, though. Surrounded by the same fucking animal heads.

Cully sat down in the chair and stared at the man. The sheriff looked back at him for a full minute and then said, "I wanted it to be you. I could taste it. You comin' in here, to my town. And all this shit breaks loose. I wanted you to be part of it."

Cully wanted to sit up. Wanted the sheriff to repeat what he'd just said, it had sounded so good. It was what Cully had been waiting thirty-six hours to hear. But he made himself sit quietly.

The sheriff said, "I was getting ready to charge you. Gonna do it and then come up with the evidence."

Cully spoke for the first time, saying, "Sheriff, I got a record, yeah, but you and I both know," keeping his face serious, "I had anything to do with this, I would have been long gone."

"Maybe."

Cully shook his head. "There's no maybe about it."

The sheriff waited and then said, "We picked up Earl Marsh. He was drunk enough that he didn't make much sense. But we got the story."

"What'd he say?"

The sheriff looked somewhere above Cully's head and said, "Seems he followed his brother the whole time. Went into the house after him and saw what had happened."

Cully asked, "And what was that?"

"Benny went on a rampage. Killed Billy Eagle and then Herb Dorrance. When Earl walked in, Benny killed Michelle. Right in front of him. And it was too much for him. He said he just snapped. Like something inside of him went crazy. Told me he didn't even remember it, the gun was in his hand and then Benny was on the floor."

Cully looked at the sheriff. "Seems a waste. All that tragedy going on."

The sheriff made a face. "Yeah, I'd guessed you'd be all broken up."

Cully looked at the sheriff and said, "See, you're always doing that. You want to think the worst of people. I'm sitting here, you know where I've been. And to you, it leaves a mark. I'll never look right in your eyes."

There was a silence in the room and then the sheriff said, "Yeah, well it comes with the job." He stood up and said, "You can go."

"Just like that?"

"Uh-huh. Unless you want to make a fuss over me dragging you in here and locking you in that cell for a day and a half."

Cully smiled for the first time and said, "No, something like that, seems to me it would be a waste of time."

The sheriff smiled, too. "At the very least."

CHAPTER

28

HE HITCHHIKED THE whole way. Standing at the bridge over the Beaufort River until a car with two Marines in it picked him up. They were drinking beer and offered Cully one but he didn't want it. He sat in the back, quiet, watching the houses go by, and then, when they got near the place he told them, "Anywhere along here would be fine."

They let him out a quarter of a mile away and he used the time, walking slowly, to try to figure out what he was gonna say. Feeling weird, because he'd never felt this lucky. Get involved in a bunch of shit, it could've turned out much worse for him. But still, he wasn't feeling that good because what he needed to hear was something from Kristin.

He got to the Shrimp Boat and walked across the lot, seeing the restaurant was closed and wondering, was she even gonna be there? But when he got near the house, still maybe twenty feet away, she opened the front door. He wondered, maybe she'd been waiting for him. Stopping where he was and looking at her, seeing her like it was the first time. Thinking, Jesus, was it possible she'd gotten better looking while he'd been in jail? Because she looked haggard, that was true, but she looked real good to him, too.

They stood there, staring at each other, with Cully too scared all of a sudden to say anything, until she spoke. Asking, "You're all right?"

He nodded. Cleared his throat and said, "You?"

"Yes."

And then he said it, the thing he'd been thinking ever since he'd been picked up by the cops. Sitting in the cell and deciding, no matter what happened, if he got lucky he was gonna come on out here and tell her how he felt.

He said, "Kristin . . . I gotta tell you this"—stumbling over the words but getting them out—"I don't want it to end. I don't want to not see you." Waiting for what seemed like an eternity because it was the best he could do. The only way he could tell her he loved her.

He spent the next thirty seconds standing there. Just looking at her. Not moving when she began to walk towards him. Motionless, while she came up next to him and touched his face where it had been hit. He was feeling something inside of himself, something he'd never felt before. Listening to her say, "I love you, too."

And then he felt her hand in his and let her lead him into the house, hearing her say, "I've got something for you."

She stopped when they were just inside the house and she turned to him and said, "Back there, in Michelle's house, with all those bodies. And you left the room. I thought I was going to lose it. Go nuts right there by my dead sister."

He said, "I had to do it. I didn't want to leave you, but I had to."

She nodded. "I know." And then she looked at him and said, "But I was in the room all alone. And you were gone for a long time." She reached into the pocket of her jeans. "And I walked over to the desk." She paused to look down at the hand in her pocket, but then looked back up at his face and said, "And I saw these." She pulled her hand out of her pocket and showed him what was in it. A little velvet bag.

He said, "Jesus."

She told him, "I don't even remember it—picking them up. It was like somebody else did it. The whole time, driving back here in the car, I had them and I didn't even know it." She undid the string and held the bag upside down over her hand. Both of them, transfixed, watched the stones spill out.

They stared at them, neither speaking, until she looked up at Cully and said, "The stupid thing to do, with all the trouble there's been, would be to go nuts with them. Try to convert them all at once. Make people sit up and wonder."

He smiled. "It would be dumb."

"But if we did it slowly, one at a time, when we needed them. That would be all right, wouldn't it?"

He nodded. "Somebody once told me, I should've saved all the money from my scores." Thinking about Michelle for a second and the talk they'd had out by her pool.

She looked at him. "Run the restaurant. If we needed some money, we could use these. But only if we needed it."

Cully was grinning. Looking at her, seeing the whole thing and smiling, because for the first time in a long time, since before he got caught back in Miami, he knew what he wanted. Thinking about it, remembering what he'd told Bobo, his cellmate down in Raiford: "Maybe what I could do, I could open a restaurant, something like that." Looking at Kristin and saying, "Yeah, we could do that." Hearing a scream over his head—a gull gliding over the house and heading out to the bay.

He looked at the restaurant and the house behind it. And then back at Kristin. Knowing it was all right, he could spend his life here. Eat shrimp and make love to this woman.

He could do that.